SPIRIT BEASTS UNLEASHED

THE SPIRIT BEAST SAGA
BOOK 2

A.P BESWICK

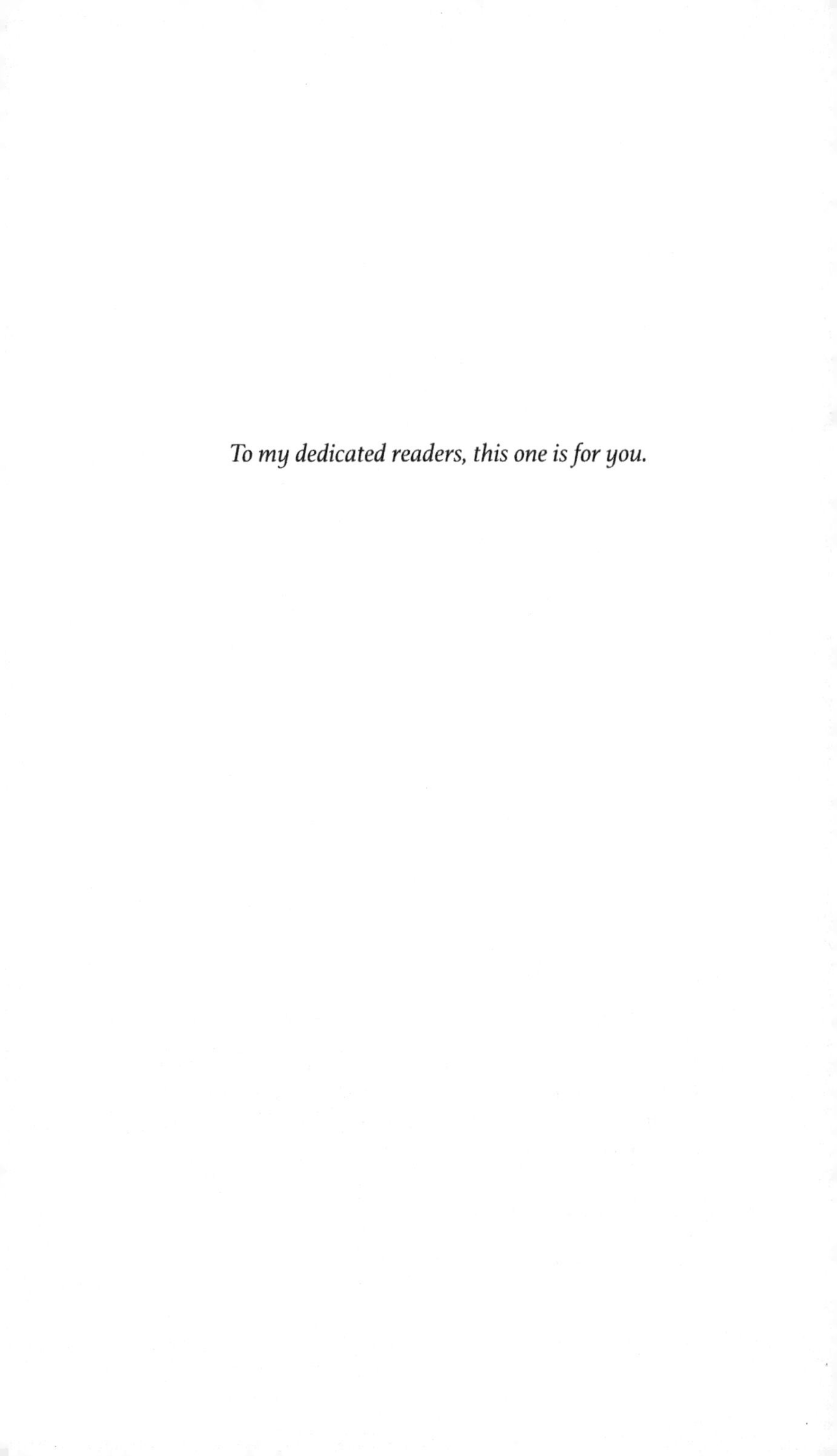

To my dedicated readers, this one is for you.

Editing - Quill & Bone Editing

Cover Design - Donn Marlou Ramirez

ISBN - 978-1-916671-12-6

SPIRIT BEASTS UNLEASHED

CHAPTER 1

The sun beat down on him with intense heat as he swung a large wooden stick against a towering oak tree, practising the latest moves that he had been shown a few days previously. The heat was just about bearable for his frame to manage, his hair matted with sweat and his clothes wet from training. The shadow cast by the old oak tree offered him just a small amount of comfort. Other than the nearby wooden hut where the boy slept, there was not much else around him beyond the woodlands and fields. An unnatural haze filled the landscape, a haze that the boy had become accustomed to in his short life so far.

He knew what the consequences would be if he was not prepared like last time, and he was not going to spend any of his time locked inside the wooden hut again, not after he was left there for six days before being let out. It was the worst experience he had ever been through.

He continued to beat the makeshift weapon against the tree, his small hands stinging as his calloused palms began to blister. He was trying to perfect his skills and was beginning to feel his confidence grow as he slowly improved.

When he felt an uncomfortable throbbing in his hand accompanied by a sharp pain, the boy decided it might be best to have a short rest and take a look at what the damage was.

Taking a seat on a large boulder that protruded from the hills, he felt a sharp burn against the back of his legs from where the sun had warmed up the rock, but he didn't flinch.

The boy had become accustomed to pain, and it didn't really impact him as much as it used to. He took a drink of water, the only reprieve from his harsh training. It had been warmed by the heat of the sun but he savoured it nonetheless, the liquid refreshing against his dry, cracked lips. The throbbing sensation in his hands brought him back from his moment of solace and he put the bottle down before inspecting the damage.

The blisters on one hand had burst and all that was left behind was small flaps of white skin where the fluid inside the blisters had escaped. The pain from these was bearable, but knowing they could become infected, he decided to return to his hut and clean them up.

Stabbing the stick into the ground, he walked back to his hut, slowly, the sweat dripping off him onto the ground. It was getting even hotter now and the boy was looking forward to getting back inside to escape the intensity of the blazing sun above.

When he opened the door to the hut, he was greeted by a wall of stale, sticky air, and he knew instantly that he should have left the door open to allow what little air there was to circulate inside. He didn't know which was more uncomfortable – sitting outside letting his skin blister from exposure to the sun, or sitting inside the stale, claustrophobic space. A space that brought him nothing but misery and loneliness.

Occasionally he was visited by a woman, but he did not look forward to these visits. These visits usually ended badly, with some form of punishment for himself, the thought of which sent a shudder down his spine.

The floor beneath him creaked as he moved across the room to the sink. The tap was stuck, requiring him to apply extra force to jar it free and spin it to release some much-needed water. The pipes grumbled as the water made its way down the copper track and slowly trickled out of the tap into the basin beneath it. The plumbing groaned and grumbled as if it fought to work, and the boy added checking the system to his mental to-do list.

It had not rained for over a month, and to the boy's annoyance, the water stopped running abruptly. This meant there was minimum water left in the tank behind his hut, and now he needed to choose between saving it to drink or cleaning his hand. He sighed to himself at the mere thought of having to refill the tank. The river – his only water source – was a mile away.

The boy decided that he really wanted to avoid a painful infection, so he placed his hand into the basin to wash it, knowing it would soon mean a trip to the river under the beating sun.

The water changed crimson, infused with the blood from his hand. The throbbing grew worse but he knew that in the long term it would be better, so he gritted his teeth and accepted that this was going to sting like hell. But it was no worse than the last time.

After cleaning his hand, he wrapped it in a small towel to allow it to dry, wishing for a moment that someone was here with him. After all, he was far too young to be left on his own to look after himself, even if he had become used to it. For once it would have been nice if someone could help him rather than him having to figure this all out by himself and wing it through trial and error. The boy had spent such long periods of time alone, apart from the occasional spirit beast that would pass by.

A sudden thud outside jarred his attention. It was as if something large had landed on the ground.

It's here, he thought, beginning to panic. It was too late to run; the moment he stepped outside the hut, it would see him. He'd been so focused on treating his wounds that he hadn't heard it approaching.

The boy's heart raced. Why would it be back so soon? What did it want? His thoughts went into overdrive and his body was going into fight or flight mode. He hated feeling like this, he hated her visiting. He wanted to be ready so that one day, he would be able to fight her off and be free from this life.

A large shadow took form outside, blocking the light that crept into the hut through the cracked and broken front door. He knew from the shape of the shadowy wings that it was outside, and in some way or another, it was going to hurt him. The heavy breathing and grunting from the creature as it gathered itself from its landing was unmistakable.

The boy's heart thumped, his body trembling from terror and adrenaline. His head grew dizzy and the room around him spun until he could no longer concentrate. He closed his eyes, hoping to steady himself, but the spinning and swirling inside his head did not subside, only got worse. The disorientation was unbearable as the room became a series of swirls and colours until he felt himself crash to the floor.

Instead of landing on the wooden floor as expected, though, the boy felt spongy earth beneath him, and he could taste the dirt in the air. Opening his eyes, he looked up to see the orange of the sun above him, even hotter than usual.

How am I outside? he thought to himself, his eyes stinging as his vision came into focus. His head felt like it was split open, such was the force of his headache, and his nausea made him heave a little. He brought his hand up to his head just to make sure he had not cut himself from the fall and his panic consumed him again.

Where is it?

He jumped to his feet to look for the beast, but it was nowhere to be seen. He surveyed his surroundings in confusion. His hut was gone. The grasslands where he had spent his life had vanished and been replaced with a busy, bustling market street. Weirder still, the haze had vanished, making everything appear so clear to him. The air felt more breathable, a refreshing experience the boy was not used to.

He was surrounded by people – actual, real, breathing people. Unfamiliar smells and loud noises filled the air, overloading his senses. He needed to allow himself time to acclimatise to his surrounding and figure out where he actually was. He walked down the street and was surprised by how no one had noticed that he was there. Instead, they chose to walk past him or rather, through him, like they could not see him. Being knocked from side to side, he tried to steady himself, just about managing to keep himself upright. He looked over at one stand to see someone selling some strange powders of multiple colours and fragrances. He walked across to see what it was and was amazed at what he was looking at.

"What are these?" he asked the man whose dark skin was like nothing he had seen before.

"*Kadam ladka*," the man replied, looking irate at the boy and gesturing wildly for him to move away.

Not understanding the language but very much aware of the body language, the boy moved away, knowing from experience that he was likely to get a clout if he were to hang around. He was amazed by everything that he could see, the people the smells, the sounds. It was so much different from what he was used to, and he knew already that he liked this place more than where he lived. He didn't know how he got here, but he was happy to be away, somewhere different.

Enthralled but disorientated, he continued to make his way down the street, realising that he should stand out like a sore thumb given that he looked completely different from the vast majority of people hustling and bustling around him. People were talking loudly over the stalls to each other, verging on shouting. He looked at another stall, confused by the three chickens that were strung up and hanging by their necks. A woman grabbed hold of one of the birds and pulled it down, then exchanged some coin with the stall vendor.

Distracted by the sight, the boy bumped into someone and began to lose his footing. Another person walked into him, and then another. He fell forwards onto the floor, the gravel stinging his already injured hands. With a sea of legs in front of him, he attempted to stand but found himself knocked down once more by the overcrowded street. Panicking, he began to crawl, looking for a gap through which to escape. Market goers kicked him as they walked past, and nobody was offering to help him. Maybe this place wasn't so different after all.

Spotting a slight opening in the sea of boots and colourful pants, the boy crawled as fast as he could and forced his way between two stalls into a small clearing. Free of the crowd, he rolled onto his back and gasped for air, then turned onto his side to spit out the dust he had inhaled.

A warm breeze tickled the back of the boy's head and he closed his eyes, feeling refreshed. But there was something unnatural about it; it seemed to come intermittently, with short intervals in between.

He froze in fear, contemplating running away, but instead opted to turn around to face whatever it was that was breathing down his neck.

"MOOOOOOOOOOOOOOOO!"

The loud noise from the cow caused the boy to jump back, startled by the creature in front of him. His surprise quickly changed to fascination, and he gathered himself, then stared intently at the animal that was roaming freely just behind the markets. He had seen plenty of cows before but never one as mesmerising as this. He'd never seen a cow that was completely brown in colour, and unlike the ones he had seen in the past, this one had no glow around it. Its long eyelashes blinked as flies attempted to make a landing on its large, dark eyes. He reached out to put his hand on top of it, but the cow butted its head at his palm, rejecting his advances.

The cow walked forwards, pressing its large frame against him and pushing him backwards. The beast was stronger than it looked. The boy glanced behind him to see that he was being pushed towards a market stall. He panicked at the thought of crashing into the merchant and his heart began to race. His head throbbed once more, and the same dizziness from earlier hit him like a sledgehammer. He felt as though he could no longer stand, his only comfort that of shutting his eyes to stop his surroundings spinning around him with ferocious force. He slammed to the floor once again, and found that this time he came crashing down hard onto a decrepit wooden floor. The market disappeared, replaced with his wooden hut once again.

"Where have you been?"

The voice was soft and calm with a coldness to it that made the hairs on his arms stand on end. How would she react to him vanishing and reappearing in front of them? He had no idea where he had been but he knew it was completely different from the world in which he had grown up. He knew then that he needed to get back there somehow. He needed to escape this life, to escape this nightmare.

"It's rude to not answer."

The boy knew the menacing undertone to her words; he had experienced it more often than he cared to remember.

"I don't know," he replied, his voice trembling, dizzy from what had just happened. He sat down on a small stool to compose himself.

"Did I say you could sit down? Who do you think you are?" Her voice elevated as she became more assertive, more hostile.

The boy stood back up, looking at the floor, hoping not to make eye contact. "I'm sorr –"

Before he could finish his sentence, he was struck across the face and sent slamming against the side of the room with incredible impact, his feet completely leaving the floor. The pain in his side was just about bearable but the searing pain across his face was not. His face felt as though it were on fire, and looking down at the distracting sound of dripping, he realised he was bleeding heavily. He looked up to see the beast that had struck him dissipating back towards the woman.

"Sorry, Mum," he cried, not knowing what to say or do. He had come to accept her coldness and occasional cruelty, but it was rare that she was this aggressive towards him, and he was scared for what might happen next.

His mum walked slowly past him and brushed his dark, blood-soaked hair from his eyes. “That’s going to leave a nasty scar,” she teased, the coldness in her voice like icicles hanging from the roof of a cave. “Now, you’re going to try really hard to get back to where you were, and you’re going to find a way to bring me back with you.”

She bent forwards and tenderly kissed the boy on the head before turning to leave, her bottom lip stained with his blood. “You wouldn’t want Mum to get angry again.” Then she exited the hut, leaving the boy alone once more.

The poor boy crumpled to the floor and curled up in a ball as he tried to comfort himself, crying into his chest. His face burned like molten metal had been poured on it. He needed to find a way to escape this hell, he needed to find a way to save himself.

He had to go back.

CHAPTER 2

Staring into his phone, Arnold dialled Otto's number with little hope that his friend would answer. After all, they hadn't spoken all summer. He waited patiently as the phone continued to ring out to no avail.

"*Hey, you're through to Otto, leave a message and I'll get back to you.*"

Arnold had lost count of how many times he had tried ringing, each time hoping that Otto would just pick up the phone and speak with him.

He sighed as the phone bleeped, indicating that he could now leave a message. "Otto, it's me again, it's getting kind of difficult to keep talking to your voicemail. Hope you're doing okay, ring me back if you get this." He hung up the phone and placed it against his head, tapping it as he thought about everything that had happened just a couple of months ago.

Otto's father, Mayor Redburn, had gone ballistic at Arnold's dad following Otto's expulsion from the Spirit Wardens, even though it had been Mr. Whittaker's decision in the end that led to his removal. Mayor Redburn believed that his family's honour had been cast into doubt and that he should have known better than to let Otto join in the first place. He blamed Arnold's father, Bernard, for not protecting his son, and in some ways, Arnold felt that his father blamed himself, too.

The day after Otto's confrontation with Raine, he had left town with his family, but no one knew where they were or what they were doing.

Everett returned to the room, passing Arnold a glass of juice and sitting next to him. "Did he answer?" she asked, knowing what the response would be.

"Nope," Arnold replied, "I hope he is okay."

"He's away with his dad; he'll be fine. I'm sure he'll catch up with you when he gets back."

Everett was unaware that Otto had been expelled from the Spirit Wardens for taking a life. Arnold had not shared this information with her, fearing that people wouldn't understand Otto's reason. He fully believed that Otto had no choice but to do what he had done following Raine's betrayal. He also believed it was for Otto to let people know that he wasn't part of the Spirit Wardens anymore.

"I hope so. I didn't leave things in a good place the last time I saw him," Arnold said. The last time he had seen Otto was the night he was kidnapped and his grandad was murdered. He had stormed off after Otto managed to summon his spirit beast for the first time, something which had drawn a jealous rage from Arnold. A jealous rage that now left Arnold full of regret. He just wanted to speak to Otto, to apologise to him.

Arnold had spent all summer with Everett and George. They had helped keep him grounded since his grandad, Elwood, was murdered by Levent. He had been consumed by grief in the aftermath from the night at the tower and thrown himself into his training, the result of which now left him feeling and looking much physically fitter. Over the past ten weeks, Arnold had grown into his frame slightly more and had more of a physical presence than he had last year, and his senses had become stronger. The training he put himself through combined with Everett and George's company had kept him busy. However, deep down, Arnold knew that this was a distraction; he still had not fully grieved for his grandad or gained the closure that he needed.

There was one more week to go before they would be back at school, and Arnold was not looking forward to that. In the aftermath of his grandad's murder, the media had been intrusive to the Ethon family, not helped by the Spirit Wardens' reluctance to give them information about Levent. Arnold and his parents were told that this was to stop a widespread panic about the link to the spirit world, but he did not fully believe them; he was not daft.

Arnold felt that everyone should know what happened and he hated keeping it secret from everyone. The only people he had confided in about what really happened at the tower that night were Everett and George, who he had sworn to secrecy.

Everett sat up straight next to Arnold, the sun just catching her hair enough for Arnold to admire her prettiness. "School is next week, so I'm sure he'll be there. You'll be able to speak to him then and clear things up."

Arnold felt fortunate to have her sat with him as they waited for George to finish at her granny's shop. He just wished he had the courage to tell her how he truly felt.

"I hope so," he replied. The need to make amends with his closest friend was all consuming. Everett and George had proven good company over the summer, but he missed Otto.

"Right, enough moping. It's beautiful outside. I want an ice cream from the parlour, and then we can head over to meet George. I don't want to sit around doing nothing." There was an assertive manner to Everett's comments, which made Arnold realise that he'd had about as much sympathy as he was going to get from her for one day.

He had been here many a time through the summer and knew it was a pointless exercise to disagree, so he stood up and stretched, smiling at Everett. "Come on then, let's go."

The two of them got to the bottom of the stairs and put their shoes on, Arnold admiring Everett as she tied her laces before she raised her head and caught him looking.

"What, have I got something on me?" she asked as she inspected her jean shorts and legs.

This was his chance. Arnold thought for a fleeting moment that he should just bite the bullet and tell Everett that he liked her and ask her out. Suddenly it was as though his throat was coated in tar and he found himself unable to form words.

"Arnold, are you okay?" Everett said with concern.

As a lump formed in his throat, Arnold banished the thought of asking her out and gave her a smile that was more goofy than it was friendly. "I'm okay."

"You know if you ever need to talk, you can talk to me. About your grandad, Otto, anything, okay?"

Arnold nodded. "Thanks." He could have kicked himself for the missed opportunity. They wouldn't be on their own now for the rest of the day.

Outside, the sun was bright, and Arnold could feel its warmth against his skin instantaneously. The street was filled with children keeping themselves entertained during the holidays. Two doors down from Arnold's house, four girls were chucking a football from one side of the street to the other, attempting to hit the kerb on the opposite side. Stopping momentarily, one of them shouted, "Car!" and the four of them stopped what they were doing to let the vehicle pass before resuming their game. There were other children in the garden opposite his house screaming with joy. Arnold smiled as he saw Brandon chasing his big sister around with a hosepipe, taking their water fight to a new level.

"I used to love kerby," Everett stated. "I always beat George when we played."

"I'm not surprised," Arnold laughed, as Everett by far was the more competitive between herself and George.

The two of them started to walk down the street towards the ice cream parlour, which was just a short walk from Arnold's house. Arnold could feel a bead of sweat forming on his forehead due to the heat. As they began to walk across the park, Arnold thought about his spirit beast.

"Want to summon them?" he asked, giving Everett a slight smile.

"Always wanting to train in some way," Everett teased. "Sure, why not." She focused for a moment and the soft, purple glow of her power wrapped around her like a mist gathering at the foot of a waterfall.

Arnold did the same and focused on the power in his core until he felt a knot in his stomach, like it was being tugged by a string. A blue energy pulsated around him and it was truly electrifying, the hairs on his arms standing on end. Finding the biting point of his connection, he channelled his power and the auro around him pulsated into the ground before his eagle spirit beast appeared beside him. It let out a high-pitched squawk before flapping its wings, its energy wrapping around the two of them. In an instant,

Arnold felt invigorated as if he could run a marathon, and he savoured the buzz as the power coursed through his body. Within seconds of summoning his spirit beast Everett had also summoned hers, and her boar took up shape next to Arnold's eagle and let out a grunting noise as it bucked about energetically. Not wasting any time, it butted its head against the eagle in a playful manner, only for the eagle to flap its wings and use its energy to push it back.

Everett's boar was considerably larger than it had been when she first summoned it in the school hall, back when life was so much simpler. Its coarse fur was ladened with a pool of energy sourced from Everett's auro, its tusks growing larger and more prominent.

The boar trotted ahead of Everett and Arnold's eagle glided elegantly above, swooping down from time to time to tease the boar playfully.

"I love watching them, it's amazing," Everett said, smiling.

It was too chaotic to try summoning spirit beasts in crowded spaces, so the park gave them the perfect space to let them out for a while. Every time Arnold summoned his eagle, he felt his connection get stronger, their bond grow tighter.

"It's great, isn't it?" Arnold said as he noticed a grin forming on Everett's face. "What are you doing?"

As Arnold's eagle swooped down again, the boar stopped and hopped backwards out of the path before charging at the eagle. Arnold was quick to this and his eagle was faster. He diverted his energy back into the air, avoiding the playful attack. To Arnold's surprise though, Everett's boar continued its run as Everett struggled to keep control.

"You okay?" Arnold asked.

"I've got this under control," she said, steely determination in her eyes. She had anything but control over her spirit beast however, and it continued charging at a flock of birds that were pecking at the grass ahead. "Why doesn't he listen to me?" Everett said in frustration, huffing out air. The boar continued its charge, the birds taking flight.

"Everett, watch out!"

It was too late. The boar crashed head first into a nearby tree, and Everett winced, rubbing her head.

"Are you –"

"I'll be fine," she said shortly, but Arnold suspected she was lying.

"Try not to –"

"I said I'm fine," Everett cut Arnold off.

Feeling deflated and picking up on Everett's vibe, Arnold chose not to offer any advice. By the time they reached her spirit beast, they were at the far side of the park so Arnold concentrated on his connection for a moment before his eagle dissipated and his blue glow of power vanished.

Crouching down, Everett gave her boar a rub on the head. "I think I got the spirit beast with no brain," she teased as she continued to rub her hand over its head and down its back. It gave a grunt of approval.

Arnold wanted to remind her that their spirit beasts were linked to their thoughts and feelings but thought it wise not to share this.

By the time they reached the parlour, he was more than ready to get an ice cream for himself to cool down. Looking into the sizeable fridge in front of him, he began to scroll over the vast choice of ice scream that lay before him.

"What do you fancy?" he asked, wanting Everett to choose first before he made his choice.

"I think I will go for the strawberry and cream, please,"

she said, pressing her finger against the glass to point out her selection.

"Mint choc chip for me please, in a waffle cone," he followed on. He could already taste it.

The lady behind the counter gave the two of them a smile before making their chosen ice creams for them. They left the parlour and crossed the road, passing the pavilion which sat opposite the cenotaph in the centre of town. The cenotaph was a tribute to locals who had died during the Second World War. A bronze statue of a soldier running with a rifle in his hands sat in the centre with an angel looking over him from above. The statue rightfully took centre stage in the town, and it was a beautiful tribute to those that had made the ultimate sacrifice in Arnold's opinion. He grew up on stories of how his great-great-grandad Charlie had fought bravely in the war, and joined in the remembrance parade every year.

It wasn't much longer before they reached George's granny's shop, and by the time they entered, they had devoured their ice creams.

A bell rang gently as they entered the shop, but no one was around – just the familiar cluttered shopfront, a wide array of trinkets and ingredients, and the occasional ornamental piece.

"I'll go see if they are out back," Everett said, walking towards the counter. She vanished through the beaded doorway, leaving Arnold to his own devices.

A thick, suffocating smoke clung to the air from the incense. Arnold didn't know what it was meant to smell like, but it reminded him of his great-aunt Nora's floral perfume, and he couldn't help but let out a slight cough. It seemed that no matter how many times he came here, he simply could not get used to it.

As he waited, he inspected one of the shelves next to him, rubbing his finger through the thick layer of dust that coated the wood. He should have known better, as in an instant, he could feel it tickle his nose. Before he had time to think, he let out a forceful sneeze, and a plume of dust exploded in his face, causing him to cough and splutter. Waving his hands around, he fought to clear the air as the dust clung to the inside of his mouth. One of his hands caught something on the shelf, which set off a regrettable chain reaction as various cups and jars of powders came tumbling to the ground with an almighty crash.

Arnold's heart sank with panic as he lunged forwards to stop the shelf from falling, pressing it back against the wall before anything else fell and more damage was caused. When he was confident it had steadied, he stepped away from the shelf and looked at the mess on the floor. One jar had broken, leaving the orange roots that it held scattered on the floor. He counted one broken cup that looked more like a mug, but everything else seemed undamaged.

He had knelt and started collecting the broken mug and bits of glass when he felt a pulsation of energy from beneath the shelf. It was faint, like a slight breeze, but being connected to the spirit world now, Arnold could tell that it was something else, something curious. Lowering his head, he peered under the shelves to see an item lying on its side. It looked like some form of chalice but it was difficult to make out any detail because of the light. Realising he must have knocked it from the shelf, he reached under to grab it, but when he touched it, a bolt of energy like a static shock zapped him, causing him to snap his hand back. Tentatively, he reached forwards to try and pick it up again, this time with no shock.

It was a peculiar looking thing: an old wooden chalice,

the wood dried and cracked in places, although not broken. Carved into the sides were multiple pictures of spirit beasts which fascinated Arnold, and as he rotated the chalice in his hand, he saw a lion with a powerful flowing mane, a falcon with its wings spread wide, a large deer with antlers reaching to the top, and a crocodile with its mouth wide open. Then his eyes landed on the last image, which was unmistakable: a dragon, its mouth open, its wings spread wide. It was as if Arnold were reading a tapestry of a battle. As he inspected it closer, there was a strange ripple of energy and a red glow pulsated through the carvings. Fascinated, Arnold lost himself in the intricate details of the chalice.

"What have you broken?" George said with a sarcastic tone, snapping Arnold from his fixation.

He raised his head to see George walking through from the back.

"Everything okay?" she asked, as if she knew something was off. She wore a black beanie hat with flowers etched into the front, a short floral dress with a pair of cycling shorts poking out from underneath, and rigger boots.

Arnold glanced down at the chalice in his hand before saying, "Sorry, I knocked a couple of things over, I was just clearing up."

"Don't worry, it happens all the time. I keep asking Granny to let me clear up, but she insists she doesn't want me to as she knows where everything is." She rolled her eyes. "I'll fetch the dustpan and brush."

While George retrieved the dustpan and brush from behind the counter, Everett and George's Granny, Edith, walked into the shop, the beads that hung down in the doorway rattling against each other as they pushed through them.

"Hello, dear," Edith said. She was wearing an orange blouse with black trousers covered in runes and a thick yellow coat that trailed along the floor behind her. Her neck was wrapped with an old necklace that boasted a stone circle trinket. Her eyes widened when she looked at Arnold holding the chalice. "Where did you find that?" she asked hesitantly.

"I think I knocked it off this shelf, sorry, I didn't mean to," Arnold said, giving another look over the chalice.

"Put it back," Edith snapped, her usually pleasant demeanour evaporating as her wrinkled face threatened to implode.

"Granny," George spoke with shock, "it was just an accident." She walked over with the dustpan in one hand and a brush in the other.

"Well, I would politely ask you to take more care!" Edith scolded. She rushed past George, almost knocking her into the table beside her, and snatched the chalice from Arnold. "You may all leave," she said shortly. "I will tidy up after you."

Arnold was in shock, mortified that he had caused such offence through his clumsiness. "I'm sorry," he said once more.

"Granny!" George's face told a story of one that was not impressed.

"Go, go," Edith repeated. "I am done for the day, and I will be closing the shop soon anyway," she said, placing the chalice on the shelf and snatching the dustpan and brush from George's hands. "Deary me," she croaked to herself as if the others were not present in the room, "this simply will not do."

Saying nothing else, Arnold, Everett, and George exited the shop in shock at the reaction to Arnold's destruction.

"George, I am so sorry, I didn't mean to," Arnold said, feeling awful, his cheeks reddening. He could have kicked himself for being so clumsy, especially in front of Everett.

George gave Arnold a kind smile and patted him on his back. "It's okay, I haven't seen her like that for a while, but she is getting snappy as she gets older."

"What do you guys want to do now?" Everett asked as the three of them stood on the street just outside the shop. Through the window, Arnold could see Edith brushing up his mess and shaking her head.

Arnold was quickly distracted, however, when he saw something moving towards him that he recognised instantly: a white car with blacked-out windows at the rear was coming down the road.

"That's Otto's car." He moved forwards excitedly, almost stepping into the road.

"Woah, there," Everett said, pulling Arnold's arm back. "Are you sure?"

Arnold was sure. He had homed in on the number plate, courtesy of his enhanced vision. The car turned ahead, driving in the direction of the Redburn's house.

"I need to go," Arnold said, and he began to run, wanting to get to Otto's house as fast as he could.

"Wait!" Everett called, but her attempts fell on deaf ears.

Arnold rushed down the street, his thoughts swirling around his head. He had so many things he wanted to speak to Otto about, but most of all, he just wanted to make sure that Otto was okay.

When he reached the house, Arnold stopped, allowing his breath to catch him up. Although he felt fitter than he used to, he was dripping with sweat from the effort and the hot weather.

Once his breath had begun to normalise, he stepped

forwards to the front door and knocked using the lion head knocker, which hung in the centre of the brown wooden door. A long pause followed three short knocks. Arnold waited impatiently, watching for the frosting at the top of the door to change colour – a quick indication if someone was going to open the door.

When a few more moments passed and there was no answer, he knocked again, and this time he could hear hurried footsteps coming to the front door. Muffled shouting could be heard behind the door before it swung open.

Mayor Redburn was wearing his suit pants and a blue shirt with the sleeves rolled up to his elbows. His dark amber eyes, tinged with green identical to Otto's, stared intently at Arnold. He had the same dirty blond hair as Otto too, but his was slicked back.

"You are not welcome here, leave!" Mayor Redburn all but shouted. It was odd seeing him this hostile, as he had always been kind to Arnold up until now.

"I just want to speak with Otto, please," Arnold replied, hoping that the conversation would swing in a different direction.

"He doesn't want to see you."

"If I could just –"

Mayor Redburn cut him off once more. "Don't you think you have done enough damage? Otto's expulsion is all your fault. What's happened to him is on you."

Behind Mayor Redburn, the vestibule door opened to reveal a much smaller person – Otto's little brother, Taron. "Nold, Nold!" he exclaimed, flapping his hands with excitement as he pushed past his dad to greet Arnold at the front door. Taron was on the autism spectrum and had always referred to Arnold as Nold, as he wasn't able to pronounce Arnold's whole name.

Arnold was happy to see him too. He crouched down to Taron's level and smiled at him. "Wow, you have grown." He spoke gently and slowly, allowing Taron time to process what he said.

Taron averted his eye contact but gave Arnold a huge smile.

"Come inside, Taron." Mayor Redburn placed his hand on Taron's shoulder and attempted to steward him back into the house. However, Taron rejected his approach and let out a loud shout in disapproval.

"Nold, Nold," he said, tugging on Arnold's t-shirt, unable to understand why he was not coming in.

"It's okay, buddy," Arnold spoke gently, recognising that Taron was beginning to show signs of distress. "Listen to Dad." He smiled and stood back up.

Taron turned and walked back inside, allowing Mayor Redburn to stand at the front of the door. "Don't come back here again. You have no idea, not a clue what you have done to this family!"

Before Arnold had the chance to say another word, Mayor Redburn slammed the door shut, the door rattling in its frame. A couple walking their dog on the other side of the street turned their heads to see what was happening.

Deflated, Arnold began to walk back towards where he had left Everett and George. He could feel his frustration building up once more. Could today get any worse? He understood that Mayor Redburn was annoyed at Otto being thrown out of the Spirit Wardens, but that had nothing to do with Arnold. He'd had no say whatsoever in the final decision, and his dad had fought for Otto to be allowed to carry on his training. Unable to understand why Otto's dad was taking his frustrations out on him, Arnold kicked a stone against a wall as he continued on his journey back to the centre of town. In the distance, he could see Everett sitting on the bench outside Edith's shop beside someone that wasn't George.

Focusing his eagle vision, Arnold could see who it was, and he cursed. Today was about to get even worse.

Kaden from school was attempting to brush his hand through Everett's hair, but Everett pushed it away, looking irate. Arnold set off running towards the two of them, his blood boiling. George was stood beside them both with a concerned expression drawn on her face.

"Oy!" Arnold shouted. "Keep your hands to yourself!"

Kaden stood up from the bench and grinned at Arnold, his smug smile infuriating him further. Arnold hated this boy who in his eyes got away with doing whatever he wanted, all because his parents had the money and backed him with whatever he said. Even though Arnold had stood his ground with him, he knew by his smug impression that Kaden was not ready to give up on his rivalry with Arnold. Kaden's father was the head at school, meaning Kaden could do no wrong in his father's eyes.

"What are you going to do?" Kaden goaded, puffing his chest up as Arnold drew level with him. His blond hair was tucked into a perfect quiff. Arnold detested how arrogant he was.

The air around them was charged and Arnold clenched his fist and tightened his jaw. He had beaten Kaden once, and he felt confident he could do it again. In fact, part of Arnold wanted Kaden to push, as he was alone for a change.

"Excuse me?" Everett interrupted, standing up from the bench and looking unimpressed with the two of them beating their chests like a couple of wild gorillas. "I'm perfectly capable of looking after myself, thank you." She looked directly at Arnold, and he knew he was in for it straight away. He stared at Kaden, wanting to wipe the smirk from his face. But knowing what the consequences would be, he stood down. He had been warned by the Spirit Wardens about keeping out of trouble. Now that he was being trained how to fight, he'd had it drilled into him by his dad about his responsibility to the Spirit Wardens.

"That's right, Ethon, let this cow stick up for you again. You're pathetic!" Kaden sneered, trying to get a reaction from him.

Everett swung her arm out, punching Kaden straight in the nose. He whimpered as he fell backwards. Arnold felt the crunch of the impact and couldn't help but smile.

"That's for putting your hands on me without me saying it was okay to do so," Everett said, shaking her hand at the discomfort from the blow. She walked up to Kaden, who was on his knees, cradling his nose which had begun to bleed. "Lesson learned?"

Kaden fell to his side, letting out another groan as the discomfort from the blow set in.

"There's no need to be so rude." She spun back towards Arnold and walked past him, smirking.

George giggled as she skipped over Kaden and joined Everett's side, taking hold of her hand playfully.

Arnold turned to follow them. "Everett, that was amazing." He smiled happily at how someone had put Kaden in his place.

"That has been a long time coming," Everett replied. "I best get some ice for this."

Arnold nodded, and the three of them began the ten-minute walk towards Everett's house.

"My mum is going to flip," Everett moaned as she opened

her front door. "She hates that I am not a girly girl like she wants me to be."

"I think you're pretty great the way you are." Arnold felt the familiar redness reach his cheeks. He wanted to kick himself for how cheesy his words sounded.

George gave him a goofy grin, a smile that said she could see something Arnold and Everett could not. "Aww, cute," she said.

Arnold's cheeks blushed even more as Everett and George headed inside, leaving Arnold on his own. "I'll see you both later," he said, eager to escape his embarrassment.

When Arnold arrived home, it was to find his dad flustered and pacing back and forth in the living room.

"It's okay, Bernard," Arnold's mum, Eve, was attempting to calm Bernard down, but it was not working.

"No, it's not, Eve. It's gone, everything has gone!" Bernard ranted as he paced the room, stopping when he saw Arnold.

"What's happened? What's gone?" Arnold pressed, puzzled by his dad's behaviour.

"There has been a break-in at your grandad's house!" Eve answered, her soft and soothing voice attempting to promote calm.

"What?" Arnold felt taken aback. He hadn't been to his grandad's house since he died. He had not been ready.

"Everything from the attic is gone. There is no damage; it has all just gone." Bernard was irate. "We only went up to sort through your grandad's clothes and realised straight away that someone had been inside. They knew exactly what they wanted too, as nothing has been taken from anywhere else."

Arnold didn't know what to say. There were loads of old looking stuff in his grandad's attic, which he had discovered by accident one afternoon. It had been one of his last visits with Elwood before he was killed by Levent.

Eve lifted her gaze to see Arnold watching them and drew Bernard's attention to the fact that Arnold was home. Bernard and Eve both gave Arnold nervous looks as if they worried that mentioning his grandfather might shatter him. After all, Arnold hadn't been able to discuss Elwood since that night, despite Eve's occasional attempts to broach the topic over the summer.

Opting to keep out of the way, Arnold went up to his bedroom, wondering where the contents of his grandad's loft had gone and why someone would take them. What's more, how had they gotten in so easily? He let out a sigh as he collapsed into his bed, exhausted.

Could there be any more drama?

Arnold sank into his pillow and closed his eyes, willing his thoughts away.

CHAPTER 3

The next morning, Arnold sat at the dining table eating some cereal, not really knowing what to expect from the day. He had already heard his father explaining to his mum that he was unable to notify the Doyens of the break-in, as they would ask what the stolen items were, and Arnold knew that Elwood had been hiding illegal artefacts in his attic from when he was an Elder.

The newspaper lay on the table, having been delivered by the over-eager paperboy who had started his round far too early in Arnold's opinion. He was sure that he had heard the letterbox just after six o'clock this morning. The metal shutter slamming shut had been just loud enough to disturb him from his sleep, meaning that he was feeling grumpy as he made his way through his breakfast.

Arnold picked up the paper and checked the back page to see whether his football team had made and whether there were movements in the transfer market, but apart from a couple of players he had never heard of, there were not any decent links to players today. He spun the paper around to look at the front and was taken aback by the bright, bold headline: *Menial Uprising*.

His interest piqued, Arnold began to read the article underneath. A spike in crimes committed by menials had been reported over the last four weeks.

Arnold couldn't help but feel that this had something to do with Levent. After all, Levent had announced that he had people everywhere. He found himself gripping the newspaper tightly as he read it, his knuckles whitening. Arnold wondered if Levent would show up again, and this fear was what had motivated him to train harder than ever before.

He didn't want to come face to face with Levent again until he was adequately prepared to avenge his grandad.

"Have you seen this?" Arnold asked as his dad walked in and finished the last piece of his toast.

Bernard nodded, still looking harassed following the break-in at Elwood's house yesterday. "I'm working on it at the moment. When he appears again, I want to make sure we are ready for him. It has to be linked with your grandad's being burgled," Bernard said, showing that he had a plan similar to Arnold's. Spinning on his heels, Bernard left the room to leave for work. Ever since the night at the tower, he had been starting work early and finishing late.

When the door shut, Arnold picked up *The Oswaldtwistle Advertiser* once more to continue reading the front-page story.

"I'm off to work now, too." Eve poked her head through the door. "Can you hoover up today for me, please?"

"No problem," Arnold answered without lifting his head from the newspaper that he was deeply engrossed in. He then heard the door shut again and continued to finish his breakfast before going back upstairs to get dressed for the day.

When Arnold came back downstairs, there was a letter on the mat by the front door that hadn't been there before. The postman didn't usually arrive until the afternoon. Arnold picked up the envelope from the floor, the hard bristles from the doormat pressing against his hand during the process. He turned the envelope over to find his name scribbled in untidy handwriting.

Realising that the post must have been hand-delivered, Arnold quickly opened the front door to look outside, but no one was around. He ran his finger against the top of the envelope, breaking the seal to see what was inside.

He found a small piece of card inside carrying a message in the same style of writing that was on the front of the envelope.

Bramley Lock-up, number 127 – Do not share this with the Spirit Wardens. We have a lot to talk about.

A pang of excitement erupted inside him. The note must have come from Otto. The handwriting was certainly messy enough to be his. Maybe he wanted to connect, maybe he wanted to do this somewhere away from his father. Arnold knew that Otto would not have been keeping his distance by choice.

Bramley Lock-up was on the far side of town, but Arnold could not help but feel optimistic. Not wanting to go alone, he pulled out his phone and tried ringing Everett but got no answer. He sent her a quick text saying he was on his way to call around to her house, then locked his front door and set off, excited to share the information that he had just received.

A short walk later, he arrived outside Everett's and walked up the path before knocking on the door hurriedly.

After a few moments, the door opened to reveal a bleary-eyed George, her white bunny pyjamas a sign that she had slept over at Everett's. She yawned and rubbed her hand on the back of her matted red hair. "Dude, what time do you call this?"

"It's half ten," Arnold replied. "I need you two to see this."

"Hey." Everett popped her head on George's shoulder. "You're keen this morning."

Arnold began to blush when he saw that Everett was stood in her pink nighty, something he hadn't seen before. "Sorry," he began to bumble. "I just had this posted and wanted to see what you thought." He passed her the card, and after reading it, Everett gave it to George.

"What do you think?" Arnold pressed for an answer. He trusted both of them and needed a second and third opinion. "I think it could be from Otto." He smiled, hoping they agreed. "Thought it best if I didn't go alone, though, don't want to end up kidnapped again."

"We need to go to this address, check it out," Everett announced eagerly. "Give us an hour to get ready and then we'll head over."

"Woah, we can't just head straight there! What if it's a trap? What if it's Levent?" George intervened. "It's dangerous, Arnold. You need to tell your dad."

"It clearly says not to let the Spirit Wardens know. My dad is a Doyen," Arnold explained. "It's why I have come here and nowhere else."

"Safety in numbers, there's three of us," Everett added.

George sighed, accepting defeat in the discussion. "Right, give us an hour." She turned and headed up the stairs to get herself ready.

"Meet us at the cenotaph at half eleven," Everett said, stepping down from the doorway.

Arnold headed straight to the cenotaph as directed and

sat on the bench across from the road, then pulled out his phone and played a game to pass the time.

The weather was slightly overcast with the clouds shielding out the sun today, and there was a faint musk in the air which indicated that the local farmers had been out muck-spreading on their fields early this morning. After an hour had passed, Arnold placed his phone back in his pocket and sat looking down the road, beginning to feel bored. He contemplated going to the address by himself but then thought it was not worth the roasting he would receive from Everett if he did.

Gazing across the road, Arnold was startled to see Otto walking past carrying a brown bag. Arnold couldn't help but notice that he looked physically bigger, like he had been working out a lot. His light blue vest revealed his toned arms, and Arnold was taken aback by how much Otto had changed over the summer. Maybe he wouldn't have to wait until he got to the lock-up after all to speak with Otto.

"Otto!" Arnold called, waving his arms in an attempt to draw his attention.

Glancing over, Otto made eye contact, then turned his head away, choosing to ignore Arnold and carry on his journey. His body language was nervous. He seemed as though he didn't want to be out in town at all and his brisk pace implied that he wanted to get home as fast as he could.

Arnold felt frustrated at how he just blanked him, and shouted again. Otto continued on his path around the corner, disappearing out of sight. Arnold contemplated running after him but felt that at this point, it would be a complete waste of time. He hoped Otto would simply meet him at the address he had received on the posted card.

"I have just seen Otto," Arnold said as soon as Everett and George arrived.

"How was he?" George pressed. "Did he say if it was him who posted the note to you?"

"Ignorant and bigger," Arnold told them, then explained how Otto had rushed off and how he looked as though he had been working out a lot while he had been away.

"Looking forward to seeing him even more now," George teased playfully.

"He seemed really distracted, I am worried about him," Arnold said.

"It must have hit him hard, being kicked out of the Spirit Wardens when he was doing so well," Everett suggested.

The thought of Everett and George finding out that Otto had taken a life in self-defence gave Arnold a ripple of anxiety. He didn't want them to judge a situation they were not involved in, and he did not want them to look at Otto any differently, even if he had broken the Spirit Wardens' fundamental rule.

Arnold didn't know how to reply, instead choosing to awkwardly switch the topic of the conversation back to getting up to Bramley Lock-up. "If he did leave the letter, then we'll talk to him at the lock-up," Arnold said.

The three of them set off up the main road, taking a left turn at the bottom and walking past the old hobbit holes into an industrial estate that looked as though it had seen better days. On their right, some garages were set up with a wide range of old cars littering the dusty grounds in front of them. The garages did not look as if they were maintained well, the layout of them looking messy from the outside. The mechanics could be heard laughing and joking whilst the sound of air guns being used to remove wheel bolts punched the air.

"I wouldn't want them sorting my car out," Everett

quipped as they walked past, kicking up dust that left a small cloud around them.

"You don't drive," George laughed. "And with your temperament, I would not like to be in a car with you when you do learn to drive."

"Harsh, too harsh," Everett followed up playfully, kicking a stone and skimming it across the floor until it clattered against the metal fencing in front of them. The noise drew the attention of the mechanics from the garage, who looked at them upon hearing the racket Everett had created.

The three of them laughed, chuckling to each other as they continued up the road towards Bramley Lock-up. When they turned the corner, the lock-up came into view just off the path. It looked equally unkempt as the garages that they had just passed. The building was a single storey, and the front of it was littered with graffiti as well as parts of the stone that had been chipped away with age. A single pane of glass to the side of the door revealed an old looking vending machine, which Arnold suspected might contain out-of-date chocolates.

"Is it even open?" George asked.

"It looks derelict," Arnold added.

Everett put her face against the dirty, plate glass window, trying to look inside. "Are you sure this is the place?"

"Erm, given the sign there, I would say this is the right place." George pointed at the broken sign which had “Bramley” painted on it. "If I didn't feel this was a trap before, I definitely do now. No one is here."

Undeterred, Arnold reached for the door handle and pressed against it, but the door was locked. Everett and George looked across at him.

"It was worth a try." He shrugged as he spoke. "We should look around the back."

"Did you not hear what I just said? This is a trap!" George's protest fell on deaf ears as Arnold took the lead and continued to the rear of the building without a moment's hesitation, wanting to know what was waiting for him. When they reached the back of the building, they could see the ground behind it was surrounded by a wall.

"Need a boost?" Arnold smiled at Everett as he stood with his back against the wall, placing his hands on his knee to offer her a lift.

Looking unimpressed with this gesture, Everett ran at the wall, using one foot to run up it. She grabbed the ledge and pulled herself on top before looking down on Arnold and George.

Arnold laughed. He didn't know why he'd bothered asking. He looked at George and nodded for her to use his boost to get up the wall. "You next."

"I think I'll wait here and stand guard. I feel really uncomfortable about this." George's arms were folded in front of her as if she was comforting herself.

"We can't leave you here," Arnold stated. "We need to stay together."

"I will wait around the front on the road. If you guys don't message me every ten minutes, I will call for help. I don't have a good feeling about this."

"Are you sure?" Everett asked, looking disappointed.

George nodded. "If anyone comes around, I will ring you." She stepped back and straightened her beanie hat before heading back around to the front of the building.

Arnold stepped away from the wall to give himself a good head start at scaling it, praying that he managed this first time. Everett would likely mock him for the rest of the day if he didn't.

Running at the wall, he managed to push off against it

and pull himself up, going one step further than Everett had and vaulting straight over the top. He landed in the overgrown grass on the opposite side.

"Show off." Everett grinned as she hopped off the wall, landing on her feet next to Arnold. "Where now?"

The grounds were extensive, with multiple storage crates scattered across the courtyard, some lined up, others appearing not to form any order. The various colours of the rusted containers brought some vibrancy to the dull, overgrown landscape.

"What number was it?"

"One twenty-seven," Arnold said, creeping around one of the crates and attempting to ascertain whether or not these were numbered. "This one says number forty-three. It must be towards the bottom of the yard."

Arnold and Everett began sauntering through the overgrown grass that had taken over, the weeds giving the courtyard a somewhat dystopian feel.

"Just let me message George," Everett said once they had reached the bottom of the yard. She took out her phone and sent a quick text to let her know that they were okay. George replied instantly with a smiley face emoji, complete with a beanie hat on top.

The two of them continued to look around the crates but were unable to locate the one that they were looking for.

"Strange," Arnold said, feeling confused.

"What?"

"The last storage crate here is one twenty-six." He stepped back to look at where they had walked past, but the row they had just walked down was definitely numbered in order.

Stepping around the side of the last crate, they could see another container on its own hidden behind.

"This must be it," Arnold professed. "It looks different and is set away from the others." The crate was sat by itself, and where the others were long and thin, this one seemed smaller than the rest. Vines crept up its sides and the ground around it was overgrown except for where Arnold assumed was the entrance. "I can't see anyone around."

"Strange. Well let's not wait around all day, we need to check it out." Everett strode ahead to the front of the crate, wanting to get a better look. "Come on."

Not wanting to fall behind, Arnold followed her over, stopping when he reached the front. "Now what?"

"Was there no key with your note?" Everett pressed in an exasperated tone.

"Need a lock to use a key." Arnold sighed, unable to see any form of lock on the front of the crate. Instead, his eyes landed on a series of hieroglyphs denoting different animals.

Looking at the last symbol, Arnold noticed that it was a picture of an elk. "That's too much of a coincidence for me," he murmured.

"What is?" Everett replied, kicking some grass back away from the front of the overgrown crate.

Arnold pointed at the hieroglyph. "That was my grandad's spirit beast."

"That is a coincidence . . . but given everything that has gone on recently, I don't do coincidences," Everett replied as she glanced at her watch, then took out her phone to message George again.

Arnold and Everett continued to stare at the front of the storage crate, wondering what to do next. Everett checked her phone again, a confused look etched across her face.

"What's wrong?" Arnold asked as he pushed against the

front of the crate, hoping that it would dislodge so that they could get in.

"George hasn't messaged me back."

"Try ringing her, she probably hasn't noticed."

Everett pressed George's picture on her phone, and it began to ring out. "She's not answering. We're going to have to turn back to check on her. I'll kill her if she has her phone on silent again." Everett was about to hang up when the call connected. "Where have you been?" she snapped.

Silence.

"Are you there, George? What are you doing?"

Concerned, Everett put the phone on speaker so Arnold could hear.

“George, are you there?”

The silence was interrupted by a low growling noise, followed by a loud scream that Arnold could hear as it came from the front of the lock-up.

"George!" The colour drained from Everett's face. "It's him, it's Levent!”

Arnold's heart raced as he grabbed Everett's hand, spinning her in her track so they could get back to George. "Come on!" He set off sprinting through the thick grass, wanting to get back as fast as he could.

Everett let out a yelp as she crashed to the floor. Arnold spun to see what had happened and found her trying to disentangle the vines that caught her foot.

"No!" she shouted when he stopped to help her up. "Go help George!"

Arnold nodded and ran at the wall of the courtyard, hopping over it with ease thanks to his intense training. As he landed on the other side, he could hear the aggressive growling noise and hoped that it was a guard dog and not Levent's remaining lion.

Sprinting around the corner of the building, he arrived to see George laid out on the floor with something stood over her.

The beast had the unmistakable glow of magic around it, meaning that someone had summoned their spirit beast. But it wasn't a lion.

"George!" Arnold screamed, trying to get the spirit beast's attention. It turned around to face him, letting out a loud roar.

"What the hell is that?" he said to himself, feeling his eyes widen.

The spirit beast stood on two legs, a good foot taller than Arnold, its large, muscular body covered in a tapestry of black and gold fur. Primal green energy flickered around it wildly as if a charge of electricity coated it. Arnold had never known spirit world energy to manifest in such a way.

Its eyes were black and feral, the same green burst of energy flickering like cracked flames in the place of pupils. It snarled and growled, its back slightly hunched, with vicious, long claws protruding from its paws. It was unlike anything Arnold had ever seen.

Unprovoked, the beast ran a few steps before dropping to all fours, its speed increasing with every step it took. The static energy around it crackled with charged power as it ran towards Arnold at pace, its teeth protruding in a snarling rage.

Arnold focused intently on his core, grounding his energy until he felt his connection to the spirit world intensify. A blast of his own power engulfed him and the air around him started swirling as if he were in the midst of a storm. A blue glow coated him as his heart beat wildly. His body felt warm with the power of his spirit beast rising up from within him.

His eagle burst upward into the air above him before diving back down at the beast as it continued to charge.

The eagle let out a shriek as it dive-bombed to intercept the attack. The bright blue glow around it seemed powerful yet angelic at the same time. Swooping down, the eagle clattered straight into the charging spirit beast, causing it to bounce onto its side. It let out a grunt as it crashed into the side of the Bramley Lock-up. A dust cloud engulfed the creature, causing it to vanish momentarily. Its silhouette soon appeared in the cloud as it again stood on all fours. Frantically, Arnold wondered where its anchor was, who had summoned this thing. Another loud roar followed, one of frustration, as the creature staggered and shook its head. It let out a howl, then ran away, retreating down the road.

Arnold rushed to where George lay on the floor. The tracks around her showed she had been knocked over then dragged towards the side of the road. Arnold slid onto the ground and dropped to his knees, bringing himself level with her.

"George!" He pulled her up towards him, and she let out a groan as he helped her sit up. He hugged her tightly, giving her a once-over. Her leg was scratched, but upon closer inspection, it didn't seem too deep.

"What happened?" George asked hesitantly as she gathered her bearings.

Arnold smiled at her nervously. "I was hoping you would tell me. Are you okay?"

"Where's Everett?" George quickly asked, a sudden panic overcoming her.

Everett had just scaled the wall and could be heard running down the side of the building in their direction. When she caught up to them, her eyes were wide with fear.

With a trembling voice, she asked, "Are you okay? Where's Levent and his lion?"

"I have no idea, that was not either of them." Arnold stood up and helped George back to her feet. "I don't know what that was, but I have never seen anything like it." He whipped out his phone.

"What are you doing?" Everett asked.

"I need to speak with my dad. He might be able to help."

"But the note said not to let the Spirit Wardens know," Everett pushed.

"They don't need to know why we were here, but we can't hide what just happened." Arnold began to call his dad. His biggest fear right now was someone being hurt by whatever that spirit beast was. The call, however, went straight to voicemail.

George dusted herself down, then walked over to the side of the road and picked up her beanie hat which had fallen off during the scuffle. She stuffed it back on her head, covering her dark red hair in the process, somehow managing to pack her head of tight curls inside it.

"See, I bloody told you it was a trap!" she said, turning on Arnold. "Levent is up to something, and I do not like it one bit." Her broad accent took over her usually soft-spoken demeanour, highlighting her anger at Arnold and Everett for not listening to her in the first place.

"Who was it?" Everett pressed.

"I have no idea, I only saw the spirit beast," Arnold responded, adrenaline still coursing through his veins. "It stood up on its back legs. Spirit beasts don't do that, not that I know of anyway. It can't have been Levent's lion. And neither of his lions had bright green, glowing eyes like this thing had." Arnold tried to ring Bernard once more, but again, the phone rang out as he pressed it to his ear.

Everett gave George a warm embrace. "Maybe it's a good thing he didn't answer," she suggested, nodding at Arnold.

"Erm, what do you mean?" George was clearly unimpressed with Everett's statement. "Why wouldn't we let the Doyens know?"

"No one was hurt," Everett pointed out. "If we ring the Doyens, they're going to want to know what we were doing here. Between the three of us, we will give it away too easily. Remember, the note said not to let the Doyens know."

"She's right, George," Arnold interjected. "Give me a few days. Let me see if we can get inside that crate. If we can't, then I will tell my dad everything."

"And if that spirit beast turns up again?" George demanded.

"Then we'll let them know," Everett added.

George paused for a moment while she considered what had been said. "Fine." She crossed her arms to indicate that she was not fully onside with their plan. "If anyone gets hurt though, that's on you. Can we please just get out of here?"

Everett rubbed George's shoulder comfortingly. "George is right. Whoever summoned that spirit beast might still be nearby. Let's go."

Arnold looked at his phone once more, but having decided not to ring his father after all, he tucked it back inside his jeans pocket. "I will head to the Athenaeum and see if I can find anything that might help us get past that rune."

With that, Arnold, Everett, and George set off back towards town, wondering what had just happened. Arnold's stomach twisted with guilt; he had been so desperate to make up with Otto – so certain the letter had been from him – that he hadn't been willing to hear George's initial doubts about going to the lock-up. He was just happy that she was okay.

He also couldn't help but feel disturbed by the fact that George had been the target and not him. Surely if it was Levent, he would have attacked Arnold, not George.

Even more so, Arnold wanted to know whose spirit beast that was. All he knew for certain was that it wasn't lion, or any other recognisable animal for that matter.

It had been something much, much worse.

CHAPTER 4

Arnold slammed the thick book against the table he was sat at, his frustration spilling over. The old, worn tome was an ancient codex hidden within the walls of the Spirit Wardens. This codex contained explanations of every type of spirit beast known, going back hundreds of years. Some pages were difficult to read due to the old-fashioned handwriting, and some of the pictures were faded, but Arnold was mostly able to decipher what he was researching. The pages contained drawings, descriptions, and sections on each beast's strengths and weaknesses, but Arnold had not found any information reminiscent of the spirit beast at the lock-up, or anything about glowing bright green eyes.

After the three days he had spent reading this codex, he still had nearly a quarter of it left, leaving him hopeful that he could still find something.

Arnold placed his hands against his face as he attempted to gather himself, knowing that he needed to focus if he was to keep going. His eyes were tired and heavy from the constant reading and thinking about what had happened earlier that week. Those emerald-green eyes haunted him, and he knew that somehow, that was the key to figuring out what the spirit beast was and who it belonged to.

Although this current task had taken priority, Arnold knew that he also needed to research the symbol on the storage container and look for ways of getting inside it. There had been no further reports of the spirit beast that they had encountered so for now, Arnold had not spoken to his father about it, not wanting the Spirit Wardens to know the real reason they were there. Deep down, Arnold didn't understand himself why they were really there. He still had no idea who had written that letter or what could be inside that storage container.

Arnold's phone bleeped, indicating he had received a message. He reached into the pocket of his dark denim jeans and removed it to see who had contacted him. It was Everett, asking how he was getting on with his research. Arnold quickly typed out a message back to let her know that he had not found anything useful yet. Looking at the top of his phone, he realised it was getting late and that he best head home. Unfortunately, the codex was restricted to the confines of the Athenaeum due to its age and value which meant that Arnold wasn't allowed to take it home with him. He was tempted to disregard this rule, but after Otto's exile, he was hesitant go against any of the Spirit Wardens' rules, however minor. After all, he still wanted to be a Doyen one day, so he opted to tread lightly.

He walked across to the side of the room where row upon row of codices lay tightly compacted into their book-shelves and placed the book back into its designated place. He was about to exit the chamber when the opaque, glass double doors unfrosted and slid opened, permitting entry to

Arnold's father alongside Mr. Whittaker, the local Spirit Wardens Elder.

"I've noticed you have been spending quite a lot of time in here the last few days and not the training room," Mr Whittaker began, his well-spoken words not fitting in with everyone else's broader Lancashire accents.

"Just fancied doing some reading, sir," Arnold replied, not wanting to give anything away.

"Let's hope that's all it is," Mr. Whittaker replied, clearly not believing what Arnold was saying to him.

Arnold had taken an even greater dislike to Mr. Whittaker, as he had been the one with the final say on Otto's expulsion from the Spirit Wardens. Arnold's father had explained to him that whatever his emotions were towards Mr. Whittaker, Arnold needed to grin and bear it, as he needed to respect Mr. Whittaker's status as the Elder.

Taking this into account, Arnold returned a smile to Mr. Whittaker before replying, "Just having a break from the physical training. My dad told me to rest, as he thought I had been overdoing it."

Bernard looked at Arnold in disapproval before answering, "I did, sir."

"Very well. However, we need this room for a meeting. Given that you are resting, may I suggest that you call it a night and return home?" Mr. Whittaker spoke with a sarcastic tone, his eyes filled with suspicion.

Arnold nodded to his father as he exited the room, grateful that he had played along. He couldn't help but smirk once he had passed the pair and walked through the double doors.

As he exited the Athenaeum, Arnold waved at the new receptionist, Grace. She smiled back at Arnold as she typed away on the desktop computer that sat in front of her. Grace had been at the Athenaeum for around a month now, after they'd gone without one for several weeks following the betrayal of the previous receptionist, Raine.

After being deceived by Raine, a menial, the Spirit Wardens had decided that anybody coming to work for them had to demonstrate that they possessed a spirit beast. Grace had demonstrated this before she was allowed to begin working there. Arnold thought she seemed like a nice lady, but he'd thought that about Raine, too. Grace was in her fifties, with short grey hair and glasses that looked like they were too large for her slim face.

The truth was, Arnold felt very guarded after what Raine had done. She had been allowed to infiltrate the Spirit Wardens, to get close to everyone and kidnap him for Levent, which had ultimately led to his grandad's death.

Arnold could not forget Levent telling him that he had people everywhere. Those words had remained in the back of Arnold's mind all summer, but had resurfaced to the forefront after George was attacked by an unknown spirit beast. Could one of Levent's people have facilitated the attack?

Arnold left the Athenaeum, but rather than heading home, he had a sudden change of plan. With thoughts of Levent on his mind, he realised he needed to be more proactive in being ready for him if he returned. Against his better judgement, Arnold turned and headed back up to the outskirts of town, towards Bramley Lock-up. He wanted to check out storage container number one twenty-seven once more before he headed home. Tomorrow, he was back to school, and after school, he was at the Athenaeum, so it would be at least until next weekend before he'd have another chance.

Before long, Arnold found himself walking through the overgrown grounds of Bramley Lock-up, making his way to the far side of the courtyard to where storage container one hundred and twenty-seven was.

He could already hear the telling-off he would get from Everett and George when they learned that he had come here by himself, but he didn't want to put them in danger again. Not until he knew more.

He approached the front of the storage container, again looking at it from all angles in case he had missed something before, but the container was sealed tight with no obvious way in. Letting out a sigh, he placed his hands on the front of the container and attempted to shake it, feeling ridiculous for even trying. The container didn't move, and Arnold kicked the door in frustration. The metal container rang out with a tin-like echo that filled the courtyard, sounding like a cheap chiming bell. None of his efforts worked, and for a moment, he contemplated giving up once more and returning home.

Arnold stared at the hieroglyph of the elk, then raised his hand to touch it. When his fingers made contact, he instantly felt his hand tingle. He dropped his hand in shock, and the sensation stopped immediately. Intrigued by the feeling, he raised his hand over the hieroglyph once more to find that his hand began to tingle again. The closer his hand got, the stronger the sensation became, to the point where it felt as though he had the worst pins and needles at the base of his palm. Feeling even more drawn to the symbol, he pressed his hand against it. The sensation was strange, but it felt familiar.

It was the same pulsating sensation he had felt when his grandad had transferred his auro to Arnold just moments before he passed.

"My auro," Arnold spoke out loud. Closing his eyes, he channelled his auro, and a soft, blue glow coated him. The tingling sensation in his hand immediately subsided and after a few moments, a loud clunking, mechanical noise started as something moved behind the front panel of the storage crate. Further mechanical movement could be heard from the outside, and the door loosened. Arnold grabbed hold of the panel and slid it to the side, his heart thumping. The light behind him illuminated the front part of the container, but beyond that, he could not see anything but darkness. He quickly found a light switch, and fluorescent lights above him snapped on. They began to hum, followed by quick flickering before lighting up the container with a bright light that caused Arnold's eyes to squint.

Arnold stood frozen, utterly confused.

All around him were his grandad's belongings, everything that had been in his attic, everything that had been stolen at the beginning of the week.

Why would this all be here? This didn't make any sense to Arnold. Who would have done this?

His thoughts were whirling around his head like a cyclone. Someone had inexplicably stolen Elwood's stuff and brought it here in secret, then invited Arnold to find it.

Some of the items he recognised, others he didn't. The contents looked as though they had been hastily added, with no particular order to how they had been placed around the room. Arnold instantly recognised the large chest where he had found Elwood's macuahuitl blade, which was now at the Spirit Wardens seeing as Arnold liked to train with it. His father wouldn't let him keep it inside the house.

He also recognised a couple of the glass cases in which different ornaments were placed, and there were boxes scattered around the room of which he had no idea what the contents would be. As Arnold continued to survey the room, he noticed an envelope lying on a small stool. It had his name on it.

A large lump formed in Arnold's throat as he recognised the handwriting immediately.

It was his grandad's.

Walking over to the stool, Arnold picked it up and began to open the envelope, pulling the message out as fast as he could.

He began to read, his eyes stinging from the tears forming in his eyes.

Dear Arnold,

If you are reading this, then I am no longer here, and you are at my storage container at Bramley Lock-up. You will have many questions, and in time you will get answers. If you are wondering who has moved all of my artefacts here, then I will let you know that it is someone whom I trust with my life.

The reason they are here is because, as I explained that night in the attic, there are many an artefact I had that the Spirit Wardens do not know about, and I fear what would happen if they were to fall into their hands.

All these things laid out in front of you, they now belong to you, my boy, and I could not think of a more deserving owner. You will find some old books and journals with age-old information around spirit beasts, spirit weavers, and many other mystical theses as well as all these ancient relics and artefacts.

These mustn't fall into the wrong hands. If everything has gone to plan, then your father will believe they have been stolen, and this must remain the case. He is too by the book with the Spirit Wardens. With you, I know this will all be looked after.

Finally, Arnold, I just wanted to let you know that I am so incredibly proud of you.

All my love
Grandad x

As Arnold stared blankly at the letter once he had finished reading it, tears fell down his face onto the paper. Feeling a large lump in his throat, he cried out loud.

Arnold was finally able to feel his grief for the first time – and say goodbye.

CHAPTER 5

Although confused by Elwood's belongings being moved to Bramley Lock-up in secret, Arnold woke the next morning feeling as though a huge weight had been lifted off him and that he could finally breathe. The letter that had awaited him in the storage container had helped him clear his head about Elwood's untimely death.

Today was the first day back at school following the end of the summer holidays. A lot had happened, and Arnold was actually looking forward to being back in school, which was a first. He now felt a lot more confident in himself than he had in the previous years. He was far more physically active, he had a spirit beast, and he had Everett and George.

As he sat at the breakfast table, a sense of sadness came over him as he waited for the familiar knock of Otto calling for Arnold on his way to school, but it didn't come.

Opening the front door, Arnold exhaled with the realisation that he would not have his best friend to support him through their first year of being senior students. His uniform hadn't changed apart from the tie that he was now wearing. The juniors at school wore a black and gold diagonal striped tie, whereas now Arnold wore a completely black tie with the gold emblem of the school embroidered into the centre.

Walking the corridors of school felt different being a senior. No one tried to trip him up as he headed to his form room to register. Arnold felt this was most likely down to his more athletic physique, giving him more of a presence.

A few people whispered to one another as Arnold passed them in the hall. He noticed Kaden, Piers, and Caleb huddled together, and they stopped talking when Kaden spotted Arnold. The three of them simply stared at him. Kaden's nose and cheeks were bruised where Everett had struck him. Arnold knew that it was only a matter of time before he had a run-in with them. This year, however, Arnold was no longer intimidated by them one bit.

Arnold simply looked ahead and walked past them.

"See you soon, Ethon," Kaden said before laughing with his goons.

Arnold eventually reached his form room and took his seat, waiting for their tutor, Mr. Higgins, to come in. The girls were sat perched around a table on the far side of the room, talking about everything that had gone on in their lives over the summer. The boys were less reserved than this and were busy winding each other up about anything that came to mind. Arnold felt happy to be surrounded by giggles and laughter.

"Right, guys, why is everyone not sat in their chairs?" Mr. Higgins projected his voice into the classroom as he entered.

Everyone looked like rabbits in headlights as they quickly scattered and found their seats as fast as they could. Mr. Higgins was Arnold's favourite teacher, and he was made up that he was going to be their form tutor this year. He naturally commanded respect from students with his combination of wit and assertiveness. All the students knew they could have a laugh with him, but at the same time knew where the line was, and no would cross this with him.

Mr. Higgins walked in with his lunchbox under his arm whilst balancing a load of papers in his hands. His sleeves were rolled up on his green shirt and his tie was not fully pulled to the top. His thick, dark curly hair was swept back to keep his fringe out of his eyes, and he looked as though he had done a day's work before the school day had started.

He set the papers on his desk before standing tall in front of everyone, placing his hands in his pocket. The chatter continued until he coughed to clear his throat, and the noise quickly died down.

"That's more like it, guys. Good morning, everyone."

"Good morning, sir," the class repeated in unison.

"I hope you have all had a great summer. Ped, what have you been up to?"

Andrew Pedder responded from the back of the classroom, "I spent the summer at the football academy." His thick Scottish accent was as powerful and fierce as he was upfront.

"But Scotland can't play football." Mr Higgins laughed before he continued, "How was it?"

"Loved it, there were some scouts there from City," Andrew added excitedly.

Andrew was a talent when it came to football and was already on the books at Blackburn Rovers, but Arnold knew he dreamt of one day playing for one of the top teams in the premier league.

"Anyone else?" Mr Higgins continued while perched on his desk.

Bethany Wright's hand shot up into the air, eager to answer. "Sir, I went to Cuba with my family, it was amazing, I got to swim with dolphins." Her well-spoken voice did not echo the broad Lancashire accent that most other people had around here. Bethany was one of the more affluent kids in school, and sometimes this could rub the other pupils the wrong way.

"Wow, that sounds fantastic, Betts," Mr. Higgins responded energetically.

"Bethany, sir, I don't like Betts."

Mr. Higgins laughed before correcting himself. "Apologies. Bethany." He gave a sarcastic look to the rest of the class to acknowledge that he had been put in his place.

"Ethon, how about you?"

The room fell silent, and Arnold felt like the black spot in the room. He didn't want people feeling sorry for him because of his grandad. No one knew what had really happened to him after all. All they knew was that he had died.

Arnold stuttered with his words before answering, "I have just been training really, sir."

"Like Andrew at the academy?"

"No, sir, at the Athenaeum," he answered quickly, not wanting to make a big deal of it. By the time school had finished for the summer, people had only just stopped looking at him like he had three heads, and Arnold did not want to go back to that.

"Ah, I would ask what that entails, but I know you are not allowed to say. Or maybe I already know." Mr. Higgins smiled, his statement catching Arnold off guard.

"Have you worked with the Spirit Wardens before?" Arnold asked, his curiosity piqued.

"More heavily researched," Mr. Higgins said before spinning the conversation. "You can tell that you have been working hard, lad. You look bigger, Arnold."

Arnold felt the room spin as if all eyes were on him, analysing him and comparing him to the last time everyone saw him. For once, though, he found that he didn't blush.

He simply replied, "I've been training hard all summer."

There was a sudden knock at the door which caught the class off guard. The door opened and head of seniors, Miss Elctree walked in, stony faced, her chin raised as though she had been greeted by a bad smell.

"We have a new pupil who has just moved to the area," she spoke briskly. "He is a bit nervous, but we have decided to place him in Form H as there was room here for a new addition. May you all welcome Marrok Lowe." She beckoned the newcomer into the classroom. "Come on, boy."

When Marrok walked in, a hushed silence greeted him. With both hands firmly fixed onto the shoulder straps of his backpack, he stood nervously, his piercing dark eyes surveying the room. He had dark skin and short shaved hair. He was tall, and carried an athletic frame.

Arnold felt for him. No one wanted to be the new kid at school. It could be hard to form friendships, especially when starting in the seniors.

Miss Elctree left the room, leaving Marrok stood next to Mr. Higgins.

"Welcome, Marrok." Mr Higgins placed a reassuring hand on Marrok's shoulder and turned him to face the class. "You now need to sing a song to the class."

Marrok looked panic stricken, but was quickly reassured by Mr. Higgins's laughter.

"I'm just kidding, lad. Just give everyone a quick introduction about you and then go sit over there by Ethon." Mr Higgins pointed at the empty seat next to Arnold.

The colour appeared to drain from Marrok. Arnold again felt for him, knowing that if it was him stood up there, his face would be bright red, and he would wish for the ground to swallow him up.

"Hello everyone, I'm Marrok." His voice was slightly shaken, his soft, Liverpudlian accent coming through faintly. Arnold only recognised the accent because he had members of his family from Liverpool on his mum's side of the family.

"I've just moved here from Cheshire with my mum and my sister." He looked around the room uncertainly. "I like writing and football."

"Right," Mr. Higgins interrupted. "Welcome to H Form, please take a seat. Ethon, make sure you look after Marrok, help him settle in."

Arnold felt happy to help Marrok settle into school and found it nice to have someone to sit next to in form for a change.

Marrok walked over to the table and placed his bag underneath it before sitting down next to Arnold. "Hi," he said.

"Hey," Arnold replied. "What team do you support?"

"Liverpool," Marrok answered.

Arnold laughed. "I'm Everton."

"Well, someone has to," Marrok said with a grin, his tension visibly lifting.

"Now, need I remind everyone that you are now seniors within the school," Mr. Higgins announced. "I expect everyone that is associated with my form to set nothing but a positive example for others to follow." Removing his hands from his pockets, he picked up the pile of papers on his desk and began to walk around the room, distributing them to everyone. "Here are your timetables. Do not lose them.

There are application forms on my desk for anyone wishing to apply to be prefect."

As they were now seniors, they were able to be prefects, which would look good on their CVs when it came to looking at colleges and then universities.

Arnold didn't have any interest in being a prefect this year; he had enough to focus on with training at the Spirit Wardens. He also wanted to spend time going through his grandad's belongings at the lock-up and finding out who had attacked George earlier on that week.

Arnold looked at his planner to see what the rest of the day entailed for him.

"Sweet, sports this afternoon," Marrok said, clearly indicating which his favoured subject was.

"Me too," Arnold stated. "The first class is always the worst though, as they make us do all sorts of activities to test where we're at and who to pair us up with for the year."

After form, Arnold offered to introduce Marrok to Everett and George, so the two of them left the classroom together and headed out to the central courtyard to meet the others. Outside, students of all ages had gathered to socialise in large groups, and Arnold couldn't help but think that from an aerial viewpoint, they must look like a colony of ants with hundreds of kids doing different things in the courtyard. Some were chasing each other, some were playing catch, while others simply were congregated or playing football or basketball. Arnold used his enhanced vision to pick out Everett and George from the crowd, spotting them at the far end of the courtyard.

"They're over there, this way." Arnold pointed and began to walk in their direction.

Marrok stood squinting, a confused look on his face.

"It's my spirit beast," Arnold explained, realising Marrok didn't know about his powers. "It's an eagle, so one of the perks is I have perfect vision."

"Wow, I've never heard of that before" Marrok said, visibly impressed.

"How about you, do you have any special traits?" Arnold pressed as he led Marrok across the courtyard. He knew it was rude to ask someone directly what their spirit beast was, so he refrained.

"Let's just say I have good senses," Marrok replied.

"Hey," Everett greeted them with a smile when the two of them reached the far side of the courtyard. Her ice-blue eyes scanned over Marrok as she seemed to weigh him up. Her hair was tied back into braids, which was her preferred style at the moment.

"Hi!" George said in a strange, cooey voice with a goofy smile. She had on her beanie with a few red curls poking out at the front, and as usual, her uniform was pristine; Arnold knew that she took great pride in her appearance at school, even if she didn't admit it.

Both stood for a moment, eyes fixed on Marrok as if they were eying up their favourite food in a buffet line, and Arnold felt a pang of jealousy creep over him. For the last few months, he had been the only boy in the group. Awkwardly, no more words were spoken for a few moments.

Finally, Arnold stepped in, clearing his throat. "This is Marrok, he is new and in my form. He's just moved here. Marrok, this is Everett and George."

"Hi," Marrok said politely.

"What brings you to Oswaldtwistle?" George inquired, unable to take her eyes off him. "Bit of a random place to move to."

"That's what I thought," Marrok admitted. "If I'm honest, I had never heard of Oswaldtwistle before my mum mentioned she had an interview for a job here." He seemed relaxed in the conversation now, which made Arnold feel better.

"And what does she do?" George pried further. Arnold could have kicked her; her interrogation techniques were as subtle as a sledgehammer.

"She's a reporter. Just got a job as an editor at *The Oswaldtwistle Advertiser*."

"What?"

"George!" Everett interjected at George's persistent questions. "Sorry, Marrok, she's not very good at talking to new boys."

George glared at Everett, clearly unhappy with her comment.

"What session have you guys got next?" Arnold asked, eager to change the direction of the conversation. "We have sports. No doubt Mr. Phillips will be drilling us all as per usual at the start of the year."

"Us too," Everett added.

The first bell rang, indicating that they had five minutes to get to the changing rooms before sports.

"I'll catch up with you at dinner, fill you in on last night," Arnold informed the girls.

"No worries, see you then," Everett replied.

Arnold didn't want to give too much away, having only just met Marrok. He didn't know him well enough to talk about the storage container with his grandad's belongings.

The four of them made their way back across the courtyard and to the sports block where they split up to go to the differing changing rooms.

As Arnold stood with Marrok outside the changing rooms waiting for Mr. Phillips, Otto walked in.

Arnold looked at Otto intently, hoping that he would at the very least acknowledge him. Instead, Otto simply walked past to the back of the line that had formed and stood with his gaze fixed firmly on the door to the changing room, avoiding eye contact with anyone. He could not have looked any more disinterested in being there, staring at the clock as though he couldn't wait to get away. Arnold contemplated going over to speak to him before the session started, but he didn't want to face the embarrassment in front of everyone if Otto ignored him again.

"Everything okay with you two?" Marrok asked, his eyes switching from Arnold to Otto.

Arnold sighed. He hadn't realised the tension between him and Otto was so obvious. "We used to be best friends, now he won't even acknowledge me," he said.

The shrill sound of a whistle startled the class, eliciting groans and moans from everyone as Mr. Phillips walked past in his blue tracksuit bottoms and sweatshirt, a whistle attached to his neck. He gave the impression he wanted to be there even less, his shoulders slumped and a lack of focus or spark in his eyes. Mr. Phillips was at a guess in his mid-forties, and his hair had started to grey around his sides. As a PE teacher he was sport obsessed. "Right boys, get dressed and line up in the sports hall. We're going to start with a bleep test."

Another collective groan erupted from the line of boys. The bleep test was everyone's least favourite test, but for once, Arnold was actually looking forward to it. This was his chance to put all his training into practice and show that he wasn't the same gangly dork that he was when they did this test last year. Arnold though about how embarrassing it had been to come pretty much last in most of the tests.

Around fifteen minutes later, the boys and girls of year ten stood lined up across the bottom of the sports hall, some looking excited by the prospect of being physically pushed, some visibly dreading it, and some goofing off clearly with no intention of taking the bleep test seriously.

Mr. Phillips stood in front of them alongside Mrs. Bramble, the girls' sports teacher. Arnold was glad he had Mr. Phillips; Mrs. Bramble's personality was known to be as spikey as her name implied.

"Most of you have done this before, but for those that haven't, Mrs. Bramble will explain what the bleep test entails." Mr. Phillips blew his whistle sharply to gather the attention of the few students that were talking to each other and not paying attention.

Mrs. Bramble stepped forwards to address the sports hall. "You will all start on the line in the centre of the sports hall. Once you hear the bleep, you'll set off running to the far side of the hall before the next bleep sounds. If you have not made it before the bleep, then you are out. You'll continue with this for as long as you can with the bleeps getting closer together until no one remains. This is a test of endurance. Don't overdo it early on, and good luck."

"Boys, you're on the left-hand side of the hall with me. Girls, you're on the right with Mrs. Bramble," Mr. Phillips directed, blowing his whistle once more as he beckoned everyone to line up where he had indicated.

There was nervous talk in the room as everyone hurriedly tried to get to the right part of the sports hall before the bleep test would begin.

Arnold lined up with the crowd of other boys on the left side of the hall as directed. He felt confident that he would do okay at this today, given the amount of training he had been doing recently. Last year had been an embarrassment with him falling over just a few rounds in. Otto and Andrew Pedder had been the last ones standing, but Andrew ended up being the winner.

Arnold exhaled, bracing himself for the whistle. As long as he didn't repeat last year, he'd be happy.

The first bleep sounded and everyone set off running in tandem, save for a few students who had decided to walk and be eliminated right away in order to save themselves the trouble.

Arnold began at a steady pace and simply focused on the line at the edge of the hall, making it with plenty of time to spare before the next whistle. Those that did not make it in time were directed to stand at the side of the hall. Arnold and the others who remained turned and began to run back towards the opposite line.

Arnold continued his steady pace for around five minutes, the number of people taking part getting smaller and smaller. He had already made it past last year's stage, so Arnold was happy so far, but he felt like he still had quite a bit left in the tank.

"Last ten, keep going!" Mr. Phillips encouraged them as the next bleep sounded.

The pace was picking up now, and Arnold began to notice the metallic taste in his mouth from the exertion.

"Four left, keep going, you're all doing brilliant!" Mr. Phillips exclaimed.

Arnold couldn't believe he had made it to this point, pleased by how much his fitness had improved over the summer.

It was down to him, Marrok, Otto, and Andrew now. Digging in, Arnold gritted his teeth and sprinted back as fast as he could, but the whistle blew right as he reached the line.

"Ethon, Pedder you're out. Well done."

Happy with what he had achieved, Arnold moved to the side of the hall while breathing heavily, trying to regain his breath. At the other side of the hall, all the girls had finished, and Everett and George were hugging each other while trying to catch their breath.

Arnold's attention drifted back to the boys' side as Otto and Marrok were going for it. The hall began to erupt with cheers and shouting as everyone tried to encourage them both to keep going. Both looked determined, but Otto appeared more focused, like he had nothing else on his mind but reaching the other side before the next bleep. Arnold wasn't used to seeing such grim determination on Otto's face; while he always tended to excel at physical activities, he usually did so with his customary casual manner. Something had definitely changed in Otto since Arnold last saw him.

"Come on, guys, you've got this!" Arnold shouted, wanting both of them to win.

This time, Otto and Marrok only just made the bleep, continuing to get faster and faster each time. Arnold was amazed at their speed and the endurance. Neck and neck, the boys sprinted to the other side until Marrok began to pull ahead slightly, just making the whistle before Otto could reach the line.

"Redburn, you're done, fantastic effort!" Mr. Phillips clapped as Marrok continued his run.

Marrok put his head down and pushed himself to make it across the line one last time. Finally he stopped, breathing hard, but he had won.

Another loud cheer erupted from all around the hall at

Marrok's achievement. He had won the bleep test, and by the look of it, he had beaten the school record. Not a bad way to start his first day as a new student, Arnold thought.

The shrill whistle blew once more. "Fantastic, Lowe, absolutely fantastic." Mr. Phillips walked across to him, the noise of his clap drowning out the pupils that were talking to each other.

Otto had moved to the corner of the room and was taking a drink, isolating himself from the rest of the students. Arnold tried to catch his eye, but Otto seemed to be intentionally evading his gaze.

"Right, everyone take a break for fifteen, then come back here. Next up is the accuracy test," Mrs. Bramble announced.

Another test that Arnold had failed miserably last year: archery. Last time, Arnold couldn't even fire the bow and hadn't made it through the first round. This time, though, Arnold had been receiving weapons training at the Spirit Wardens, and although he hadn't done much bow training, he knew he could now at least fire one.

Before long, the whistle blew again, and everyone lined up into five groups in front of the targets that now lined the sports hall.

"You all know the drill," said Mr. Phillips. "You hit anywhere within the target, you go through. You miss, you're out."

"After two rounds, the targets will then be moved further back until we are down to the final person," Mrs. Bramble finished.

At Mr. Phillips's whistle, the first row of people lined up to take their shots with the bows and arrows. Everett was up first out of their group and hit the target easily. Unfortunately, George didn't, and she shrugged to herself before walking to the side of the hall to watch everyone else continue. Otto and Marrok also hit the target with ease.

When it was Arnold's turn, he stepped forwards and picked up the bow from the previous student and reached into the quill next to him to retrieve an arrow. He focused on the centre of the target and took a slow, deep breath. Pulling the arrow back against the bowstring, he let go. To Arnold's surprise, the arrow fired into the centre of the target, to the applause of Everett, George, and Marrok. Otto just looked bored.

Arnold shrugged it off as beginner's luck, just happy he hadn't made a fool of himself. When he passed the bow back to Everett, he fought off a smug smile.

After another round, the targets were moved back to the halfway point, and this time Marrok missed.

By the time the targets had been moved back into the final quarter of the sports hall, only Arnold, Everett, and Otto remained out of everyone in the class.

Arnold took hold of the bow and felt his nerves increase, aware that everyone in the hall had eyes on him. He used his enhanced vision to focus directly on the centre of the target. Understanding the trajectory courtesy of those that had gone before him, he raised his bow slightly before pulling the arrow back and releasing. Arnold exhaled as the arrow fired across the sports hall and pierced the target in the yellow zone just off the centre. He turned to smile at Everett as he passed her the bow for her second turn at this range. This time, Everett narrowly missed the target, meaning it was down to Otto and Arnold. Otto and Arnold fired at the same time, Arnold becoming more frustrated with Otto's arrogance as he squeezed his bow. They both followed up by hitting the target once more.

The targets were now moved to the far side of the sports hall and could not go any further.

"Just to make you aware, no one has ever hit the target from this range," Mr. Phillips informed everyone.

Otto stepped forwards first, pulled his arrow back, and fired it without hesitation, hitting the target with apparent ease. The students began to clap and cheer at Otto's achievement. Feeling under pressure, Arnold stepped up for his turn and again used his enhanced vision to focus on his target. He raised his bow higher up in the air and inhaled slowly, then fired the arrow across the room.

A second after he fired it, he heard the noise of it hitting the target, to further applause from the other students. Even Mrs. Bramble nodded approvingly.

Otto quickly fired his second arrow, which sailed into the red centre of the target. He was completely calm, composed, and seemed only focused on one thing: beating Arnold.

Feeling slightly taken aback by how quickly and easily Otto had taken his second shot, Arnold stepped forwards and nocked another arrow.

"Ethon, if you hit this, whoever is closest to the centre will take first place. Miss, and Redburn wins," Mr. Phillips announced from the sidelines.

Arnold took aim, focusing on the centre of his target. A deep-rooted urge to win intensified within him; Otto had been ghosting him all summer which hurt him, but more than anything, the urge to prove himself in front of his classmates took over. No longer being last or playing second fiddle, serving in the shadows of his friends. In this moment, he would show them all exactly what he could do.

Otto's shot was just off-centre, so Arnold knew he would have to land a perfect shot to win. He tried to focus on his target but found himself distracted by Otto's near-perfect hit. Taking a deep breath, he drew his arrow back, his focus torn between both targets simultaneously.

Arnold paused; he could feel the familiar tingling sensation in his hand that he associated with his spirit beast. He raised his bow once more and let go of the arrow, firing it into the air. As it set off, Arnold was confused by the sight before him.

Two arrows flew through the air. One looked normal – like the one he had just pulled from the quiver – but the other glowed a bright blue colour. With a *thud,* the first arrow flew straight into his target. The glowing light, however, hit Otto's target at the same time as his own.

Upon closer inspection, courtesy of his enhanced vision, Arnold could see that both shots were in the centre of the targets.

The sports hall didn't erupt with cheers. Instead, Arnold was met with bewildered or awe-struck expressions as everyone seemed to be trying to understand what Arnold had just done. Arnold was just confused as they were. An eerie quietness fell over the students, interrupted only by the whispers from his classmates.

"He's spirit-wielded a weapon!" Marrok said.

"Spirit-what?" Everett asked, voicing Arnold's own question.

"He's connected to the spirit world to wield a spirit weapon."

"Ethon, what the hell was that?" Mr. Phillips roared across the hall.

"I don't know, sir," Arnold replied, shaken and nervous by what had just occurred.

Mr. Phillips paused for a moment before beginning to

slowly clap, still looking bemused. "That was amazing. We have our winner!"

Encouraged by Mr. Phillips, the hall began clapping and cheering at Arnold's victory. Arnold stood frozen in place, unsure what to do. This was something he had never experienced. Not only were people cheering for him, but he had also just produced a new ability that he had no idea he was capable of.

Mr. Phillips gave a shrill blow of his whistle before saying, "That's enough excitement for now, have a fifteen-minute break, then we'll come back to do the rest of the tests."

With this, everyone made their way towards the changing rooms just outside the sports hall. Arnold received multiple pats on the back from his peers, but others stared at Arnold as though he had three heads.

Arnold was making his way down the corridor alongside Marrok, Everett, and George, when Mr. Higgins stepped into his path.

"Come with me, boy," he said, a concerned expression on his face. Arnold exchanged looks with the others, then quickly followed Mr. Higgins down the long corridor towards H block where the teachers' offices were. Mr. Higgins pushed open a door and ushered Arnold in. "Take a seat," he said.

Arnold obliged, sinking into a padded chair that sat on the opposite side of Mr. Higgins's desk. Mr. Higgins perched at the end of the table, eyeing Arnold with curiosity. "I saw what happened in there. Spirit-wielding is a rare power."

Arnold didn't know what to say. Was he in trouble? Had he done something wrong without realising it?

Mr. Higgins grabbed a notepad and pen off the top of his

desk. "Would you mind if I take some notes? For research purposes," he added, noticing Arnold's confusion.

Sceptically, Arnold said, "Sure."

"I know you're training with the Spirit Wardens. Are you aware that they will frown upon such a power? They don't like drawing on power from the spirit world other than that which grants us our connections to our spirit beasts," Mr. Higgins said with concern.

"No, I didn't," Arnold replied, overcome with a sudden sense of worry. He'd had no control over what just happened, and up until fifteen minutes ago, had never heard of the term spirit-wielding.

"Be careful who you show this power to," Mr. Higgins said, his eyes suddenly serious. "The Spirit Wardens will not show you how to control this ability. They would rather you suppressed it. I can't go into too much detail now . . ." He cast a glance at the door as if expecting someone to walk in at any moment. ". . . But I believe I can help you get a better understanding of this new ability of yours."

Everything had happened so fast. Arnold's hands still tingled as the raw notes of energy remained charged within him. "Sorry, sir, it's just so much to take in," he said.

"I understand, Ethon, but I do believe you need help to get control of this ability of yours. To leave it unbound and raw . . . it could cause some long-term damage to your connection to the spirit world."

"Really?" Arnold said, suddenly concerned. He gave a look over his hands as if they did not belong to him. Magical energy was still pulsating through his arms and hands, leaving him with a dull ache.

"I'll go through everything with you after school tomorrow. In the meantime, try not to go into too much detail with the Spirit Wardens about what happened today. As I said, they may not look on this power favourably. If they hear about it somehow, tell them there was a misunderstanding."

Remembering the Spirit Wardens' distrust when Arnold had learned that his spirit beast might be a dragon like his grandma's, Arnold had no reason not to heed Mr. Higgins's warning.

Arnold sighed as he left. More than anything, he wished that his grandad was still here. He had so many questions he would ask him.

Elwood would have known what to do.

CHAPTER 6

"How the hell did you do that?" George stood aghast and unable to process what she had just witnessed Arnold do. "You fired a light arrow out of your hand!"

Arnold, Everett, George, and Marrok were sitting in the school hall, making their way through their lunches. Everyone seemed to be buzzing about what had just happened in the sports hall. By now Arnold's firing a bow made of light had spread around the school faster than the recent fires on Rivington Moors.

Arnold looked sheepishly around the room, acutely aware that the vast majority of people within the hall were whispering to each other, making him feel paranoid. He had lasted one morning without everyone looking at him like he was different, and now it was back to like last year.

"I've heard my mum mention spirit-wielding, but I never realised it was anything more than a myth," Marrok said, looking impressed. "According to the stories, it's where you use your auro to draw energy from the spirit world to form a weapon. I'm sure my mum always said you needed an artefact to help draw the energy, but Arnold seems to have done this without using one."

"I haven't got a clue how I did it," Arnold spoke with uncertainty. He wanted to be at the Spirit Wardens now so that he could ask his father about spirit-wielding. "I will talk to my dad when I get to the Spirit Wardens, surely he will know about this." He had so much to do now, between the lock-up, finding out what had attacked George, and now learning about spirit-wielding.

"As well as the spirit-wielding, Marrok, you were fast in the bleep test." George gazed at Marrok with adoring eyes, clearly smitten with the new boy.

"Football, rugby, and track sports," Marrok replied. “It’s all I’ve ever done since I was little.”

“Still, you beat Arnold and Otto, who have had specialist training," Everett added.

"It's nothing special." Marrok was clearly trying to downplay his achievement. However, the look on Everett and George's faces implied that he had not succeeded.

"You said before about the Spirit Wardens?" Marrok spun the conversation back to Arnold, attempting to divert attention from himself.

"Arnold and Otto were allowed to join the Spirit Wardens," George responded quickly and without hesitation.

"We declined," Everett added.

Marrok looked even more interested now. "What, how is that?"

"It's a long story," Arnold finished, feeling there were more pressing topics to discuss. Turning to the girls, he said, "I need to tell you about the lock-up, too." Arnold had decided that Marrok seemed trustworthy enough. "I managed to get into it last night."

"And? What's in it?" Everett demanded.

Arnold looked around him to ensure no one else was listening in, then leant forwards to speak quietly to the others. "My grandad's stuff," he whispered. "It went missing from his house and has been moved there."

"That doesn't make any sense, why would someone do that?" Everett responded, lowering her voice.

"I don't know, but whoever has done it doesn't want the Spirit Wardens to know. I think there are artefacts there."

"What!" George spoke loudly, drawing attention to their table. Everett quickly elbowed her to tell her to keep quiet. George spoke more quietly this time when she continued, "Arnold, if there are artefacts there, you need to hand them over to the Spirit Wardens. As much as I don't agree with their ways, I don't want us to get into trouble with them."

"Ever the responsible one," Everett teased.

"The note said not to, and until I know why, they will stay in the lock-up. If we meet up after school, I will show you everything."

The school bell began to ring, meaning that they all needed to head back to the sports hall to finish the final part of the PE test. The last session of the day was a strength endurance test, and Arnold was feeling more confident than ever that he would be more than okay this time around. They headed back across the courtyard and made their way into the sports hall.

THAT EVENING, Arnold sprinted up the steep stone steps to the Athenaeum and made his way through the large, intricately detailed, circular wooden door at the entrance.

"Is my dad around?" he asked Grace tentatively as he entered.

Grace looked up from her computer, pushing her large-framed spectacles up her nose so she could get a better look at Arnold. "Bernard is upstairs in his office."

"Thanks." Arnold walked past the reception area, and when he arrived at his father's office, he walked straight in without knocking, eager for information.

Bernard was sitting at his dark wood desk, a fan pointing in his direction to cool him down from the excessive heat they were currently experiencing. He looked irritable as he quickly grabbed some papers that were just about to take flight courtesy of the fan.

"You might be my son, but you need to knock before you come in, we are not at home," Bernard said sternly.

"Sorry, Dad," Arnold said sheepishly. "I just heard about something today and wanted to ask you about it." It wasn't quite a lie, Arnold assured himself.

Looking up from his paperwork, Bernard removed his reading glasses from his face and placed them on the desk next to his pile of papers. "Go on?"

Arnold hastily began. "There is this new kid at school, well, we were just talking, and he mentioned something, something that I have never heard before." His speech was fast as he was trying to offload all this information to his father so he could get the answers he wanted without saying too much. "He said it's called spirit-wielding, have you heard of that?"

"What?" Bernard looked surprised. "Spirit-wielding?" There was a sudden panic in his eyes.

"It's real then," Arnold said, sensing his father's concern.

Bernard shuffled some papers on his desk before placing them in a neat pile and moving them awkwardly to the side.

"Dad!" Arnold prompted.

"Yes, it's real. It is very rare but also very dangerous. For that reason, the Spirit Wardens forbid the use of it. To even speak of it would be frowned upon by the higher ranks."

Arnold mused on his father's words. Mr. Higgins had been right in his warnings about how the Spirit Wardens would react, then.

"Besides, you would need an artefact to help you control the power in its rawest form. As far as I know, the Spirit Wardens are in possession of most, if not all, of them."

"Why is that?" Arnold asked.

"Because of how dangerous spirit-wielding is. Spirit-wielding requires one to pull raw energy from the spirit world. To do so risks ripping open the dimension entirely. So much so that the Wardens have long tried to hide its existence. Where did you say you heard about this phrase?" Bernard picked up a pen as if he were going to scribble down some notes.

"Just the new kid at school," Arnold said, opting not to share Marrok's name as his mind went into overdrive. Both Marrok and Arnold's father had said one needed an artefact to spirit-wield, but as far as Arnold knew, he hadn't used one, and he was fairly certain that his school probably didn't own an ancient artefact right under the noses of the Spirit Wardens.

"Is there more to this, Arnold?" Bernard asked sceptically, his eyebrows lowering in an untrusting manner.

"No, I just never heard of it before, that's all." Arnold shifted awkwardly where he stood, "How would the Spirit Wardens know it would risk ripping open the dimension to the spirit world?"

"Because that is what has been passed down from Elder to Elder," Mr. Whittaker's cold voice interrupted their conversation from the doorway, startling Arnold and Bernard. "What is going on here, Bernard?"

"Nothing, sir. Arnold was just asking me about spirit-wielding, having heard the term mentioned at school today."

Mr. Whittaker looked down his nose at Arnold as if he were repulsed by a foul smell. "Perhaps we need to pay a visit to school and check exactly what they are teaching children. To have such knowledge of spirit-wielding is dangerous in its own right, never mind if one was able to actually form a connection with the spirit world." He looked down at his wrist, revealing a large, very expensive looking watch. "I have a meeting in five minutes. Bernard, can you come and see me afterwards?"

"Yes, sir."

"Very well." Mr. Whittaker left, the heels of his finely polished shoes echoing loudly in the corridor.

"You know you can talk to me, Arnold," Bernard said. "You know, if anything has happened."

"I know, Dad." Arnold needed a way out before his father delved in any deeper. "I need to go and train, I best be going."

"Don't overdo it with your training, son. I know why you train so hard. Things haven't been the same since your grandad was killed."

"I could say the same for you with work," Arnold fired back more sharply than he intended. A wave of guilt consumed him when he saw how his words had washed over his father.

Arnold spent the next two hours alone in the training room, practising with his grandad's macuahuitl, which he had been using all summer. He was finally starting to get used to the weight of it and knew he was a lot more effective with it now than he had been when he needed to defend himself against Levent at the tower.

When Arnold finished for the day, he placed the macuahuitl in the weapons rack, then grabbed a quick shower in the changing room, all the while pondering his newfound ability. Levent was more powerful than Arnold. Perhaps if Arnold could master his new power, it would tip the scales in his favour and help him avenge his grandad once and for all. Arnold was certain that at some point, Levent would return, and when he did, Arnold planned to be ready.

Arnold quickly changed into the spare clothes that he left at the Spirit Wardens, itching to meet the others at the lock-up as planned. Dressed in his dark grey jogging bottoms and his sweatshirt, Arnold tugged on his trainers and headed out of the changing rooms. When he exited, Mr. Whittaker and Mayor Redburn were walking into Mr. Whittaker's office. Mayor Redburn noticed Arnold and shot him a look of utter disgust.

Arnold didn't understand why Otto's dad now hated him so much. He also wondered why Mayor Redburn would be having a meeting at the Spirit Wardens, as he'd expressed nothing but animosity for them since Otto's exile.

As frustrating as this was, Arnold pushed this to the back of his mind as he made his way out of the Atheneum, a more pressing issue taking priority.

Who had taken his grandad's artefacts and why had they left them in a storage container for him to find?

CHAPTER 7

Arnold arrived at the lock-up to find Everett and George. Everett was fanning her face for a reprieve from the heat, and George clung to the shadows as if she were a vampire whilst examining the runes etched into the side of the container in amazement.

"Did you see your dad?" Everett asked, leaning against the storage container with her arms folded.

"Yeah, he didn't really go into that much detail." Arnold walked up to the front of the container and held his hand over the elk hieroglyph. Like before, his hand began to tingle again. The mechanism behind could be heard unlocking and Arnold pulled the door back to reveal the contents to the others.

"Wow!" Everett took her hands out of her pocket while admiring the items that were stored inside. "This is pretty cool." She stepped inside the container to take a closer look.

"Pretty strange, more like." George didn't look impressed. "It's too easy, why would someone move all this stuff here?"

Everett cast George a sceptical look as she picked up an old vase and inspected the painted image on it. She squinted before pulling her sleeve over her hand and rubbing the dust away. "What is all this stuff?"

"Things my grandad accumulated over the years from different countries," Arnold told her. "I know there are artefacts in here." He picked up a misshapen bowl and blew the dust off it to inspect it closer. As far as he could tell, it was just a normal dish, so he placed it back on the shelf. "The question is, which ones?"

"What is that?" Everett said, pointing at one of the glass cabinets.

On a little table stood a worn, stone figurine with a large head. Its squinted eyes and thin mouth seemed to denote anger or sadness. Symmetrical raised lumps protruded from the sides of its head, which Arnold assumed were meant to be ears. "I've never seen this before," he said. "It looks like it's wearing a hat."

The small statue's hands were clasped together in front, but the carvings on it were not clear, having been worn with age.

"It's a headdress," George explained. "Looks really old, Arnold. Headdresses usually mean it's of high ranking from wherever it's from."

"It's giving me the creeps," Everett said. "Can we not turn it around so it's not looking at us?"

Laughing, Arnold walked over to the peculiar item and turned the old, worn statue around so that it was facing the opposite way. "Better?"

Everett smiled at Arnold and began rummaging through some of the boxes.

George brushed off a cardboard box, covering her mouth to protect herself from breathing in the dust as she opened it. "Books!" she exclaimed. "These look really old, too. Guys, I really think we should be handing this stuff over to the Spirit Wardens."

"No!" Arnold said. "My grandad kept this stuff for a reason, away from the Spirit Wardens, and we need to find out why."

"Sounds good to me," Everett nodded.

"If you insist, but it doesn't mean I am happy," George finished.

With everyone in agreement, they continued to look through the varying boxes, drawers, and shelving units in the container, eager to see what else Elwood had been collecting. Not that any of them actually knew what the items were.

During their search, they mainly found what appeared to be ornamental items, including the strange statue, various bowls and vases, and a couple of large chalices.

Arnold opened the final box that remained unexamined in the corner of the container. He unfolded the interlocking cardboard to reveal more books, even older looking than the ones George had found. On the top of the pile lay an untitled leatherbound book with a gothic border imprinted into the leather. Within the centre of the leather cover sat a turquoise stone.

Arnold removed it from the box, drawn to the contrast between the dark brown leather and the turquoise. The book had a strange feel to it, and Arnold could feel his hands throbbing slightly, much like the sensation he felt when placing his hand on the hieroglyph outside. Intrigued by the design, he took a large gulp of breath, blowing on the book.

Everett and George peered over his shoulder in hushed silence, as if they, too, could feel that it was significant somehow.

Arnold opened the book and began to carefully flick through the pages. It appeared to be full of journal entries, penned in an outdated handwriting style. Detailed sketches and drawings of different spirit beasts, emblems, totems, and hieroglyphs adorned the pages.

"Any name on it?" Everett asked.

Flicking the book back to the front, Arnold skimmed over the first couple of pages, then flicked to the back, but couldn't find anything. Something seemed familiar to Arnold, however, as he looked intently at the scribed words within the journal. A spark ignited in his head, and he walked over to one of the cabinets, opened a drawer, and removed the letter he had found in the lock-up when he first managed to get inside. He unfolded it and placed it next to the journal, linking the handwriting together.

"It's my grandad's," he confirmed, his heart racing.

No wonder why he had been drawn to it. Arnold loved that he had something that his grandad had written when he was younger, and he wanted to get home as quickly as possible so that he could read it.

"What's that noise?" Everett asked suddenly, perking her head up.

Arnold had been so distracted by the book that he hadn't noticed the low grumbling noise coming from outside of the storage container.

The noise grew louder as it approached.

George froze. "It's – it's back." Her already pale complexion looked as though it had been drained of all blood.

Everett ran to the entrance of the container and pulled the door shut, quickly locking the three of them inside. There was a loud roar followed by a bang as the spirit beast threw itself at the container, the noise echoing terrifyingly around them. It was quiet for minute, and then there was another loud bang.

The beast was trying to get inside.

"What are we going to do?" George's voice trembled as she spoke.

"We need to ring the Spirit Wardens for help," Everett said.

"We can't," Arnold said defensively. "They will find this place."

There was another loud bang from outside, and Arnold realised with alarm that if the thing succeeded at breaking in, they'd be completely cornered. He could have kicked himself; he had brought Everett and George here, he had put them in danger. With a steely grit, he knew he needed to take responsibility, he needed to protect his friends. He scanned the room, desperate for anything he could use as a weapon, his eyes landing on the old coat stand in the corner. Mind racing, he walked over to it and snapped the end off, creating a makeshift spear.

"We are going to open that door," he said. "As soon as I get out there, you shut the door behind me, okay?"

"Are you mad?" Everett snapped.

"I agree with Everett, you can't go out there!"

"I would rather face it out there than in here," Arnold said, his mind made up. "Open the door, shut it behind me," he repeated, a steeliness in his voice.

He nodded to Everett and George and the two of them reluctantly slid the door back. Arnold leapt outside, bracing himself to come face to face with the feral spirit beast as the container quickly shut behind him.

But the beast wasn't there.

Arnold brought his makeshift spear into the air and held it in a defensive position as he cautiously stepped forwards through the overgrown grass. Feeling supercharged with adrenaline, Arnold walked slowly around the grounds. He knew that whatever this spirit beast was, it was in here with him. He could feel its presence, could sense that preying eyes were on him. The sun had nearly dipped below the horizon, casting dramatic shadows around the grounds. There was an eerie quietness as a gentle breeze rustled the tall grass.

The sound of rapid footsteps exploded to Arnold's left. The spirit beast was upon him within seconds, the force of its collision sending him crashing into the side of the storage container behind him. Arnold jumped back to his feet, raising his spear.

Standing in front of him was the same spirit beast that had attacked George, its green, glowing eyes and auro unmistakable. It stood on two legs, its enormous frame slightly yellow in colour with black, circular markings dotted around its skin. Large, jagged teeth protruded from its mouth as it stood growling at Arnold, its large claws visible from its opened hands.

This didn't fit the profile of any spirit beast Arnold had ever heard of, and it was not clear to him what animal this beast even was. It almost seemed more human than animal, the way it stood on its hind legs.

The beast ran at him once more and drew its clawed hand out to swipe at Arnold. Arnold dived to the side, narrowly evading its strike, and the creature clawed down the side of the container instead, drawing sparks from the impact. Arnold spun around and swung his spear, hitting the creature on the back with as much force as he could muster. The impact snapped the frail weapon as soon as it struck the creature's muscular back. Arnold jumped back to avoid another swipe, but the large claws caught his arm, cutting him. He winced and instinctively clutched his arm, knowing he needed to find another weapon, and fast. He grabbed the broken spear and began to motion his bloodied arm in the air to summon his eagle.

The soft, blue glow of his auro began to emit, and within a moment, his spirit beast had appeared to aid him. Sensing that he had an injury, the eagle stood in front of Arnold and fully extended its impressive wingspan, shielding him from view. Moving forwards at speed, the eagle took flight at the strange beast and sank its talons into its shoulders, then took off into the air.

Using its momentum, the eagle let go, sending the spirit beast crashing into the side of a storage container. The incredible force created a significant dent in the side of the metal casing. The beast climbed up from the floor and with a frenzied snarl, began to slice and swipe at the eagle. The eagle used its enormous wings to bat its arms away before jumping on top of a storage container out of its reach. The beast climbed up after the eagle, vaulting the unit with minimal effort and continuing its a volley of attacks.

The eagle launched back into the air and attempted to grab the beast with its talons for a second time, but the beast grabbed its feet and spun the bird through the air as if it were an Olympic hammer thrower.

After spinning a few times, the beast let go, launching Arnold's spirit beast through the air. The eagle bounced off the uneven ground before eventually sliding to a stop in front of Arnold. Arnold dropped to his knees as his eagle's pain became his own, searing down his back and sides with a dull, throbbing ache.

A tingling sensation erupted in Arnold's hands, and they began to glow with latent energy. Unarmed and desperate, Arnold focused on drawing the raw power from the spirit world as he attempted to spirit-wield once more. His knees trembled as he tried to get to his feet, his legs threatening to buckle beneath him.

Nothing happened.

The feral beast dropped down from the container, dirt and dust rising around it as it hit the ground with force. It ran at Arnold once more with relentless speed, throwing itself through the air and landing a dropkick in the centre of Arnold's chest, sending him tumbling backwards.

Arnold gasped for breath, trying to pull himself up, but instead he collapsed back on the floor, unable to pick himself up again. He could hear the feral snarling of the spirit beast as it continued to walk over to him.

Arnold caught a glimpse of the razor-sharp teeth that threatened to tear him apart right before he was scooped into the air as if he weighed nothing. The beast pulled him towards its face with its clawed hands, shredding his sweatshirt in the process. Arnold looked into the green, glowing eyes of the beast and could see nothing but feral rage within them.

The realisation struck him: this spirit beast had no control over what it was doing.

Feeling its warm breath on his face, Arnold felt like his fate was now out of his hands. If only he had been able to spirit-wield, he might have stood a chance.

The loud shriek of his eagle pierced the air as it clattered into the back of the beast, causing it to loosen its grip on Arnold. Sensing his opportunity, Arnold managed to wriggle from its grasp and drop onto the floor. He kicked out at the beast's legs, toppling the creature to the floor. His eagle retook flight, flying high up into the sky before turning and diving straight back down. It hurtled towards the beast, divebombing straight into it.

A plume of dust exploded around them, making it difficult for Arnold to see. When the dust eventually settled, his eagle lay on the floor, its breathing laboured through exhaustion.

The beast stood beside it. However, it seemed different now, calmer almost. It turned its gaze from the battle-worn eagle to Arnold. Its eyes had stopped glowing, and its green auro was gone.

The creature released an ear-splitting roar, then turned and ran towards the far wall of the courtyard. Dropping to all fours, it picked up pace quickly and vaulted over the wall.

Just like that, the spirit beast was gone.

Arnold limped across to his eagle and crouched down next to it, placing his hand on its side. A warm sensation came over him, and the pain in his arm and back began to subside as the eagle's auro wrapped around him like a warm blanket.

Behind him, he heard the storage container open.

"Arnold!" Everett cried as she ran over and wrapped herself around him. "Look at you, that was so stupid." She squeezed him tightly, tears streaming down her face.

"Are you okay?" George asked as she offered her hand out to help him to his feet.

"Yeah," he responded, trying his hardest to downplay his injuries. He grimaced as he climbed back to his feet with George's assistance.

"We need to get you checked over," Everett said, seeing his arm covered in blood.

"We can't hide this spirit beast from your dad, Arnold," George insisted. "He needs to know."

Arnold couldn't help but agree with her. Whatever that thing was, it was dangerous. If he didn't report it and it hurt someone else, he would never forgive himself.

Everett and George stood on either side of him to help prop him up as his eagle began to dissipate back into him.

"What was it?" George asked as she and Everett helped Arnold across the courtyard of the lock-up.

"Like a wild animal. Whatever that spirit beast was, it was not in control. It looked . . ." Arnold frowned, knowing how ridiculous he was about to sound. ". . .It looked kind of human."

That wasn't what concerned Arnold the most, however.

Something else was bothering Arnold even more, something he wasn't ready to share with the others.

The beast had felt familiar, somehow. And now he needed to find out why.

CHAPTER 8

"Where's my son?"

Arnold could hear his mum outside the cubicle where he sat with Everett and George at the hospital.

"He is in bay three, Mrs. Ethon," came the softly spoken voice of one of the nurses.

Eve yanked open the curtains and let out a gasp when she saw Arnold sitting in the hospital bed with his left arm bandaged. Bernard was standing beside her, looking equally concerned.

"Was this him? Was this Levent?" Bernard asked in a panicked state.

Eve rushed over to Arnold and squeezed him tightly.

"Mum, you're hurting me, I'm okay," he gasped, feeling as though he might lose consciousness if his mum hugged him any tighter.

"I don't think it was him," Arnold answered his dad's question. "It was like it was wild, Dad, like it didn't have an anchor. Is that even possible?"

"This doesn't make any sense," Bernard said. "Why would it attack you if it wasn't linked to Levent?"

"I don't know, I just saw these wild green eyes and the way it moved around." Arnold glanced at Everett and George, who gave him encouraging nods to continue. "It was as though it was human," he finished.

"Human?" Eve's tone rose as she spoke.

"I know it sounds crazy," Arnold hastily added.

"Arnold was so brave," Everett announced. "I dread to think what would have happened to us if Arnold hadn't fought it off." She rested her hand delicately on his arm.

Arnold blushed, embarrassed by the fuss being made over him.

A doctor walked in and explained that Arnold needed to have some stitches in his arm, but apart from that, he just needed to rest for a couple of days, and he would be fine. Once the discharge papers had been signed, they left the hospital, dropping Everett and George off at home on the way.

At home, Arnold hobbled up the stairs and entered his room where he collapsed onto his bed, falling asleep almost immediately.

He was at the tower. He wasn't flying, but he was high up on a branch on a nearby oak tree. He hadn't been here in his dream for some time, but once he got his bearings, he soon felt accustomed to being in the form of an eagle once again. As Arnold began to spread his wings to take flight, he was stung by a sharp pain. He quickly re-folded his wings in close to his body, the feeling knocking him sick.

Flying, it seemed, would not be an option. Something like this had never happened to Arnold in his dreams before, and he didn't like it.

He woke to the unwelcome noise of his alarm clock,

feeling as though he had only been asleep for a few moments when it had been seven hours. He pondered the dream, deducing that he must have been feeling the pain his eagle experienced from the fight with the feral spirit beast the day before. Arnold was convinced that when he had these dreams, he was somehow connected to the spirit world.

He slowly sat up in bed, realising he had slept in his ripped, blood-splattered clothes all night. He was lying on top of his quilt, having passed out as soon as his head hit his pillow. Dragging himself up, he got undressed and jumped into the shower to freshen up. His arm was aching from the slash received in the fight and subsequent twelve stitches that he had received to patch him back up.

After his shower, he got himself dressed and ready for school before heading downstairs where he found that the ever-eager paperboy had already been. He picked up the paper from the doormat and took it with him to the dining table to peruse over breakfast.

The headline on the paper caught his attention immediately, the bold letters filling the top half of the paper.

The Beast of Oswaldtwistle – Panic as Local Boy Left Fighting for Life.

Arnold stared at the headline with disapproval, feeling that he had been far from fighting for his life.

A local boy has been left fighting for his life after being attacked by multiple-murder suspect known as Levent. The attack, which took place near Bramley Lock-up, has left the boy in critical condition due to the frenzied encounter. Questions are being asked of why the Spirit Wardens failed to keep a member of the community safe from such an attack.

Earlier this year, Elwood Ethon, a retired Elder, was brutally murdered after the Spirit Wardens were unable to apprehend Levent, despite months of investigations. It is unknown at this time whether last night's victim will make it through the next few days. Questions need to be asked about the Spirit Wardens' ability to keep the town safe from this highly dangerous man. The Spirit Wardens have declined to comment at this time.

Arnold stared at the paper long after he finished reading the article. Whoever had written this had added two and two together and made ten. Not only was he okay aside from some minor injuries that he knew he would recover from in the next week or two, but he was certain that Levent had nothing to do with the attack.

"Dad!" Arnold shouted from the bottom of the stairs. "There's something in the paper that I think you need to read."

When Bernard walked down the stairs, Arnold wordlessly handed him the paper, uncertain what his reaction would be.

Bernard scanned the page, his expression becoming more and more annoyed. "What a load of rubbish," he vented. "This is a way to cause unrest against the Spirit Wardens. Who on earth leaked the attack? Mr. Whittaker ordered a media blackout!"

"It says the attack was Levent, but it wasn't, it was something worse," Arnold insisted, concerned that the creature that attacked him was still on the loose. "What if it attacks someone else? They're pointing fingers in the wrong direction!"

"We have a lot of people out looking for it," Bernard said. "There's no way that it won't be found and killed by the end of the week."

"Killed?" Arnold was shocked. He wanted to put a stop to the danger to be sure, but this seemed to be taking things a bit too far. "What happened to 'capture not kill'?" he demanded.

"This thing is not human. It doesn't need capturing, Arnold; it needs killing!"

"What if it is human?"

"It's not human, it's a spirit beast. You said so yourself."

"Something doesn't seem right," Arnold spoke with certainty. "There was something familiar about it. I don't know what, but I want to find out."

"You need to keep away from this. You're lucky to still be alive."

"Managed to hold my own against it, didn't I? I'm still here because of me and my spirit beast."

"Yes, you have grown stronger, and if not for your training, this could have ended so differently. Don't go looking for the fight though, Arnold!" Bernard said, his voice stern. "I mean it. Just because you know how to fight doesn't mean you actively seek one."

"Who said anything about looking for a fight?" Arnold snapped back. "I want to find out who this is."

"Don't you mean what, not who?"

"I meant what I said," Arnold replied curtly. With this, he threw his bag over his shoulder and walked towards the front door, wincing at the pain that erupted in his arm. He left the house and headed to school, frustrated that his father wasn't listening to him.

Outside, the weather was unusually warm, promising another scorching day. Arnold made his way to the cenotaph in the centre of town to meet up with Everett and George. He could see them already waiting for him from the top of the road, courtesy of his enhanced vision.

When he reached them, Everett ran over to him and launched her arms around him, hugging him tightly.

Arnold winced from the pain of her strong embrace, yet found himself savouring the moment nonetheless.

“I am okay, Everett,” he laughed, “although I’m not sure my arm will be if you hug me any tighter.”

"Sorry." Everett stepped back, allowing Arnold to breathe and giving him an awkward smile. "How are you feeling?" she asked, looking uncharacteristically bashful as she brushed her hair behind her ear. “I can’t believe you managed to fight that thing off.”

"I can't believe you are coming into school," George said. “We saw the paper.” Despite the heat, she still insisted on wearing her favoured beanie hat.

"Yeah, and how wrong have they got it. Levent wasn't even there,” Everett said. “Do you think he had something to do with what happened?"

"Who knows. I do want to find out, though." Arnold spoke with conviction, determined to get to the bottom of this.

"Tell him your idea, George,” Everett said excitedly as they began to walk to school.

George nodded. “I’ve been researching with my granny. I think that with the right remedy, we may be able to make a connection.”

“Connection to what?” Arnold asked.

“To your dreams," she said. "We need to use your link to the spirit world to find him, to find out if he is behind all of this. We need to find Levent.”

CHAPTER 9

After Arnold's grandfather was killed, he'd dreamt of his grandmother and Levent at the tower. Arnold felt certain that his grandma was still alive and trapped in the spirit world, where Elwood had banished her because of how dangerous she had become when her dragon spirit beast corrupted her.

Arnold could remember all too well how Levent had hoped that Arnold himself would have a dragon spirit, and how he had planned to exploit Arnold's anger and hatred for him to let it manifest so that he could take it for himself.

Elwood had simply been collateral damage in Levent's twisted plan. Even worse was the revelation that Levent was Arnold's uncle. Elwood had been murdered by his own son – a son he didn't know he had.

The hatred that Arnold felt for Levent was still eating him from the inside. As for his grandma, she had been trapped in the spirit world for a reason. Arnold had no intention of exploring how she was still there, or how she hadn't appeared to age a day while trapped there, if his dream had been anything to go by.

Anger erupted inside of Arnold. "You want me to use my connection to the spirit world to contact Levent? He's a murderer, George! Or have you forgotten?"

"Hear me out – "

"I haven't got time for this." Arnold set off towards school. He had no intention of making any contact with Levent. Not until he was ready to do what needed to be done to avenge Elwood.

"Arnold!" Everett scolded him. "There's no need to be like that with George! She's only trying to help."

Arnold sighed and reluctantly stopped in his tracks to allow George to finish.

"In the dream you told us about, you saw them, and they saw you," George continued.

Arnold nodded; he could still clearly remember how his grandma had appeared to shift her gaze directly towards Arnold in his dream.

"She interacted with you. What if you could do the same?"

To give her credit, George had a point, and Arnold did agree that if his grandma were able to spot him, then maybe he could communicate with them when he was dreaming. From what Arnold could tell, he was somehow linked with the spirit world when he dreamt of seeing through his eagle's eyes, feeling what it felt and sometimes controlling its movements. He had always felt these were more than just dreams, but after his last experience, Arnold was even more confident that he was directly connecting to the spirit world somehow.

"Even if I wanted to contact them, which I don't by the way, I haven't had any dreams about flying for the last three months." Last night had been the first time in many months that he had dreamt of being in his eagle's body, but he hadn't been able to fly.

He was correct the dreams had stopped abruptly. Although he missed dreaming of that sensation of flying, he didn't want to come face to face with Levent or his grandma given everything that had happened. As much as Arnold wanted revenge on Levent, he was not ready for a confrontation. He needed to be stronger and at full health in order to challenge him.

"I believe there is a remedy we can use," George replied. "Granny will know how to make it."

"I suppose it's an idea," Arnold said. "And at least it gives us something to aim for." He dreaded the thought of coming face to face with Levent again, but at this moment in time, he felt it the only option given that they had nothing else to go off.

As the three of them continued their journey to school, Arnold couldn't help but feel that at some point, their plan was going to backfire on them. Yet, he felt he had a responsibility to locate whatever it was that had attacked him at the lock-up, before anyone else got hurt.

They reached the school grounds and its usual early morning bustling. Many students stood huddled in groups, catching up on the latest gossip. Some were clutching copies of *The Oswaldtwistle Advertiser*.

After leaving Everett and George, Arnold made his way down the winding corridors, exiting one building to take a shortcut he knew, feeling that he'd rather avoid the gossip and curious gazes of his classmates that morning. It was a pathway not meant for students, but he occasionally made the shortcut with no one noticing.

"Ethon!" a voice bellowed from behind him.

Arnold recognised the voice straight away.

"Ethon!" Kaden called again.

"What now?" Arnold snapped back, turning to find Kaden, Caleb, and Piers approaching. He wasn't in the mood for this.

"Where's Otto?" Kaden sneered. "Not around to fight your battles."

"Pretty sure I fought my own battle last I saw you," Arnold said smugly, although in truth, he was ashamed of his actions during their last encounter. Regardless, he had proven in their last confrontation that he was more than a match for Kaden.

Kaden stepped threateningly into Arnold's personal space in an attempt to intimidate him. His dark green energy rippled around him, causing Arnold to take a step back in surprise. Arnold realised he wasn't the only one who had been training over the summer holidays.

"Kaden, you can't summon your spirit beast here," Arnold protested. "If you're caught, you'll be expelled." Getting into a schoolyard quarrel was one thing. Intentionally summoning one's spirit beasts to fight was another.

"Don't tell me what I can't do." Kaden had a look of hatred as he continued to channel his auro. Arnold looked on with a feeling of unease. Surely one of the teachers would pick up on the energy he was emitting.

It seemed that Arnold was on his own, however. He stared Kaden down, refusing to be intimidated by him or his goons. He was stronger than he had ever been and was not going to be pushed around this year.

"Something funny, Ethon?" Kaden growled.

"Nothing really. Just, your nose looks even funnier this close up."

Piers and Caleb stepped forwards, and with ripples of

power, they began to draw on their own auros. Piers's was a dark purple and Caleb's was a turquoise colour.

Arnold took another step back. This was more than a schoolyard grudge, he realised – they truly intended to hurt him.

Before he had a chance to move, Kaden shot forwards and shoved Arnold in the chest. As he did so, his viper spirit beast shot out from his arm, its mouth wide as it attempted to bite Arnold.

Arnold swung his shoulder back, barely dodging the attack, but the movement caused him to grimace as pain from last night's injury engulfed his arm. Piers and Caleb sprung to either side of him and grabbed his arms, restraining him. Arnold struggled against their firm grips, but his right arm was too weakened.

Kaden grinned as he stepped forward. "This should knock you down a peg," he growled. He launched a volley of punches against Arnold's chest and stomach. His viper started to coil itself around Arnold's legs and waist until it had begun to constrict him.

Arnold heaved as the wind was knocked from him, sucking in what air he could through rasping gasps. "Stop!" he yelled, his sides aching and his chest getting tighter as the viper moved higher towards his chest. He desperately tried to loosen his arms, but Piers and Caleb had a firm hold of them. "I can't breathe!" he gasped as Kaden glared at him with pure hatred.

Kaden gave a mirthless laugh. "Is this all you have? Let's face it; you're still just as pathetic as last year." This time, Kaden struck Arnold across the face.

Arnold had no option but to summon his energy from the spirit world, panic overcoming him as he continued to struggle. He drew on enough power to send out a warning ripple as his auro activated and he became shrouded in his own power. It was enough to cause the viper to loosen its grip and that was just the opening Arnold needed. He used Piers and Caleb's weight to lift his legs from the ground and kick Kaden backwards away from him, knocking him to the floor in the process.

Using his momentum, Arnold swung his legs back to the floor and pulled Piers and Caleb down together in front of him, releasing a grimacing, pain-filled roar. As Kaden scrambled back to his feet, Piers swung a haymaker at Arnold, but Arnold quickly manoeuvred out of the way and pushed him backwards into Kaden, knocking the two of them over once again. Caleb attempted to land a punch, but Arnold dodged this with ease. Caleb's large frame meant he was considerably slower than Arnold was.

Arnold landed a blow across Caleb's face, knocking him straight to the floor.

Kaden climbed back to his feet and ran at Arnold, spearing him to the ground, knocking the wind out of him in the process. Arnold knew he was stronger than the three of them individually, but it was three against one and he was limited by his injury.

Kaden began to rain down blows on Arnold's body, clearly determined to prove a point. Arnold braced himself as Kaden swung both arms into the air to deliver a blow, but suddenly he was lifted off of Arnold and slammed to the floor.

Marrok stood there with his arm outstretched. "Need a hand?" he smiled.

Arnold gratefully took Marrok's hand and pulled himself back to his feet.

"Three against one isn't really fair, is it?" Marrok said confidently. He walked over to where Kaden lay on the ground and kicked him in the side, leaving him sprawled out on the floor.

"Now three against, two, I like those odds better." Marrok smirked.

Kaden furiously jumped back to his feet. "Come on, then," he growled.

"What on earth is going on here?" a voice roared from the doorway.

Mr. Higgins was standing there, looking livid. "Follow me, now. All of you."

The charged atmosphere dropped like a stone in a well.

They all scowled but did as they were told and followed Mr. Higgins across the courtyard. Arnold knew straight away that they were being marched to the office of their head of years, Mrs. Elctree.

Mr. Higgins dragged Kaden, Piers, and Caleb into the office first, instructing Arnold and Marrok to sit on the chairs outside.

"Listen," Marrok spoke under his breath. "I know how the Spirit Wardens works. If you get in trouble for fighting here, you will be punished there, too."

"I can't let you take the blame."

"I'm the new kid. After this, everyone will leave me alone, and you won't get reprimanded at the Spirit Wardens. Win-win, really. Just follow my lead, okay?"

It didn't sit well with Arnold, but he felt that Marrok had given him little choice in the situation.

A few minutes later, Kaden and his goons scurried out of the office, and Mr. Higgins led them away to another room.

"You two in here, please," Mrs. Elctree's stern voice called. "Sit there." She gestured to the chairs on the other side of her desk, then sat forwards with her fingers interlocked, her glasses perched on the end of her pointed nose. "Tell me what happened."

"They jumped Arnold, miss. I got there, and the three of them were beating him up. So I ended it." Marrok spoke before Arnold had the chance to say anything.

"You're saying you caused all three of their injuries because they were beating Arnold up? Is this true, Arnold?"

Arnold didn't know what to say, so he simply nodded in agreement even though this didn't feel right to him.

"Fighting is forbidden at this school, whether or not it is justified in your eyes. I'm sorry, Marrok, I am going to have to call your mum. You are suspended for the rest of the week. The same goes for Kaden, Piers, and Caleb." She pushed her glasses back up her nose before continuing. "Arnold, I suggest you go to class, if you are okay to do so."

“Maybe Ethon would benefit with the rest of the day off, given the current state of him?” Mr. Higgins said. Arnold hadn’t noticed him hovering outside the doorway.

"Very well. I will contact your parents."

When Arnold stood up to make his way out of the office, he glanced back to find Marrok discreetly giving him the thumbs up. Arnold knew he now had the rest of the day to look into the creature that attacked him.

“Wait outside until your parents come to pick you up,” Mrs. Elctree said, using her eyes to sternly point at the door. “I do not expect to see this from any of you again for the rest of the school year!”

Mr. Higgins held the door open for the two of them to leave and Arnold and Marrok obliged, walking back out into the hall where Kaden, Piers, and Caleb all sat silent and stoney faced.

“Perhaps you two can come and wait at my office,” Mr. Higgins said as he closed Mrs. Elctree’s office door behind him. "It is quite clear you boys cannot be trusted to be left with one another."

Kaden stared into Arnold as if he wanted to rip him apart. Arnold simply stared back; he wasn't intimidated by him anymore.

"Now," Mr. Higgins said as he continued his walk towards his office. Not wanting to get into any more trouble, they both quickly followed.

When they reached his office, Mr. Higgins opened his door and sternly said, "Inside, now." It was a side to Mr. Higgins that Arnold had not seen before, and it made him nervous. After he and Marrok entered, Mr. Higgins slammed the door shut behind him.

"Do you two take me for an idiot?" Mr. Higgins demanded. "It's quite clear you were involved in the fight, Ethon, I could see your bloody auro when I arrived!" He walked to his desk and sat down, exhaling deeply. "If I had told Mrs. Elctree, you would have all been expelled, and there goes your education. I am sure the Spirit Wardens would not have been thrilled, either."

"But – " Arnold began to argue his defence.

"Save it. You really have let yourselves down, boys." Mr. Higgins looked at Marrok. "Can you give us a moment?"

"Yes, sir," Marrok said before leaving as instructed.

"Are we still on for practising this spirit-wielding?" Mr. Higgins asked. Though he still looked frustrated, his tone had changed, and Arnold suspected he was trying to hide his excitement.

Arnold had completely forgotten that he was meant to be sitting with Mr. Higgins tonight, after everything that had been happening.

"I've been reading up, and I think I can help you," Mr.

Higgins continued. "Take the rest of today to rest and we will go through what I have found on Friday."

"Yes, sir," Arnold said.

"Now, go wait outside with Marrok, and try to keep yourself out of bother." Mr. Higgins look exasperated. "I dread to think what would have happened if it was another teacher who caught you all fighting."

"Thank you, sir," Arnold replied sheepishly before leaving the room.

Arnold, however, dreaded to think what would have happened if Marrok hadn't shown up.

AROUND LUNCHTIME, a text came through from George: *Heard that you got sent home I'm at Granny's shop as planned you should come here G x.*

Quickly getting changed out of his uniform, Arnold made the ten-minute walk to Rushton's Remedies. The bell rang as he entered though the wooden doorway, and George and her granny looked up straight away.

"How are you?" George asked. "I heard what happened. As if they suspended Marrok."

"I'm fine, just a little achy. I should have been suspended, too. Marrok took the fall, insisted on it." He brought his hand up to his aching arm. "I don't suppose you have anything that can help with this pain?" he asked. He didn't care how foul the concoction tasted if it helped reduce his pain.

George's granny was standing with her back turned to the two of them. Arnold could see her motioning her hands, and what looked like steam or smoke rose in front of her, casting a floral smell around the room. By the usual standards, it was quite pleasant. She then leant over slowly to pull out a flask which she placed on the worktop, her arched back reflective of her age as she continued to tinker and toil with her brew.

While waiting, Arnold looked around the shop. It was as ramshackle as the first time he had visited, and he still found it fascinating that they were able to find anything in here amongst the clutter. His eyes searched over the cabinet he had knocked over last time he was in here, and he noticed the chalice was gone.

Panicking, he asked, “Where’s the chalice? I didn’t break it, did I?”

Edith didn’t look up from grinding up some herbs with a pestle and mortar, which she then added to another bowl in front of her. Using a small step that she could move around the shop given her short stature, she reached for a ladle from the rack above her. She then used this to scoop the liquid from the bowl, transferring it to a flask.

Finally, she said, “It was just an old thing, don’t worry,” then handed the flask to Arnold. "Here, drink this dear."

Reluctantly, Arnold accepted the flask, unable to decide whether it was smoke or steam rising from the concoction within. As nice as it smelt, it looked awful, like a mud pie fused with petals. He drank it as quickly as possible, hoping to evade the foul taste. Three large gulps in, he gagged as he struggled to finish it. It tasted exactly how it looked – like thick, grainy sludge.

George's granny laughed. "What did you expect, lemonade? That's a family remedy that my mother taught me when I was just a young girl. Tastes terrible, but those aches and pains you are feeling will slowly subside soon, I promise."

It was telling how much Arnold trusted her, given that

he had just drunk the vile liquid without even asking what it was first.

"Georgina tells me you can connect with the spirit world through your dreams?" she asked as she walked back around to the other side of the counter. "Very rare indeed, if it's true."

"I used to have dreams that I was flying. Then my spirit beast turned out to be an eagle. Since then, my dreams have mostly stopped."

"I see. It may be that now the connection is complete, there is no need for these dreams or visions." She began to putter about, picking up different herbs and remedies and putting them into a fresh bowl. "Now, it might be that you just experienced dreams. However, if there is a true connection, you need to be very careful not to interact with anything on the other side." The tone of her voice changed as she continued to grind and add herbs to her latest remedy. "If you interact with something that is in the spirit world, you run the risk of it trapping you there."

Knowing their plan was to contact Levent in the spirit world, Arnold did not like keeping this from George's granny.

As if reading Arnold's mind, George cut him off before he could say anything. "We just want to see if it's a dream or if it's a true connection."

Arnold was surprised at George's omission of the truth, given how close she was with her granny. If Arnold felt unsure about contacting Levent, he felt even more uneasy now that he had been warned he could get trapped in the spirit world.

Edith cast her a look that implied that she didn't fully believe the words that had just come out of George's mouth.

"I trust you, Georgina." The way she said it almost seemed like a warning.

"George, Granny, not Georgina," George corrected her.

"That is not the name you were given at birth. It's not the name I will be using for you." She gave George a quizzical look. "No matter how many times you ask me." She finished what she was doing and poured the fine powder that she had created into a little brown bag before sealing it and passing it to Arnold. "Here you go. Just add some boiling water before you go to sleep and inhale the vapours that it produces. If there is a connection, you will know about it by the time you have woken up."

"Thank you," Arnold said gratefully. The remedy he had just drunk seemed to already be kicking in, as his aches seemed to be quickly subsiding.

Edith simply smiled as she grabbed a broom and began sweeping around her worktable. "You're going to be late back, Georgina," she said, not looking up.

Arnold walked George back to school and saw her off at the gates before heading back to his house with the powder that her granny had given him. He planned to follow her instructions and use the powder before going to sleep that night. But a new concern pressed down against him the more he ruminated on what George's granny had said. There was a risk of him getting trapped in the spirit world. Was that a risk he was willing to take?

CHAPTER 10

It had been a long and tedious afternoon and evening with Arnold lying on his bed staring at his clock waiting for time to pass by. Edith's remedy had worked wonders, and he felt so much better after drinking it. What it didn't help with was the lecture he had received from his parents about his fight at school. Even if the school believed Marrok's story, Arnold's parents were not daft. They knew that Arnold had been more involved than he let on. He could still hear his dad's patronising voice reminding him that he needed to walk away from those situations, but it felt so good to show Kaden and his goons that they wouldn't be able to push him around anymore.

Yet, Arnold couldn't help but feel guilty about Marrok being suspended when he should have been as well, but Marrok was right; he would have received a further reprimand by the Spirit Wardens for fighting, and it could have jeopardised his future with them.

Finally, it was half past nine, so Arnold headed downstairs to the kitchen with the powder and boiled it into a tea as instructed. Once back in his room, he placed the bowl on top of his drawers and leant over it to breathe in the vapours which smelled like Parma Violets. He exhaled too quickly at first, the steam scalding his throat. Arnold coughed, then tried again more carefully this time.

After a few minutes, the vapour began to fade as the liquid cooled. Taking this as a sign he had inhaled enough, Arnold sat on his bed and waited for something to happen. He didn't feel any different and wasn't sure what to expect. Finally, he lay down on his bed, and before he knew it, he had drifted off into the deepest sleep.

The sensation of soaring high was just as exhilarating as he remembered. He had missed that unique chill from the wind as it pushed back against his feathers, the vibrations soothing the strain he felt from the wings keeping him in flight. Looking down, he could see the shimmer from the sun reflecting on the lake beneath him. The pine trees around it and the mountain range looked familiar, and he knew that he recognised the area. He changed his flight path accordingly and began to fly in the direction of the tower, which he knew lay just beyond the mountains in front of him.

He had missed this feeling and wow, did it feel good. He felt free. Up here, he was invincible. Nothing could touch him. He wished he could stay like this forever, with the picturesque landscape below like something one would see in the most detailed oil painting. It was so beautiful that it didn't seem real.

Arnold rode wave after wave of wind. Rising high in the sky, he would dip suddenly, the rush of which would spike his adrenaline before using the pressurised force to push himself higher in the air. He repeated this process over and over until eventually, he could see a familiar building in the distance at the top of a hill. It was the tower where he last saw Levent and his grandma conversing, when she had seen him perched on a tree watching them.

Arnold had never mentioned this dream to his father. He feared it would be too painful for Bernard to learn that his mother might still be alive, trapped in the spirit world, and Arnold didn't think any good could come from opening that can of worms, not after everything he had learned.

He wondered if they would both be there again, and if they were, how he would communicate with them. He was in the form of an eagle, and last time he checked, eagles couldn't talk. It was an obstacle he hadn't even considered.

Gliding gracefully, Arnold landed on a window ledge of the tower and peered through the glass, looking for a sign that someone was around. He spotted movement around through a doorway at the far corner of the room. Jumping out from the window, Arnold glided further around the tower to land on a windowsill, eager to get a better look at the figure.

Levent was laid out on the floor doing press-ups, wearing a black tank top. Arnold had never seen him without his large black overcoat on.

He must have been training for a while, given the amount of sweat that was pouring off him. His focus appeared undeterred. After around five minutes, he stopped and picked up a glass of water from the table, taking a long drink before placing it back down. His face had the same look of anger etched on it that Arnold remembered from their last encounter.

Just as Arnold was wondering if this look was permanently fixed on Levent's face, a crooked smile overcame him. Without turning around, Levent said, "I wondered when you would come back again." His voice was as menacing as ever, a hostile undertone to his words.

Arnold's heart sank. Levent had noticed him, and he hadn't thought about what to do at this point.

Levent's gaze settled directly on Arnold. Then he began to slowly walk towards where Arnold was perched on the windowsill.

Arnold panicked and jumped backwards, quickly realising that there was no hard surface behind him. He flapped his wings to regain his balance and stop himself from falling.

Levent gestured for Arnold to come in through the partially opened window. "You have come a lot closer than you did last time I saw you here. Either you are feeling a lot more confident, or you're here to confront me." His wild grin intensified as if he relished the thought of a confrontation.

Arnold had come here to talk, not fight, but he couldn't speak the words in his eagle form. What's more, he didn't trust Levent at all, and knew if he stepped through the window that he would be in Levent's territory, and Edith's warning weighed heavily on his mind.

Having had the displeasure of being trapped in the basement within the tower when he was kidnapped by Raine just a few months earlier, Arnold knew deep down that he never wanted to step foot within those stone walls again.

With no other way to communicate, Arnold began to tap over and over on the window. He moved his head in the direction away from the tower.

Levent laughed. "You should know you can be trapped here. That wouldn't be of any use for me. I have a bigger plan for you." He turned around and began training once more, lashing out at a makeshift mannequin. "She, however . . ." he looked over his shoulder past Arnold.

A large shadow began to form around Arnold. He spun round to see a large, dark creature hurtling towards him at speed. Not having much time to take in any details apart from the large, intimidating wingspan of the creature before him, Arnold dropped from the ledge and then stretched out his wings to glide up into the air as quickly as possible.

Their trajectories crossed, but Arnold whipped away, feeling a blast of wind from the large creature's movement. His heart was pounding. Another moment later and who knows what would have happened to him.

Arnold continued to fly as fast as he could, not even wanting to think what would happen if the spirit beast behind him were to catch up.

He barrelled towards the mountains, to safety, but the wind was pushing against him. He decided he had to turn slightly and use the power from the wind rather than fighting against it. Seeing a pine forest not too far away, he realised that this would be his best chance for cover. He reached the wooded area quickly and flew between the trees at speed, not waiting to see if the monstrous creature was close behind him. He soon realised that he had flown in too fast. He narrowly managed to dodge one tree before clipping his wing against the branch of another. He went crashing down to the ground –

Arnold sat bolt upright in bed, cold sweat pouring from his face. He knew straight away that that was far too close for comfort, and he didn't want to do that again any time soon. He had interacted with Levent in the spirit world and narrowly escaped from what he presumed was his grandma's dragon spirit beast.

Arnold's chest pounded. He began to breathe through his nose and out through his mouth, attempting to calm down before heading to the bathroom to wash his face. After getting a glass of water from downstairs, Arnold returned to his bedroom and lay back down on his bed.

It was half past four in the morning. Arnold did not go back to sleep for fear of crossing back over to the spirit world, terrified of would happen if he were to come across his grandma once more.

Arnold hadn't learned anything about the feral spirit beast that had attacked him. But he had learned one thing: Levent had a bigger plan for him.

And that scared Arnold more than anything.

CHAPTER 11

"Never again," Arnold spoke with conviction as he headed to school with Everett and George.

"You look shattered," Everett said, squeezing Arnold's hand tightly.

"Granny did warn you."

"He said he has a bigger plan for me, that he had no intention of trapping me in the spirit world," Arnold said, still shaken. "He also said he hadn't seen me since my grandma spotted me three months ago, so I don't think he has anything to do with the creature that attacked me."

"Don't forget that he has an army of menials out there, Arnold," Everett highlighted. "He could just as easily be getting one of them to do his dirty work. Like he did with that receptionist at your Spirit Wardens."

Arnold knew that Everett was right. Levent could be getting one of his menials to attack him with the use of an artefact. However, deep down, he just didn't believe this, and he couldn't shake the feeling that he knew the feral spirit beast somehow.

"What now?" George asked. "We haven't got anything to go off."

"I have a feeling that Levent will be paying a visit soon," Arnold said. “I reckon it's only a matter of time.”

"That's a dangerous game to play, Arnold," Everett expressed her concern. "Don't forget, this guy has murdered people."

Arnold’s anger flared. "I don't need reminding, thank you!" he snapped.

A sad looking Everett let go of Arnold's hand as they continued their journey.

"Sorry, I didn't mean to," Arnold replied quickly, overcome with guilt.

"It's okay, but you need to realise you can't bite everyone's head off every time they mention your grandad."

Arnold knew that Everett was right, as usual. However, he couldn't help but feel the rush of anger that overcame him every time he thought about what Levent had done to Elwood.

Arnold had been tied up and made to witness Levent and his grandad fight to the death. Elwood had been surprisingly strong and was able to hold his own against Levent and his two giant lion spirit beasts, even managing to fell one off the lions during the battle. It was then that Levent revealed a stunning truth: Arnold’s grandma hadn’t been destroyed by her spirit beast the way Arnold thought she had. Instead, Elwood had trapped Arnold’s grandma in the spirit world when her dragon spirit beast had corrupted her. Not only that, but she was pregnant with Levent at the time, meaning he had grown up in the spirit world, his existence completely unknown to Elwood or anyone else. Somehow, Levent had managed to find a way to travel between there and here.

Arnold's stomach churned as he thought about being powerless from stopping Levent from burying his blade into Elwood's side. The anger it caused him had given Arnold the strength to break free and harness the power of his eagle spirit beast for the first time.

If only Arnold had been able to summon it just a few seconds sooner, maybe Elwood would still be alive. Would still be around to talk Arnold through his worries, to wind him up about girls.

Arnold just wished he could see his grandad one more time.

But Elwood was gone, and he wasn't ever coming back. Being part of the Spirit Wardens meant that Arnold had to abide by their laws. If he were to take Levent's life in revenge, he would be kicked out of the Spirit Wardens, dishonouring himself and his family. Arnold loved every second of being involved at the Spirit Wardens, and knew he couldn't compromise his future with them.

And yet, Arnold couldn't get past his deep need to avenge Elwood somehow.

After a pleasantly dull day at school, Arnold headed towards the Spirit Wardens to continue with his training. He often found that the physical aspects of training were a great way of relieving any stress or frustration he was feeling, and it was exactly what he needed today.

As Arnold walked down by the canal that ran down the side of Oswaldtwistle, he remembered an afternoon when he'd walked down this very road with Elwood. Elwood had launched into a history of the factories, and at the time, Arnold had found the story insufferably boring. Now, though, he'd have given anything to listen to Elwood drone on about the good old days.

With fresh eyes, Arnold suddenly found himself admiring the old, abandoned factories that followed the other side of the canal, smiling to himself as he remembered Elwood's tales.

Back in the day, Oswaldtwistle had been front and centre for various trades given its convenient location, with access to land and ability to join onto the canal that passed through it heading to Leeds one way and Liverpool the other. The factories were ideal points for manufacturing things such as cotton, as they could be traded between the two cities, maximising profits. Oswaldtwistle's other primary source of income had been the coal mines that ran deep below the town. However, after the mining strikes, the tunnels became desolate.

All that stood now was nothing more than empty shells around the town, with smashed windows and graffiti-covered walls.

When Arnold arrived at the Spirit Wardens, he could see that the new receptionist was busy typing away. Not wanting to interrupt, he quietly followed the checkerboard floor to his left, put his finger on the pressure pad next to the training room, and waited for it to bleep to give him access. Once it did, he quickly got himself dressed into his training robes and headed across to the weapons room to take out his grandad's old macuahuitl, which Elwood had acquired when he was younger and still working as a Doyen for the Spirit Wardens.

Arnold picked it up and began to move it slowly through the air, its intricate carvings blurring in front of him. Over the past three months, he'd become intimately aware of its weight as well as how best to balance it when wielding.

Unlike most weapons, the macuahuitl was heaviest at its hilt, making it quite tricky to balance, but Arnold had slowly gotten used to this. He held the blade in both hands and began to move back and forth, practising different moves that his father had been teaching him. He spent around half an hour honing his defensive stances and blocks before switching to another thirty minutes of offensive strikes.

When he trained with this weapon, Arnold somehow felt connected to his grandad. Knowing that this had been Elwood's weapon of choice brought Arnold comfort and focus while training.

That was when Arnold suddenly remembered the journal he had found in the lock-up. He'd been so distracted by the attack that he'd completely forgotten about it.

Arnold checked his watch. He wouldn't have time to retrieve Elwood's journal this evening, as he was supposed to meet Mr. Higgins at school about spirit-wielding. He made a mental note to get it as soon as he could as he headed to the school.

It was strange walking through the grounds of the school when it was empty. It gave Arnold a real end-of-days feeling as he traversed the eerie, quiet grounds.

When he arrived at the entrance to Mr. Higgins's office, he gave a light knock.

"Come in," Mr. Higgins said.

Arnold entered to find Mr. Higgins dressed in sweatpants and a sweatshirt with an old book opened in his hands. It was odd to see Mr. Higgins in such casual attire.

"Ah, Ethon," he started, "I was beginning to think you had forgotten again." He closed the book in his hand with a prompt snap.

"Sorry, sir, I had my training first."

"If you've already trained, you may be weakened for our session?"

"Our session, sir?" Arnold asked, puzzled. "I thought we'd just be doing research and stuff."

Mr. Higgins looked down at his slightly plump physique and let out a chortle. "Because teachers in my shape don't do any exercise?"

"That's not what I meant, sir."

Mr. Higgins laughed again. "Don't worry, no offence taken. Follow me."

After a short walk through the school, they arrived at the sports hall where Mr. Higgins opened up the book he had been reading and started flicking through it.

"What book is that?" Arnold asked. It didn't look like a textbook. It had a leatherbound cover similar to his grandad's journal, Arnold realised.

"This old thing is where I find the information that the Spirit Wardens are less inclined to share," Mr. Higgins said. "I always believe in widening your knowledge on sources outside of those where we are directed. It is often in those spaces where you obtain the truth."

Arnold simply blinked, unsure what Mr. Higgin was getting at. "Okay, sir," he said simply. "What do you want me to do?"

"Now, did your grandparents ever mention possessing the skill to spirit-wield?" Mr. Higgins asked.

"My grandparents?" Arnold asked, startled by the question.

"Maybe even your parents? From what I have read, you have to have a very specific connection to the spirit world to be able to spirit-wield. That type of connection is usually only passed on via bloodline."

"How do you know that?" Arnold asked. His parents

wouldn't have kept something like this from him, would they? Arnold frowned, remembering how his father hadn't wanted to tell him about the possibility of his spirit beast being a dragon. Was there more his parents were hiding from him?

"This very book," Mr. Higgins replied. "I believe I can help you channel this raw power you seem to be able to harness." He put the book down and rubbed his hands together as if in anticipation. "Now, this is not going to be easy by any stretch, and it is dangerous. After all, you're going to be allowing your body to flood with energy from the spirit world. At any moment if you want to stop, we stop." There was a sudden seriousness to his tone. "You will have to push yourself harder than ever before. Is this something you feel up to?"

"It is," Arnold said confidently. After all, if he could spirit-wield by accident, how hard could it really be to do it on purpose?

"You managed to fire an arrow with raw spirit energy, unharnessed. This shows the powerful connection you have to the spirit world. In that raw state, however, you could have caused more damage to the surrounding area. Normally, you would need the use of an artefact to help harness the power, to anchor it."

"But we don't have any artefacts," Arnold pointed out.

"Exactly," Mr. Higgins said in an almost frustrated tone. "We have the Spirit Wardens to thank for that. You managed to spirit-wield without an artefact that first time, so I have every faith that you could do so again." He walked to the centre of the sports hall and beckoned Arnold to follow him.

"Now, from what I have read, artefacts help you wield specific weapons. If you have the hilt of a sword, you would be able to use it to anchor a blade. If you had the pommel of an axe –"

"I'd be able to summon an axe," Arnold finished. "And that's why I summoned an arrow. Because I was holding a bow."

"I would go as far to assume you forced out a blast of energy," said Mr. Higgins, beaming as though excited by the prospect. "Are you ready to begin?"

Although nervous, Arnold felt up for the challenge. He nodded, awaiting further instruction.

"First you need to focus on your spirit beast, focus on its power, the energy that it creates."

Arnold began to focus on his spirit beast until he felt a surge inside; he knew from the feeling that he had linked with his eagle. He nodded at Mr. Higgins to tell him that he was ready to proceed.

"That's the easy part. Now, focus on the trait that your spirit beast intensifies."

"What do you mean?"

"Keep focused, Ethon. Think to when you summoned your eagle for the first time. The feelings you experienced are what triggered your connection and finally enabled you to connect with it."

Arnold went back to when he summoned it for the first time and again felt a surge of anger as he recalled being tied up while his grandad was killed.

No sooner did he feel the rush of anger, Arnold was disabled by what felt like an electric shock. He cried out as he dropped flat to the floor, his muscles tightening up as though he had a horrendous, all-body cramp.

"Break your connection, Ethon!"

Arnold was trying but continued to writhe on the floor in agony. The pain was immense. He could not break the connection, he didn't know how. It was as though he was magnetised to it and unable to break free from the raw energy of the spirit world.

Mr. Higgins knelt and grabbed hold of Arnold. "Accept the energy that is coursing through you. You need to learn to harness it. Look at me, accept that pain, Arnold."

Arnold opened his eyes and looked at Mr. Higgins, but it was too difficult. His body continued to convulse. He didn't know how much longer he could stand this. After a few moments, he could hear Mr. Higgins's words becoming more and more muffled as he slipped into unconsciousness.

When he woke, Arnold was unsure how long he had been out. What he did know was that his body was aching even more than ever.

"Here, drink this." Mr. Higgins passed him something that looked and smelt similar to the remedy George's granny had given him.

Arnold sat up and accepted the drink. Remembering the foul taste, he drank it in one go.

"Let's try again," Mr. Higgins pressed.

"What?" Arnold spoke, alarmed at what was being asked of him.

"I told you this wasn't going to be easy. You need to develop your strength so you can maintain that energy without crumpling to the floor like you just did."

Arnold didn't like the idea of doing this, but understood that to get stronger, he needed to keep trying. He reluctantly climbed back to his feet and gathered himself.

It was going to be a long night.

CHAPTER 12

Arnold spent the next two months settling into the new school year after having a rough start. He was intent on putting his head down and keeping a low profile. Things seemed to have quietened down following his fight with Kaden and his goons, with Kaden opting to leave him alone for the moment.

Marrok's plan had worked. He had risen quite high in the popularity rankings at school after news soon spread about him taking on Kaden, Caleb, and Piers by himself, and Arnold didn't betray their secret.

Arnold had not had any further dreams, nor did he want to after his last experience. Most nights Arnold struggled to get to sleep, worried that he would slip across to the spirit world.

What he had been doing was training intently with Mr. Higgins nearly every night to further hone his spirit-wielding skills. He was still violently convulsing on the floor with raw energy from the spirit world surging through him whenever they practised, and Mr. Higgins had told him that it would be some time before he was able to channel this effectively.

Every night he would do as Mr. Higgins had instructed and focus on what he felt when his grandad had died. Every time he did this however, his body just could not cope with his auro, and it would resort to him becoming a groaning heap on the floor.

Arnold, however, was determined to succeed, no matter how painful or embarrassing the failed process was. He had failed to spirit-wield when the feral beast had disarmed him at the lock-up, and Arnold knew that things could have ended very differently then. He needed to be prepared for what was to come, whether it was Levent or another attack by the unknown creature.

Arnold had racked his brain about the strange spirit beast, but the only person he could imagine being behind it was Levent. And yet, he believed Levent when he claimed not to have seen Arnold in months.

Tonight, Arnold had been doing his usual training at the Spirit Wardens, but between dividing his time between physical training here and spirit-wielding training with Mr. Higgins, he was exhausted. Knowing his body was at its maximum threshold and feeling as though he could vomit at any moment, Arnold decided to call it a night. He took a seat on the bench at the side of the room while gathering his breath, sweat dripping down his face. After a short break, he packed up his bag and exited the training room for the night, walking ever so gingerly down the corridor due to his aching muscles. He was getting used to the aching now, but it did not mean that it hurt any less. His pain threshold was increasing, though.

It was later than when he usually left tonight. The sun had begun to set and his rumbling stomach reminded him that he was still yet to eat anything substantial this evening. He could already hear the lecture his mum would give him when he finally returned home.

As Arnold made it to the bottom of the corridor, he began to hear an echoed conversation coming from the offices. Initially, Arnold didn't think anything of it, but then he recognised one of the voices.

It was Mayor Redburn, conversing with Mr. Whittaker again. Once again, Arnold found it odd that Mayor Redburn was here at all.

"I will ensure that no one asks any questions," Mr. Whittaker's words echoed down the corridor.

Arnold stopped in his tracks, intrigued. He decided to loiter around for a while to listen to what was being discussed. They must have thought that the Spirit Wardens was empty, given how brazenly they were both talking.

"Remember, this benefits both of us," Mayor Redburn responded. "People will start to whisper if they find out. The last thing we want is the paper get wind and cause a panic."

"I would suggest that you take care of this operation, Mayor Redburn," Mr. Whittaker said. "We need proof of" – he cut himself short before continuing – "not everyone will agree with us."

"As soon as we get access to the coal mine, you'll be the first to know. It's only a matter of time."

The coal mine? Why would they be trying to access the coal mine after it had been shut for over forty years? Arnold was equally confused as to why they were trying to keep this a secret, but they clearly thought they were alone.

Arnold made for the door quietly, trying his hardest not to let his trainers squeak on the finely polished floor and betray his presence. He slowly exited the Spirit Wardens, wondering what Mayor Redburn and Mr. Whittaker were up to.

Arnold was not Mr. Whittaker's biggest fan, but he was pretty certain that Mayor Redburn hated Mr. Whittaker, given that he had thrown Otto out of the Spirit Wardens with no chance of ever returning, exiled like he was a traitor or a criminal. Arnold was surprised that he had heard the two of them in the same room, making plans to work together.

He continued his journey home trying to think why they would want to re-open the mine. He could not come to any conclusions.

Making the short journey home, Arnold hung his bag up in the hallway before heading to the kitchen to see what his mum had prepared him for tea. It was enchiladas tonight. They were cold, so he put them in the microwave to heat them up. He stood there waiting patiently while the microwave continued to make its loud humming noise.

He placed them on a plate and moved through to the dining room to tuck in, the smell of the enchiladas making Arnold even more hungry than he was before.

"You should start getting back at a decent time."

Arnold sighed. He had been waiting for his mum to surface and begin her lecture about making sure he was eating correctly to keep his energy levels up. Too tired to argue, he began making his way through the cheese-covered delights at an impressive rate.

"Slow down. You will give yourself indigestion," Eve told him disapprovingly.

Arnold took the advice and slowed down, not wanting any more lectures. "Sorry, Mum, I didn't realise what the time was."

"You have been at the Athenaeum a lot this week. Maybe have a rest tomorrow?"

Arnold hadn't told either of his parents about his extra training at school with Mr. Higgins.

"We'll see," Arnold responded, knowing that he had no intention of having a day off. "There is one thing."

"What's that?"

"The coal mines, where do they run underneath?"

"Why?" she asked, apparently puzzled by the random question.

At this point, the front door opened, and Arnold's dad walked into the dining room, his weary face showing the signs of tiredness from his busy day at work.

"Arnold was just asking me about the coal mines," Eve told him.

"Why?" Bernard asked, sounding suspicious.

"Erm . . ." Arnold wasn't sure if he should disclose the conversation he had overheard, but decided it couldn't hurt. "I overheard Mayor Redburn and Mr. Whittaker talking about the coal mines. I think Mayor Redburn wants to re-open them."

Judging by his reaction, Arnold knew straight away that his father didn't know anything about the deal he had overheard being struck.

"I am sure Mayor Redburn has his reasons," Bernard added. "Perhaps there is more work to be done down there that can fetch some much-needed money to the town." He started moving around awkwardly. Arnold couldn't help but think his dad wasn't being entirely honest with him, and one thing he already knew was that his dad was a terrible liar. He thought back to the offence his dad once caused when he tried to tell his mum that the dress she was wearing suited her. The awkwardness he was showing now was the same, if not worse, than that day.

"Where do they run?" Arnold pressed, asking the question again. "The mines, where do they run?"

"They run for miles and miles underneath the town. It is one of the reasons we closed them down. The deeper you dig, the more chance there is of something going wrong." Bernard gave Arnold a steady look before saying, "Leave this, Arnold. Don't dig around in things that you don't need to."

Bernard's reaction confirmed that there was definitely more to this than he was letting on, however Arnold didn't think he would get any more from his dad.

After his parents left the room, Arnold sat and finished his tea, pondering what he had heard. He knew that his father wasn't telling him everything he knew about the coal mine, but one way or another, Arnold intended to find out. He finished his tea and headed up to his bedroom and worked on some of his homework. He felt as though all his spare time was spent on school or training, and that he couldn't catch a break at the moment.

After pushing himself so hard at training, he felt as though he had little energy left to work out the various math equations that he needed to do by the morning. Arnold hated algebra more than any other subject at school. He found it a pointless exercise. Who on earth used algebra in real life?

Arnold scribbled down a few answers before eventually losing his patience with it and putting down his pencil. Looking down at his desk, he felt that he could just put his head down and go to sleep, he felt well and truly drained.

Trying to juggle the two was catching up with him, and he was only two months into the new school year. If he had to choose, he would simply focus on his training at the Atheneum with the Spirit Wardens, but they had made it clear that if he was to remain with them, he had to continue to pass his classes at school. Whether he liked it or not, he was going to have to learn to focus on both.

CHAPTER 13

With a bang, he clattered into the side of the wooden hut with considerable force, which knocked him sick instantly. His head felt fuzzy from the blow, but he refused to stay on the floor. Refused to show any weakness.

He had been through this process many times as the woman continuously beat him, but he didn't know why. It had been like this for a few years now.

Often for long periods, he would find himself left to fend for himself. He had even learned to grow vegetables throughout the year, and he had managed to bring back tins of food from time to time from the other world, but he still didn't have any control over when he went there. He especially liked the tinned peaches in syrup and bacon grill that he had managed to get his hands on. He was a survivalist even though he was only fifteen years old. He had needed to learn. Otherwise, he simply wouldn't be here.

Then she would arrive, sporadically, out of the blue and when not expected. During these visits, all she would do is inflict pain and suffering on him, tell him how disappointing he was, then leave. This was a process he had gone through time and time again for as long back as he could remember. Sometimes it would take a few days to recover from his injuries, sometimes weeks. The horrific scar he had on his face had taken months to heal fully. Even though it was from when he was a boy, it still burned every day as though a red-hot poker was pressed continuously against his face. It was a sensation that he had become accustomed to, one that he had to accept and learn to get on with, just like these intermittent beatings.

He hated her with every ounce of his being, but he never tried to run, never tried to fight back, because that just made things worse, the beatings more severe.

His legs were buckling, and he recognised the familiar feeling of being winded. The woman grabbed him by the scruff of his already tattered clothes and lifted him towards her as if he weighed nothing. Her strength was unbelievable. Someday, the boy aspired to be as strong and as powerful.

"You're pathetic," she growled. He never understood her intense anger towards him, given that he hadn't done anything to her.

His gaze did not move from hers as he tried to show that he was stronger, that he was not afraid. This didn't stop her. She slapped him across the face, then tossed him to the ground. He bounced off the gravel and ground to a slow, painful stop.

"Come on. You have had long enough, show me!" she ordered, appearing more impatient at his apparent uselessness. He knew that there was only one reason she had allowed him to live this long: she wanted him to show her the ability he had shown many years ago, but the boy had no control over when he appeared in that other world or when he came back to this one. That's what all these beatings were for, to try and trigger a reaction from him. Despite her best efforts, it had never worked.

During these beatings, the boy would close his eyes and count to ten in an attempt to distract himself. It rarely worked; he felt everything. Every blow, every claw mark of the dragon that was etched into his back over the years.

She had kept him alive, not out of want but out of need. His very flesh and blood were what she needed to escape this place. It was becoming apparent that she was going to have to wait longer given that at fifteen, the boy was still unable to summon a spirit beast, a failure she loved to remind him of.

The longer this went on, the more likely that he was a menial. If he were a menial, then he had no idea where he drew that power to drift across to the other side. One way or another, she had told him over the years, she was getting back to where she came from.

The boy attempted to climb to his feet once more, but he felt his body pinned to the floor immediately. The pressure was so intense that he realised it was the dragon that had slammed him down, its large foot grinding him into the ground. He hadn't felt this power or force for many months. She must be furious for her spirit beast to have finally shown itself.

The boy hid his grin. He had been waiting for this moment, biding his time. Taking beating after beating for all these years purposely so that from time to time, he would be confronted with this magnificent spirit beast. His opportunity now was to study it intently, how it moved, how it breathed, how it reacted to its surroundings. She had played into his hands and lost her temper. The one thing that he was certain of was that he wanted a dragon spirit for himself, and he was determined to achieve this, no matter what it took.

If he succeeded, no one could ever hurt him again, including her.

The boy realised he must have been knocked unconscious because the last thing he remembered was that he had his eyes tightly shut and was counting slowly in his head to counteract the clawing, burning sensation down his back. The pain was unbearable. When he had come round, she was gone, along with her spirit beast.

He lay there on the ground battered and exhausted as he stared up at the clear blue sky above him. He was aware of the sun shining brightly, but his eyes had swollen shut, having received numerous blows to his face.

This was one of the worst beatings he had received, and the boy turned his head to discharge the blood from his mouth. He had put everything he had into not passing out as he was tossed about by the spirit beast like a rag doll.

He lay on his back in the worst pain he had ever experienced. A manic smile erupted, and he began to laugh to himself. It had been worth every ounce of pain that he was now feeling.

He reached down and pulled his ripped t-shirt up slightly. It was still there, tucked unto the front of his pants. He had managed to grab it when she had scooped him up in the air without her noticing, like a seasoned pickpocket.

He pulled the item out and lifted it above him to look at it. It was the dagger that she had always carried with her. One that he was sure was an artefact and had a unique ability. All he had to do now was figure out how to use it, and quickly, because as soon as she found out that the blade was missing, she would be back.

Staring intently at the decorated hilt, he noticed that the

base was made from ebony and the blade from ivory, the darkness of the blade looking like the night itself. When he was younger, he had seen her studying the blade, chanting various incantations, but up until now, she had been unable to use it. She had remained unsuccessful all these years in getting it to work, whatever it was that it did.

Knowing what may happen should she return, he closed his eyes once more and began to count to try and get through the immense pain he was feeling. His back felt like it was on fire, and he knew that he couldn't take another beating, not one more blow.

At this point, a tremendous wave of sadness came over him. What had he done to deserve this life? He had been an innocent baby when he had been born in this world alone with no one looking out for him other than that evil woman. How he hated her for what she had done to him throughout his life.

The boy felt a knot in his stomach, and suddenly struggled to swallow, feeling as though he had eaten glass. It was at this point that he released an emotion he had not shown since he was a little boy. Tears began to stream down his face, leaving streaks of clean skin where they had removed the dirt. His sorrow felt as though it would never end, and he contemplated using the knife in his hands to end it all.

Then he noticed something through his stinging eyes. The blade was emitting an orange glow around it. He could feel its warmth, and it felt as though the unbearable misery he was feeling had started to lift, calming him. He stared at the blade, mesmerised by its illuminated beauty. Then the feeling intensified. He felt his grip tighten around the blade as though he couldn't let go. He sat upright and began to get to his feet, something that five minutes before he did not feel strong enough to do.

The glow around the blade became bigger and began to draw up his arms, engulfing his entire body like flames. The more the flames wrapped around him, the more he felt as though he were wrapped in a warm blanket. It was the warm embrace that he had craved his entire life, and the pain he was feeling dulled. It was like the blade was listening to him and soothing his internal and external pain all at once.

He continued to emit a bright orange glow until he felt something connect with him inside. It was a feeling that he couldn't quite recognise, but for the first time in his entire life, he didn't feel alone. From within his body, something escaped. Through the light, a large animal stepped outward from his very body, followed by a second one. They stood in front of him, both looking powerful and majestic at the same time.

When the boy had found himself warped into a zoo once a few years ago, he had seen lions there. He was certain that the two animals in front of him were lions, but they did not quite have the same appearance as the ones he had seen before.

Neither of them had manes around their intimidating heads. They both stood there looking at him with intense focus. The one on the left was slightly smaller than the other and carried a massive scar on one of its cheeks. It stood in front of him, its very frame intimidating to look at from so close. It released a loud growl which made his heart flicker as the magnificent beast began to walk towards him slowly.

The creature then bowed its head to him. The boy reached forwards, slowly placing his open hand on its head. Suddenly the connection he had felt before intensified and he could feel the lion's feelings and thoughts as if they were his own. It was the strangest sensation, one that he immediately craved more of. Within moments he felt strong and powerful, but he wasn't stupid; he knew he would not be powerful enough to take on her and her dragon spirit beast. But at least now he finally stood a chance. At least now he finally had not one but two spirit beasts to call his own.

He looked at the two giant lions and was mesmerised by their beauty. They sat there calmly looking at him, their tails flipping and slapping the floor sporadically as the larger one of the two let out a giant yawn.

Then the boy could feel another strange sensation, one that he had not felt for some time, and he knew what was coming. Next to him, the air became distorted, and the frosted portal opened, a force of energy blowing out around it with more power than usual. He felt a magnetic pull towards it, and he had no control over it. The portal was drawing him in, and he began to slide towards it until he fell inside.

Suddenly the boy became disorientated as the feeling of weightlessness came over him, like he was falling. He had come through mid-air at the top of a steep hill. He fell around eight feet before landing on the wrong side of the hill, where he began bouncing down violently, feeling every rock, shrub, and tree that he collided against on his way to the bottom. When he stopped, he lay on the floor staring up in the sky, his body aching and throbbing from head to toe. He wondered what he must have done to deserve this. His happiness at suddenly having two magnificent spirit beasts had been short-lived with suddenly being catapulted down a steep hill. He didn't know where he was, and he had no idea how long he would be here.

CHAPTER 14

It was a Saturday, and Arnold took refuge in the fact that at least for the next two days he didn't need to go to school. It also meant he could take a rare break from practising spirit-wielding and let his body rest.

He still hadn't had any success, but Arnold was determined to succeed. He was still no nearer to finding out anything more about the mysterious creature that had attacked him at Bramley Lock-up, either.

He had his plan for the day which was to spend some time at the lock-up with Everett, George, and Marrok. Arnold had made the decision to invite Marrok after the fight at school. In defending him and taking the fall, Marrok had earned his trust.

Arnold wanted to go through some of his grandad's old books to see if they could find out anything about the spirit beast that had attacked him. Arnold was already at the lock-up and searching for a specific book he had thought he had seen when they first found his grandad's belongings. He had just finished rummaging through some old boxes when the door to the lock-up began to slide back.

"Hey." Marrok walked into the room. "Just you here?"

"Everett and George are on their way."

"What are you doing?"

Arnold picked up one box and placed it on top of another to create a bit more space for the four of them. "I'm looking for some old books. I saw one that looked like a scrapbook with drawings in it of different spirit beasts. I want to find it. I haven't seen it since we were attacked here." There was a frantic tone to Arnold's voice.

"I'm sure we will find it," Marrok said, moving to the far side of the lock-up and opening one of the drawers at the bottom of a cabinet.

"It's just, if this spirit-wielding is hereditary, maybe there is something inside that will help me." Then Arnold thought, could his grandad spirit-wield?

"I can help. What did it look like?" Marrok said with a smile.

"It was like an old leather book with a stone in the centre of the cover, like a pale blue colour."

"Random, it can't be that hard to find."

The two of them continued rummaging around looking for it for a short while, rustling through different boxes and cabinets like burglars ransacking the room.

"You know you really should take more care of the things in here, boys."

They both turned around to see Everett and George stood at the entrance to the lock-up. Everett was looking particularly pretty today. She was wearing some dark jeans and a white vest top. George had a fifties-style dress on with little red roses all over it, along with her boots and her beanie hat.

"Arnold wants to find a book, leather thing with a bluish stone in the centre of it."

"Your grandad's journal? Oh, I think it's over here." George walked over to a cupboard and pulled out a drawer to reveal the book stored away inside.

"Brilliant!" Arnold walked across and took the book from her and began to flick through it. On each page of the journal, he found different sketches of spirit beasts and a small explanation on the opposite side to describe each spirit beast's traits. The first page had an outline of an elk which had been his grandad's spirit beast. The next page had a giraffe, then a hippo followed by an owl.

Everett peered over Arnold's shoulder to catch a look. "Wow, your grandad was good at drawing."

"He was, wasn't he? This has got loads of information in it." On the page with the hippo, he noticed that Elwood had scribbled *Charles Grey* at the top of the page. "Looks like he has written down some of the names of people that have these spirit beasts." He turned the page. There was a detailed sketch of a dragon. Arnold's heart began to race. He instantly recognised this spirit beast as the one that had chased him in the spirit world, its razor-sharp teeth matched by its pointed scales which stuck out at the bottom of its wings. At the top of the page, he saw the name *Helen Ethon*, confirming to him that this was, in fact, his grandma's.

He continued to turn the pages until one made him stop, catching his attention instantaneously as he recognised the spirit beast he could see. It had sharp fangs and pointed ears and a mouth that protruded from its face like a cat or a dog, more feline. Then he looked at the patterning of the spirit beast and could see it had rounded dots all over it with a darker outer edge. The spirit beast resembled what he had come face to face with outside of the lock-up. This spirit beast looked more humanoid in form than any Arnold had ever seen, and this was what had been puzzling him. As with the other pages opposite the sketch, there was a handwritten entry.

"Night-Sun?" Arnold spoke as he read the words at the top of the page.

"What do you mean?" George looked just as puzzled as everyone else in the room.

"That's what it's called, the creature that attacked me! It's called Night-Sun."

"I've never heard of a spirit beast that goes by that name," Everett pointed out. "That sounds more like a name than an animal. What else does it say?"

Arnold started to read the page out loud to the others. "*Worshipped by the Order of the Aegis, Night-Sun is seen as the reincarnation of an ancient deity, the Were-Jaguar.*"

"Were-Jaguar?" George repeated loudly.

At this point, it clicked into place, why the creature had felt so familiar, particularly those eyes. How could he have been so stupid and not realised this sooner? The markings matched that of a jaguar. He had the information all along and just not realised it.

"It's Otto! The thing that attacked me, its Otto!"

"What? How is that even possible?" Everett said in disbelief. "Why would he? How is he?" The questions were coming out of her mouth faster than Arnold was thinking of them himself.

Arnold was in shock. How had this happened to his best friend? He had a jaguar spirit beast, so what had happened for him to turn into that ferocious creature? The wildness in its eyes was something that had stuck Arnold during their confrontation.

"I don't know how, but it's him, I just know it is." Arnold was sure of it.

There was a noise outside, like scuffled footsteps in the dirt.

"Damn it," the voice from outside cursed.

Marrok shot to the front of the lock-up to see who it was outside. "Otto?"

Arnold moved to the entrance to see Otto sat on his backside as if he had just fallen over. "It's you, how could you?"

"It wasn't me, Arnold, I promise," Otto said in a panicked voice. "Well, it *was* me, but not me, if that makes sense?" he continued to stutter.

Arnold didn't know what to think or feel. He didn't know if he was angry at being attacked by his best friend or upset that Otto hadn't told him what was happening to him.

"You're Night-Sun?" Arnold asked, hardly able to believe it.

"Night what?" Otto stood back to his feet and dusted himself down.

"Why are you here?" Everett interrogated.

"Want to go another round, is that it?" George followed up.

"Wait, no, why would I?" Otto sputtered, not appearing to understand what he was being accused of. "I don't know what is happening to me, what has happened to me."

"You attacked me!" Arnold explained angrily.

"And me!" George added.

Otto's eyes filled with tears. He looked desperate for help. Arnold had never seen him look so frightened before, so vulnerable.

"It wasn't you though, was it, Otto?" Arnold asked, more softly this time. "You changed into something. It was your jaguar spirit beast, but you had turned into it."

"It first happened about a week after the Spirit Wardens

threw me out. I had no one to go to, Arnold. My dad took me away to see my family. They see it as a possession and tried to do things to remove my spirit beast from me. Horrible things, all summer."

Otto's eyes began to well once more and he looked as though he was ready to burst into tears. "It's the dagger. It did something to us. I can't control it; it just happens."

"Where's the dagger now? I can ask the Spirit Wardens."

"No," Marrok interjected. "If you go to the Spirit Wardens, they'll take Otto away."

"I'm not a lab rat. I don't want to lose my spirit beast. I don't want to be a menial."

"We need to help him, Arnold." Everett walked across and threw her arms around Otto and gave him a huge hug.

Otto began to sob, sinking into her embrace. Arnold walked over and wrapped his arms around the two of them, followed by George.

"We're here for you, Otto, whatever we can do."

Otto might be in a bad way, but Arnold had his friend back, and he needed their help.

"Where is the dagger? We could maybe ask your granny, George." Arnold knew that she had the knowledge given that she was a shaman and might have more information for them.

"I don't know. That's just it, I can't find it," Otto said. "After everything that happened, I don't know where it is."

"Right, if we head to Granny's shop, we can go see if she can help us," said George.

Arnold walked to the lock-up and placed his hand on the side, triggering the locking system to secure the container. "Come on, let's go, you're going to be okay, mate."

It wasn't long before the five of them had made the short journey across town and found themselves at Rushton

Remedies. The town was quite busy today given that it was a Saturday, and everyone was taking the opportunity to get their shopping done. Car after car passed on the main street with people coming in and out of the different shops. The quietest shop on the road was their destination.

Technology had changed, and people were happy to take tablets to cure different ailments rather than remedies, and because of the development of technology, not that many people went to see traditional healers to help them with pain relief.

As they opened the door to the shop, the old bell above them rang with the old technology favoured by George's granny.

"Granny?" George called out. "It's me!"

They waited at the front of the shop for Edith to come out from the back, but she didn't appear. The shop seemed eerily quiet. Arnold was always surprised they didn't have more customers, given how much the remedy he had been given had helped him with his pain relief.

George walked through the shop and lifted the folding part of the counter over to walk through. The door to the back had a multi-coloured beaded door blinds preventing anyone from looking through. George pulled them to one side, the beads clattering into one another.

"GRANNY!" George cried as she shot through the doorway.

Arnold quickly followed, bursting through the beads after her.

George's granny lay out on the floor, her skin pale, almost colourless. George was kneeling by her side and had begun crying hysterically. Arnold walked over and placed his hand on her granny's wrist; her skin was cold to the touch.

There was nothing they could do for her.

Arnold knelt next to George and wrapped his arms around her.

Everett and the others came to the doorway and were shocked at what they could see.

Arnold turned to face them. "Someone call an ambulance and the Spirit Wardens," he requested. "George's granny is dead."

CHAPTER 15

Arnold stood at the side of the coffin along with the rest of his friends as they paid their final respects to Edith. The ceremony had been beautiful, with George reading a poem she had written during her eulogy.

George stood on the opposite side of them with her dads on either side of her. She was wearing a black lace dress, and she looked distraught. Her granny had been her best friend who she spent most of her spare time with, and now George would never get to see her again. Arnold understood how she felt, but he had not had a chance to speak with her following Edith's death as she had spent the last four days at home with her family with her phone off.

The coroner's report had said that she'd had a heart attack. With everything that had been going on, Arnold had initially questioned whether something more sinister had happened. However, he was relieved to find out that she had died of natural causes, and he wondered if he was becoming too paranoid.

But she had been the only shaman in town, the only

person they could think of to go to for answers about Otto, and now she was gone. They were all back to square one.

The coffin was lowered into the ground slowly, and George leant into her dad as her crying intensified. Her other dad hugged the two of them together to comfort them. They were such a close family, and it was hard for Arnold to see the pain they were all going through. After George and her parents stepped forwards to throw soil onto the coffin, they headed back to the cars together, George's head tucked firmly into her dad's side.

"I hope she is okay," Arnold said to the others.

"She will be. She appreciates us all being here, I know it," Everett answered. "I'll call round in the morning to see her. We best head back to school."

George's family had chosen to have the wake at the house with only immediate family. The school had allowed Arnold, Everett, Otto, and Marrok to attend the funeral, but had requested that if they felt okay to, for them to go back to school in the afternoon.

Arnold watched sadly as George and her dads headed to their car to leave. That was when he noticed what looked like the mayor's car. He used his eagle vision to zoom in on it, and was surprised to see Mayor Redburn sitting in the back of the car looking out at them, with Mr. Whittaker beside him.

"Why would your dad be here, Otto?"

"Huh?"

"He's down there in his car with Mr. Whittaker."

"I don't know." Otto frowned. "Strange, that. My dad hates Mr. Whittaker for throwing me out of the Spirit Wardens."

Everyone else had left the funeral and were getting into their cars to leave, so the four of them headed across the field towards the school. They were partway across the field when Otto suddenly stopped and bent over, holding his stomach.

"You okay?" Arnold asked.

Otto didn't respond. He had his eyes closed and began to breathe heavily. "It – it's happening!" He dropped to his knees in agony.

"What's happening?" Marrok asked.

"You all need to leave, now!"

Arnold realised what was happening. "We can help you."

"I don't want to hurt anyone. I can't control this. You all need to get away from me!"

Otto was gasping for breath, clearly in agony. His body started to contort violently which he had no control over. "Go!" he growled at them. "Why are you stiiillll heeeeere?!" He was struggling to talk through the horrific pain.

"We want to help you!" Arnold yelled. He hated seeing Otto in all this pain.

Otto's bones began to make cracking noises like large tree branches snapping. His bones were breaking, and Otto began to scream. When he looked up, his eyes appeared different, as if the Otto they knew was disappearing before their very eyes. His face had started to change shape, and the jaguar markings began to take form on his skin.

He reached forwards and grabbed hold of the ground in front of him. They could all see his hands changing shape as large claws began to protrude from his fingertips.

Otto then stood taller than all of them. His body had completely changed. He had become his spirit beast.

He had become Night-Sun, the were-jaguar.

He let out a ferocious roar towards the group, but none of them moved.

"It's okay, we're here," Arnold said, putting his hands up

to be as unthreatening as he could be. He stepped towards Otto slowly.

Otto let out another roar. His breathing was heavy and produced a growling noise in itself. Arnold continued to walk towards him slowly to show he wasn't frightened and that he wanted to help him. It seemed to be working, but suddenly Otto backhanded him with full force, knocking him to the ground. Everett and Marrok quickly helped him up, and the three shuffled backwards, away from Otto.

"Arnold, what do we do?" Marrok asked. "Someone is going to get hurt!"

"We need to stop him," Everett said, acting fast. She stepped forwards and began to emit a soft purple glow, and soon her boar appeared before her. It had grown in size and now had larger tusks protruding from its mouth, its large body showing that it had increased in power.

Arnold concentrated, and his light blue auro engulfed his body as his eagle spirit beast flew out from within him. It landed on the ground, its large wingspan spread out in a show of power.

Marrok nodded and followed suit. An orange glow began to generate through his auro, and seconds later, a white wolf ran from inside him and stood on all fours next to the eagle and the boar. It had a thick mane of hair with red eyes that contrasted against the beast's ice-white colour. It let out a shrill howl as it fixed its gaze upon Otto and bared its teeth.

"A wolf, that's awesome," Arnold said, impressed. "Trust, is that right?"

"Yeah," Marrok confirmed without shifting his eyes.

Otto jerked and growled in his spirit form, but he seemed scattered and unfocused. Saliva dripped from his open mouth where his razor-sharp teeth were on full display, his stare switching between the three spirit beasts that stood before him.

"What do we do now?" Marrok asked, seeking direction from Arnold.

"We can't let him get away, no matter what!" Arnold commanded.

Otto charged at them, but the boar and the wolf ran to meet him with equal speed. Arnold's eagle took flight and flew in the same direction as the others. The boar reached Otto first, but Otto hurdled over it, dragging his claws down the boar's back in the process. Everett winced as the boar made a shrieking noise.

Using his momentum, Otto vaulted the boar and hurled itself head-on into the wolf. The two of them grappled with each other on the floor, but Otto was much stronger. He bit down on the wolf's neck which let out a pained yelp.

Arnold's eagle swooped in, but Otto was quick to its pattern of movement and jumped out of the way. The boar came charging from the side and crashed into the beast, breaking its firm bite on the wolf and knocking it back. The were-jaguar let out a growl and launched itself at the boar, grabbing it with both of his hands and embedding his claws into its sides as he rolled over the top. Using his momentum, Otto lifted the boar into the air and slammed it down to the ground.

Everett dropped to her knees, feeling her boar's pain in her own body. "He's too strong!" she cried as she crumpled into the ground.

The eagle swooped down at Otto again and grabbed at his shoulders with its dagger-like talons to lift him in the air and drop him to the floor. Otto reached up and grabbed hold of the eagle, slamming it straight into the ground below him. Arnold held his side, but his pain threshold was higher than the others'.

Otto continued his run towards the group. Arnold stepped in front of Everett and Marrok and braced himself for the impact from the were-jaguar, but moment later, he realised that the impact hadn't happened as expected. Otto had run past them and was charging across the field.

"What's going on?" Everett shouted.

"We can't let him run through town in that form!" Marrok yelled. "Someone will get hurt, and he's going to be captured." He set off running after the out-of-control spirit beast. "Come on!"

Arnold immediately followed even though they didn't have a plan for what to do once they caught up with him. Otto was faster than the three of them, but they were still quick and they both covered ground quickly, managing to keep Otto in their sights.

Otto had almost reached the main street that led into town where Arnold was sure disaster awaited. His eagle flew overhead, following Otto into town. It swooped down and clattered into Otto's back, knocking him over. Arnold and Marrok made up some ground whilst Marrok's white wolf overtook them and volleyed itself into Otto's side, delaying him from climbing back to his feet. Everett remained in the distance, her spirit beast slower and less powerful than Arnold and Marrok's.

They managed to catch up, and a few moments later, they were level with him.

"Otto!" Arnold called, trying to get his attention. "You need to stop!"

Otto continued to grapple with the eagle and wolf, not responding to Arnold's pleas.

"Listen to me, listen to my voice," Arnold continued to

try and get through to him.

Otto began to rain down blows on Marrok's spirit beast, his wildness taking over him.

"Otto, stop!" Arnold cried. "You're going to kill him!"

Marrok had fallen to the floor, unable to cope with the pain he was sharing with his spirit beast. His connection was strong, but he didn't appear experienced with it.

Arnold grabbed hold of Otto from behind and tried pulling him away, but a flailing elbow to the ribs was his reward. "Come on, listen to me!"

Otto looked up, and suddenly his eyes looked different. His wild gaze had softened, and there was sadness in them. The sorrow evident in his eyes only solidified what Arnold already knew: his best friend was not in control of what he was doing.

"Come on, Otto. I know you are in there!" he yelled desperately.

Otto stopped and stood there calmly, his violent, scatty movements slowing as an air of control came over him. He moved away from the wolf which lay injured on the floor and walked slowly towards Arnold.

Arnold's eagle moved next to the wolf and wrapped its wings around him, creating a half-dome shield around it while using its energy to help it recover from its wounds.

Otto continued his steady walk to Arnold.

"Can you hear me?" Arnold asked, standing his ground.

The beast nodded.

"Can you understand me?"

The beast nodded again.

Arnold couldn't believe it; Otto had regained control of himself.

But then Otto began to stagger and shake his head, his movements becoming erratic once more. He started to grunt and growl, then turned away from Arnold and set off running, dropping onto all fours as his speed increased dramatically. Otto collided with the eagle head-on, which was still wrapped around the wolf. Both the eagle and wolf lay injured on the floor as Otto continued his run beyond them.

They had failed. Otto was about to hit the main street where everyone would be able to see him.

"Stay with your wolf!" Arnold shouted.

He set off running after Otto, desperate to stop him, but he had no idea where Otto was going or what he was doing.

He kept Otto in sight using his enhanced vision, but unless Otto stopped, it would be impossible for Arnold to catch up with him. Otto was too fast.

Otto finally hit the street and straight away, Arnold heard the screams begin to ring out as Otto barrelled into the busy crowd of shoppers. His heart raced as he sprinted after the were-jaguar. His dad had told him that the Spirit Wardens planned to kill the beast if they caught it – but they didn't know the truth. Arnold had to stop him before it was too late.

When Arnold hit the street, Otto was way ahead of him, running down the main road. Crowds of people screamed and ran as he hurdled over car after car. A loud, metallic scratching noise pierced the air from where his claws sliced the rooftops of the vehicles as confused drivers honked and swerved.

Arnold knew it was only a matter of time before the Doyens arrived, and he could feel his stomach churning with what might happen when they turned up. Head pounding from the adrenaline coursing through him, Arnold kept running, knowing that Otto's life and the lives of innocent bystanders were at stake.

Otto suddenly stopped in the middle of the road and began staring directly at one of the shops, as if he recognised it.

It was Rushton Remedies, George's granny's shop.

After a short moment, he smashed through the window, the glass shattering as he climbed inside the building.

Seizing his opportunity, Arnold put every ounce of his energy into catching up, and he was outside the store before he knew it. Whilst running, his eagle dissipated back into his body as he saw a crowd of people were running away from the vicinity, and Arnold could see people on their phones, most likely making hurried calls to the Spirit Wardens. Arnold ran and hurdled through the broken window, the glass crunching below his feet as he ground it into the floor when he landed. He could hear Otto in the back of the store crashing around and grunting.

Why would Otto be in this store, of all places? He had seemed to specifically target this shop as if he were looking for something in particular, which made Arnold think that he was at least somewhat lucid. This gave him hope that he might be able to get through to him.

"Otto!" Arnold called.

The grunts stopped, and Arnold could hear a growl start to call back to him from the backroom aggressively.

"I just want to help!"

"You need, get away, no control!"

It took Arnold a moment to realise that the deep, husky voice had come from Otto.

"What are you doing?" Arnold asked, slowly creeping towards the back of the shop.

"I . . . feel the pull . . . like magnet. No control," came Otto's staggered speech in the same, nearly unrecognisable voice.

Arnold heard the back door open to the rear of the building and was sure there were more than one pair of footsteps, along with a murmured voice. Confused as to who Otto was talking to, Arnold had stepped towards the back of the shop to see what was happening when he heard the call from behind him.

"Whoever is in there, you need to come out!" the voice bellowed. "This is the Spirit Wardens!"

Arnold froze, recognising his dad's voice instantly. He could no longer hear Otto, which made him think he must have already exited the building. Arnold decided to exit out of the rear of the building to try and trail Otto again.

"I'm coming in," Bernard announced.

Arnold made it into the back room of the shop just as his dad entered through the front. He could hear Bernard's footsteps slowly crunching the glass on the floor.

Arnold moved to the back door.

"Don't move!" Bernard bellowed once more as he caught up with him. "Arnold?" he asked, a look of shock and surprise on his face.

"Dad, I can explain."

Movement outside caught Arnold's eye: Otto vaulted the wall at the back of the yard before escaping down the alleyway.

"What is that?" Bernard said while channelling his auro. "Arnold, get behind me!" Bernard gave chase after the were-jaguar, oblivious to the fact that the beast was Otto. Arnold knew he needed to protect Otto from the Spirit Wardens, from his dad. He was running as fast as he could to reach the bottom of the alley, navigating down the uneven cobbled floor beneath him.

"Stop!" Bernard yelled.

Arnold knew he wasn't going to outrun his dad, but he

needed to keep him distracted so that Otto could getaway.

He could hear fierce growling ahead, and Otto stepped out from the bottom of the alley in front of him. His height and frame were physically imposing. His clothes were heavily ripped, displaying the intricate pattern of a jaguar hide that was now all over his fur-covered body. He was baring his teeth, and saliva poured from his face as he began to growl wildly.

Otto vaulted past him and headed towards Bernard at pace on all fours once more. Arnold whirled around just in time to hear the roar from Bernard's bear as he summoned it.

The bear charged towards the were-jaguar, and the two slammed into each other. Razor-sharp, jagged teeth and claws began gnawing at each other in a flurry of motion. The powerful grizzly knocked Otto into the wall with such force that the siding cracked from the impact.

"Dad, no!" Arnold yelled, running towards them.

"Arnold?" Bernard looked puzzled, "What are you –"

The grizzly bear snapped its jaws around Otto's side, and Otto let out a roar in anger as he began to pummel the grizzly bear from above, repeatedly slashing it with his claws. The grizzly tightened its grip and flung Otto sideways who went skimming off the floor before crashing into the wall on the opposite side of the alley.

The grizzly stood up on its hind legs, its intimidating size standing at around seven feet tall. It let out a roar that shook Arnold to the core.

Arnold threw himself forwards in between Otto and the bear.

"Stop!" he yelled again, his arms outstretched as he tried to make himself as big as possible.

"Get out of the way, Arnold, what are you doing?"

Arnold stared at his father with no intention of moving. He didn't want either of them to get hurt. "You need to trust me, Dad. He doesn't know what he's doing."

Otto jumped up from the floor and let out an equally deafening roar, splattering Arnold with slimy drool. Arnold could feel the heat from the were-jaguar's breath on his cheeks as he stood there, shaking with fear.

He slammed his hands against Otto's chest and put all his weight into pushing him back against the wall.

"You need to stop!" he cried. "Look at me!"

Otto cast his gaze downwards. He was so much taller than he usually was, and his eyes still looked wild. He began to push against Arnold's hands, and Arnold slid backwards from the force.

"Please, Otto."

Otto shook his head, and his eyes became recognisable once more.

"Focus on my voice," Arnold tried once more.

Otto stood still for a moment, more human-like than before, his breathing laboured as he seemed to try and collect himself. The grizzly bear dropped back to all fours, a slow grumble emitting from under its closed mouth.

Otto looked at Arnold with great sadness once more, and his bones slowly began to crack back into shape. The jaguar markings all over his body changed back to normal skin as Otto dropped to his knees and slumped back to the wall.

"Otto?" Bernard called as his spirit beast began to dissipate back inside him. He raced to Otto's side, looking stunned.

Arnold knelt next to Otto to check on him. He looked ready to pass out.

"How?" Bernard seemed unable to process what he had

just seen. "You're a –"

"Were-jaguar," Otto grumbled as he attempted to get back to his feet.

"I'm going to have to take you in, Otto."

"You can't, Dad!"

"The whole town has seen him. If I don't, then they're going to send more people from the other Spirit Wardens to find him."

"They'll kill him," Arnold proclaimed.

Otto looked scared, as if it was slowly dawning on him what had just happened. "I didn't have any control over myself," he said.

"Even more reason for me to bring you in, Otto, it's not safe."

Otto began to shake. "Please, Mr. Ethon, I'm scared."

"We need to help him, Dad. If we take him to the Spirit Wardens, who knows what they'll do to him?"

A siren could be heard from the other side of the building, its noise echoing down the alleyway.

"That will be Mr. Whittaker."

"Dad, you need to help him, us. Please, just until we try and figure something out."

Bernard looked at the back of the shop before looking at the two of them "Go," he commanded to the two of them, looking unsure of his decision.

Arnold breathed a sigh of relief and hooked Otto's arm around his neck, and the two of them began to make their way down the alleyway and out of sight. Away from danger, away from the Spirit Wardens.

The question now was: how were they going to stop anyone finding out Otto's secret?

And why was he transforming into the were-jaguar in the first place?

CHAPTER 16

"What does it feel like?" Arnold asked after he and Otto had made it back to his house. Arnold was sitting on his beanbag with Otto sprawled out on his bed, still recovering from his transformation into the were-jaguar.

"It hurts like hell. The pain is like nothing else. I feel my bones breaking as I am transforming. Then it goes dark, and all I can feel is emptiness, loneliness." Otto breathed out a huge sigh. "What do we do now?"

"I don't know. I'm hoping my dad will know what to do."

Arnold heard the front door open, and footsteps came straight upstairs before his dad walked into his room.

"What on earth. How are you? Are either of you hurt?"

"All I know, Mr. Ethon, is that when Raine stabbed my spirit beast with her dagger, something happened to me when I tried to pull it out of him. That's when all this started."

"Why didn't you come to us at the Spirit Wardens?"

"Because I was thrown out, disgraced for my actions," Otto said. "Raine was going to take my jaguar, and there was no other way of stopping her. I went to my dad, but he told me to keep quiet, and took me to spend the summer with my family to try more traditional ways of healing me."

"That worked then." Arnold felt annoyed with Mayor Redburn. If Otto had been able to come to them sooner, they could have maybe helped him.

"I was told to distance myself from everyone when we came back. My great-uncle said that I had become fused with my spirit beast. When I touched that dagger, I reabsorbed him, but in an unnatural way."

"Like a form of corruption. This is not good, Otto," Bernard added, looking as concerned as ever.

"My great-uncle said that it has happened before, but a very long time ago. My dad has reached out to a group of people called the Order of the Aegis."

"The Order of the Aegis? Otto, you do not want to get into bed with those fanatics."

Arnold remembered that the Order of the Aegis was mentioned in his grandad's journal. "They worship the were-jaguar as a deity. Night-Sun," he blurted out.

"How do you know that?" Bernard asked.

"I read it."

"Read it where?"

It was beginning to feel like an interrogation. Arnold didn't want to tell the truth, so instead, he decided to answer with a question. "Why?"

"Because the Spirit Wardens keeps any texts about the Order of the Aegis. They are kept at the Grand Atheneum in London for a reason. Somewhere that you do not have access to."

This confused Arnold. Why would his grandad have kept information from the Spirit Wardens when he was a Doyen and then an Elder working for them?

"You know what, we have bigger things to deal with. What were you doing at that shop?" Bernard switched the target of his interrogation.

"I honestly don't know. When I transform, I am not in control. It's like I am a passenger. There are times when I can break through, but it's not me."

"So, you have no control, or someone else is controlling you?" Bernard pressed.

"Like a spirit beast," Arnold concluded.

"You mean I am now a spirit beast?" Otto looked dejected at this information.

"You're corrupted. If I had to make a suggestion, it would be that whoever has that dagger is the person who is controlling you."

Otto frowned. "Whoever it is . . . they seem really familiar."

"Your dad. Otto, I think your dad has the dagger." Arnold was sure of it as soon as he said it, but why would Mayor Redburn control Otto and make him transform before breaking into the remedy store? It just didn't make sense to him. "He was there, wasn't he? You gave him something at the back door?"

"I don't know, I don't remember." Otto said, struggling with his thoughts. "Why would my dad do this? He is trying to help me. He is looking for a way to free me from this." He looked over his hands with a tinge of sadness. "Whatever this is."

"If it was your dad then he had you attack me," Bernard said, looking unimpressed with the idea.

"I'm so sorry." Otto cut a sad figure. He looked tired and weary from everything that had been happening. He did, however, look better for being able to share his secret with someone and offload.

"This wasn't you," Bernard reassured him.

"He's trying to help me," Otto insisted. "My dad. He told me there might be a way to separate us. He just needs somewhere with a high connection to the spirit world."

"Why not use the tower?" Arnold asked.

"Because it's not powerful enough."

"The coal mine," Bernard muttered, the realisation dawning on him. "He wants to use the deepest part of the coal mine which is right in the centre of town. The energy levels there are astronomical, it's the real reason why it was shut down."

“I knew there was more to those mines,” Arnold said. Suddenly it all began to make sense to him. Mayor Redburn wished to secretly open the mine so that he could try and separate Otto from his spirit beast. The main question now was how he planned to do it.

"Do you remember what you gave him at the shop?" Arnold asked.

"I don’t remember anything about the shop."

"It's most likely linked to what your dad has planned. It must be . . . but why the remedy shop?" Bernard was thinking out loud.

The Spirit Wardens, at some level, were involved. Mr. Whittaker and Mayor Redburn had been meeting up and discussing the opening of the coal mines. Did Mr. Whittaker know the real reason for Mayor Redburn wanting to open it? Arnold didn't know what the best option was to do now. They could go to the Spirit Wardens for aid, but risk them locking Otto up for his “safety". Or, they could go to Mayor Redburn to try and see what his plan was in its entirety. The problem with the latter was that Mayor Redburn was incredibly hostile towards Arnold. He certainly wasn't going to want to talk to him, and deep down, Arnold was aware of what the Spirit Wardens would most likely do to Otto, so he didn't want to go down this path either.

"What do we do, Dad?"

"I don't know, son. For now, I think we need to sit tight. People have seen you and the Spirit Wardens are now looking for you. You need to ensure that if you are to transform again, you will not be seen, for your safety and others'. At least until we have a plan. I can't know where you are, Otto. Because if this were to happen again, I would have no choice but to take you in."

"I understand, Mr. Ethon. Thank you."

Arnold felt proud of his dad for helping Otto, but he also knew the position both of them were in with the Spirit Wardens. If they were to find out that Arnold and Bernard had helped Otto escape and hide, then his dad's career would be over, and Arnold would never be able to become a Doyen as he had always dreamed.

"I need to head back to the Spirit Wardens now," Bernard said. "Mr. Whittaker wants my report on his desk by the end of the day. Remember, lie low until I know what to do." With this, Bernard left Arnold's bedroom, and within a few moments, the house was empty again apart from Arnold and Otto.

Arnold went downstairs and got himself and Otto ham sandwiches and glasses of orange juice. They sat and discussed their next course of action. Arnold already knew where the best place for Otto to stay hidden was. He just hoped that Otto felt the same.

"You can stay at the lock-up," Arnold started. "I don't know where it came from, but someone moved my grandad's things there."

"I know." Otto looked sheepish. "I followed you guys there, the last two times I have been there I have blacked out and transformed." Cutting a forlorn figure, Otto finished his sandwich and took a large gulp of his drink. "I feel famished. Transforming does take all my energy."

Arnold felt amazed at how easily Otto was distracted, having shifted from following them at the lock-up to being starving within the same sentence. It felt like he had his friend back which felt fantastic. No matter how different he was physically, he was still Otto.

"My lock-up, you can only get in and out with me, so if we get some supplies, you can stay there. If you do change again, I'm pretty sure you won't be able to get out. It's the best we can do."

They left Arnold's house and walked around the corner to Mr. Shah's shop to get some basic things for Otto for the rest of the weekend. They walked in and could smell the alluring scent of his freshly made samosas which lay by the side of the till. Mr. Shah did not sell these, he simply gave them away throughout the day to his customers as a thank-you for their custom.

The shop was small, as it was initially a terraced house before Mr. Shah's family converted the front into a shop some years ago. Walking in the shop felt cramped, with shelves on either side of them and the counter directly in front of them. A rack lay just to the left-hand side of the stand that was filled with a wide variety of chocolate bars, ranging from Mars Bars, Snickers, and Arnolds personal favourite, mint Aero. The two of them went to opposite sides of the store to collect what they would need for the rest of the weekend. Arnold grabbed some chocolate bars and a couple bags of crisps. There were tins of beans and other canned goods, but the lock-up did not have the facilities for cooking these, so Arnold didn't bother with them.

It did, however, give him food for thought about whether

he would be able to upgrade the container so that it was more hospitable than its current state.

Otto met him at the counter with a couple of comics, some gum, and far more pop than he could ever drink. They bought their supplies and accepted a couple of Mr. Shah's samosas before carrying on to the lock-up, taking extra care not to be followed by anyone.

As they approached the courtyard to the lock-up where the container was, it felt more like a desert than anything, the heat from the sun was that intense. Arnold suddenly thought that maybe it wasn't such as bad thing that Otto had chosen to buy so much pop.

When they reached the container, Arnold placed his hand on the door to unlock the intricate mechanism that guarded his inherited belongings. He opened up the door, the loud sound of grinding metal echoing through the grounds and startling some birds that were perched on the outer perimeter wall.

Inside the container, the heat slapped Arnold in the face like a wet flannel. The air he breathed in felt hot, and suddenly he had second thoughts about Otto staying here.

"I'm going to be like a dog left in a car, aren't I?" Otto sighed. "Except this car doesn't have any bloody windows."

Feeling sorry for him, Arnold passed him a chocolate bar as a peace offering. "It's the best we have at the moment."

Otto looked around the container and gave an expression of disinterest in all the ancient texts and parchment that lay scattered around the room. He certainly did not share the same interest in reading that Arnold had. However, he did seem keen to look at the different artefacts and small selection of weapons that were inside.

"I will stay as long as I can. That way, we won't need to shut the door," Arnold said. The truth was, Arnold thought

Otto could not last long in the airtight sealed container for more than an hour in this heat, but there was nowhere else to go.

Otto took out one of the comics he had bought and began to skim through it while Arnold sent a quick message to Everett to let her know where he was, hoping she and Marrok were okay after the altercation earlier.

A short time later, Otto and Arnold were sat reading, Otto making his way through his comic while Arnold perused his grandad's journal.

"Otto, what are you doing here?" came Everett's voice from the entrance to the storage container. "Would have taken two seconds to let me know you were okay!" Everett was furious, her eyes wide with frustration as she stomped towards the two of them.

Instinctively Arnold stepped in front of Otto to shield him. "I am sorry but we had to deal with my dad trying to catch Otto. Is Marrok okay? Where is he?"

"He is fine, a little banged up but he is at the store helping clean up with George and her parents."

"You need to sit down. There's a lot to get through," Arnold said.

Otto and Arnold spent the next hour explaining what had happened behind the shop while Everett listened intently. Once she was up to date, the three of them continued puttering about the container looking through more of his grandad's ancient texts.

Arnold had found another handwritten journal which he was making his way through. This one was more like a diary. It was amazing to be able to sit there reading his grandad's thoughts around different assignments and cases he'd had during his time in the Spirit Wardens. Arnold had learned a lot in his life but never anything like this, nothing so personal that no one else had read, and it made him feel as though his grandad was there in some capacity.

16TH JANUARY 1985,

Life has not been the same since we lost her. I am unable to concentrate at work. Bernard has been acting out asking where his mum is. He is too young for me to explain the complexities of what we had to do to trap her in the spirit world. It by no means was what I wanted, but the Spirit Wardens wished to capture her like she was some form of animal and they would have used her like some lab rat, and I could not let that happen. Eventually, she would have been killed, and this was the only way to keep her alive and everyone else safe.

I have been tasked with looking into some intelligence that the Order of the Aegis has resurfaced recently.

This is the last thing I need right now. Another day in the life of an Elder, how I do miss being a Doyen.

ARNOLD COULD FEEL himself welling up as he finished the paragraph. Being able to read his grandad's thoughts resonated with Arnold even more than he had expected.

"You okay?" Everett stood looking at different items in the cupboard in the corner of the storage container. She took out an old bowl and blew off the decades-old layer of dust that had collected on the top of it to reveal a decorative pattern underneath.

"I'm fine," Arnold told her. Remembering that other people were in the room, he shook his head before closing the journal and putting it back in the box.

He decided he would carry on reading this later when he was on his own.

CHAPTER 17

He stared up at the open sky as he attempted to regain his breath after falling to the bottom of the steep hill in an unknown land. He noticed the air was hot, burning as he took short, sharp breaths. He acclimatised himself to the pain he was experiencing all over his body. Not only had he fallen badly down this hill, but he had been tortured by her and the dragon that controlled her.

The sun was incredibly bright, and an occasional bird surveyed the sky above him. He could hear shuffling nearby and turned his head to see where the noise was coming from.

He was startled to realise that a girl was staring down at him. His eyes were swollen from his beating, but he could make out her dark skin as it shimmered in the sun, and her lengthy hair which was decorated with beads and braids. His attention, however, was caught straight away by her big, amber eyes which looked mesmerising.

Her smile was innocent as she tried to reassure him, and

she knelt next to him. "Are you okay?" she asked in a softly spoken accent which was not one he had heard before.

"I've had better days."

The girl looked around the same age as him, and as she helped him up, he instantly felt a connection between the two of them, and his stomach knotted as he didn't know what to say. She stepped in front of him and pushed his hair to one side, noticing the large gash on his head that was pouring with blood.

"Come with me," she said, taking hold of his hand and pulling him to follow her. Her hands felt soft in comparison to his own calloused ones. "What's your name?"

"I don't have one," he replied. He had met people before when he had travelled into this world, and he knew other people had names. However, for him, he had merely been born. He was an item, a belonging. One that hadn't been nurtured or been given the basic gift in life of receiving a name so as to be able to have an identity.

"No name?" The girl shook this off and continued the walk through the harsh terrain. The ground was a combination of rocks, dirt, and dried grass. It was clear there had been no rain for some time here. "My name is Kaliska. We go to my tribe. My father is a shaman. He can heal you."

It was a ten-mile walk to Kaliska's home, and as they walked, Kaliska explained that she had grown up with her tribe in these harsh surroundings. The boy wondered what that must have been like, living and growing with a family, something he never had.

It was hot, and his head grew fuzzy from his injuries and dehydration. Noticing this, Kaliska stopped by a small stream, allowing a short break to rest and rehydrate themselves. She sat him down on a rock and pooled some water in her hand. She wiped this across his face to remove some of the blood that had curdled around his swollen eyes, pausing for a moment when his scars were revealed from beneath the blood and dirt. She slowly brushed her fingers across the scars before gently running them down the natural cracks that had formed across his eye and face. "How?"

He turned his head away, feeling like a freak and uncomfortable with anyone being so intimate with his scars. He felt hideous, and he hated the scars that he had, scars that were inflicted on him when he was so young. A memory flashed into his mind. A memory that would often wake him in the night with cold sweats and night terrors.

Kaliska turned his head back to face hers and smiled at him. He could not understand why she was so kind to him.

"You grow with your scars. You accept your scars; they are part of you. You grow stronger." She didn't seem fazed by his disfigurement in any way, which surprised him.

"We are not far now, come." She took hold of his hand again, and he followed her until eventually they made it to a heavily forested area.

They continued their journey through the dense wood before eventually stopping, having reached her village.

"This is home."

About ten huts dotted the area around them, constructed of a combination of wood, mud, and large leaves from the trees. There was one larger hut that sat at the top of the village, and in the centre lay a large shelter where people were sat underneath at different tables, some talking, some sorting through what looked like clothes. On another table a group of children were playing a game, judging by the laughter coming from them.

He instantly felt at home and fell in love with the relaxed environment, enjoying being in a populated area that wasn't overcrowded. He couldn't see anyone trading, no one trying to get richer than the others. From what he could see, everyone was helping one another.

Following Kaliska, he could see different people busy getting on with their day. There was a group of women walking back to camp carrying water, and some men were working on the roof of one of the huts, pulling a large leaf over the top of a small gap. Children were running around chasing after each other, laughing and smiling at one another. No one stopped to look at the stranger that had walked into their village with Kaliska and most notably, no one had stopped to gawp at the scars on his face. Kaliska pushed open the door to a large hut that sat at the back of the village overlooking all the other huts. The door opened, and the two of them walked inside one after the other. The hut was poorly lit with only a couple of candles providing any form of lighting. He could see the frame of a man sitting in a tall chair, his face half covered from the shadows in the hut.

"Father," Kaliska started. "I bring this man to be healed."

Picking up a torch, the man raised it over the torch to the side of it, and the flames ignited, providing brighter light in the hut. He walked in front of the boy and began to look him up and down, taking in every detail of him like he was a builder surveying a blueprint.

"I sense great pain and anguish." The shaman placed a firm hand on the boy's shoulder, the cracks in his skin showing he was slightly older than he would have expected for a daughter of Kaliska's age. The boy instantly felt calmer and more relaxed, and strangely, his throbbing head and aching body began to fade.

"Come, sit." The man gestured to the very chair that he had been sitting on when the two of them entered.

Feeling obligated to do so, the boy limped across to the chair and took a seat as directed.

"Fetch my things, Kaliska."

Kaliska disappeared into the darkness of the hut and returned with a satchel which she passed to the shaman before nodding to him and leaving the hut. The shaman walked over to the boy and stared at his head for a moment before pulling out a tiny metal hook.

"This needs sealing." He pointed to the top of his head. "First, it needs cleaning."

At this point, Kaliska returned with a bowl of water and some dressings which she began to use to clean the open wound. The boy didn't flinch as she scrubbed at the gash in his head. The pain was minimal compared to what he had been through in his past. After cleaning his head, she stepped back to allow the shaman in who had been tying some thread into the hook. He used this to pierced the boy's skin, then began to stitch the torn skin back together. After a short while, the stitches were done, and the shaman stepped away from him. He walked to a small table and picked up a mortar and pestle made of wood and stone, and began to grind different herbs together until he had formed a thick, green paste. He scooped some of this up in his hands and smeared over the freshly sealed gash.

"Kaliska, dress his head and meet me outside." He walked away from them and left the hut, leaving them alone inside.

Kaliska stepped in front of him and began to delicately wrap a dressing around his head. His heart fluttered as she stood over him. He had never been this close to a girl before, and he didn't know where to look or what to do, so he sat there awkwardly in silence.

"Your cut should be healed in the next week or two." Kaliska placed her hand on his cheek once more, rubbing her thumb over the bottom of his three sizeable, clawed scars that carved his skin. Her sensitivity and soft hands calmed him even further, and he wondered whether she had the same healing abilities as her father. In that moment, he didn't feel sad or empty, he didn't feel lonely. He didn't feel pain.

At this moment, he felt happiness.

"Come." Kaliska turned to leave the hut, and so he quickly followed outside. A small gathering had formed around the large shelter in the middle of the village. The shaman stood in the centre, waving his hands around while he conversed with the villagers that stood around him.

He followed Kaliska over to the central shelter where he was summoned up by the shaman. "Tell me, what is your name?"

"He has no name," Kaliska called out from within the crowd that had formed.

Gasps rang out around them. This was most strange for them to meet someone of his age without a name.

"Interesting," said the shaman. "Tell me, what is your spirit beast?"

"Lions," the boy answered, not wanting to go into the complexities of what had happened earlier that day with the blade he had stolen.

The shaman began humming and chanting to himself while he poured a mixture of herbs and liquids onto a bowl, which he then passed to the boy. "Drink."

Lifting the bowl, the boy drank the contents and was

pleasantly surprised by the sweet, honey-like taste, a far stretch from the bitterness he had braced himself for.

The shaman closed his eyes and began to chant once more. "The spirits, they speak to me," he whispered. "They say your name, your name means 'lion'. It means brave, and honoured. It means 'protector'." He walked across to the boy and placed both his hands on his shoulders, squeezing tightly.

The boy had never felt so welcomed anywhere, and he wished he could stay here for the rest of his life. He bowed his head to the shaman as a mark of respect to him.

"Your name is Levent," the shaman announced.

FINALLY HAVING A NAME AND AN IDENTITY, Levent felt on top of the world. Over the next few months, he became ingrained as a member of the tribe. He spent a large portion of his time out with other members of the tribe developing his hunting skills and providing for the village by catching and killing wild animals that lived around the forest. It was his way of contributing to the village that had accepted him with open arms and offered such kindness to a stranger in need. He felt prepared to spend the rest of his life happily repaying them. This was the safest he had ever felt. He finally had somewhere to call home.

In his first few weeks, the people helped Levent build his own hut within the village, one he could call his own. It was here where he stored his blade away. He wasn't ready to share that it was through this weapon that he was able to summon his spirit beasts, in case they treated him any differently.

He was happy.

Late one afternoon, Levent had helped capture a wild boar which had been hogtied around a large wooden pole. He was helping carry it back, an extremely strenuous job given the weight of the creature. This boar was large enough to feed the entire village for at least two days, and that night while the boar roasted on a spit, the village celebrated their life and their families before all sitting down together to feast.

Feeling full from his share of the boar, Levent decided to call it a night and head back to his hut to get some rest. His injuries had healed well, and the scar on his head was barely noticeable. Having acquired the boar, he knew there would be no need for hunting tomorrow, and he wanted to make sure he got a good night's sleep so he could have a good exploration of the nearby areas, something he had not done yet.

He snuck off to his hut quietly so as to not cause any offence for leaving early. He stepped inside and sighed. He was tired after today's work and could not wait to get in bed.

It was at this point he heard something and realised that he was not alone in the hut. He turned to his side to see what the noise was that startled him.

A shadowy figure ran towards him, and Levent braced himself. Kaliska wrapped her arms around him, and the two of them shared a warm kiss.

"I missed you today," she said.

"I missed you too."

They continued to kiss for a while, enjoying the moment while they could. They had been meeting up like this for six weeks now in the darkness away from everyone else.

"I need to speak with your father. I can ask his permission."

"I'm not eighteen yet. Be patient. He will allow it but not until then. He is bound by the rules of the tribe."

She kissed him on the cheek and left the hut, turning to smile at him from the doorway. Levent lay down on his bed and let out a huge sigh. He hated having to hide this. He just wanted to be honest with everyone in the village, to be honest with the man who had welcomed him into the tribe with open arms.

Levent was in love with the shaman's daughter.

CHAPTER 18

It was six o'clock, and Arnold was heading to the Athenaeum. He went every evening after school to train at some point, and with everything that had been going on, he didn't want to draw attention to himself by not going today. Everett had already headed home, and Arnold had secured Otto in the container for the night. He was starting to get nervous; they'd expected Mayor Redburn to reach out at some point, demanding to know where Otto was, but the mayor had not been in contact. Surely Otto's dad would have heard about the were-jaguar sighting in town by now.

The sun was beginning to set, and the temperature was cooling, which Arnold was grateful for, given that Otto was now holed up in an airtight storage container.

Arnold arrived at the Spirit Wardens and headed straight to the changing room to get dressed into his training clothes. He planned to train until eight and then head back to the lock-up, not wanting to leave Otto alone for too long.

When Arnold came out of the changing rooms, the

Spirit Wardens seemed different. Quiet. Usually he would be able to hear his dad or some of the other Doyens around, but today, it appeared empty. Arnold headed back to the reception and noticed that Grace wasn't there, either. Thinking back, he couldn't recall if she had been sitting at her desk when he entered, as he'd been preoccupied with his worries about Otto.

Arnold headed to the training room and started practising with his macuahuitl. It wasn't the best training session he had ever had, given that he could not concentrate today. Arnold took a short break, then put away the macuahuitl and began working on his physical strength, making his way through a routine of press-ups, sit-ups, squats, and planks.

Arnold was packing up when one of the hilts he had used in training with Mr. Higgins fell from his bag. He thought for a moment before deciding he would give it a go and have another try at spirit-wielding. No one else was around so a little practice could help.

He picked up the hilt and focused his energy, concentrating like Mr. Higgins had told him to, time and time again. Each time that he had tried, he had failed, but for some reason, he felt more confident this time. He continued to focus, and his hands began to glow with his auro. His hand started to tingle, then he fell to the floor convulsing as though he had just stuck his finger into a plug socket. All his muscles tensed tightly as raw sprit energy coursed through his body. It was a horrible experience, but Arnold knew he needed to get his body used to the spirit energy. Previously Mr. Higgins had assured him that each time he did this process, it would hurt a little less as his body became used to the process. At this moment in time, however, as Arnold lay convulsing on the cold floor once more, he did not feel as though anything had gotten easier since last time. He was struggling to concentrate on getting up from the floor.

Then, to Arnold's amazement, he suddenly had some control over his body, and he began to climb to his feet, his muscles still tensed. Through stubbornness and gritted teeth, he managed to stand tall, and it took everything he had not to allow his body to fold upon itself and slam back against the floor. He was determined to do this. He managed to hold his ground for two seconds before he crumpled up on the floor again, letting go of the hilt to break the connection, allowing him the release of not having the raw energy flow through him. He panted on the floor as he regained his breath and waited for his muscles to stop tingling before getting back to his feet.

He stared at the hilt before shaking his head in disbelief. Arnold knew how much of a glutton for punishment he had become. He picked it up and went through this process repeatedly, each time managing to climb to his feet and stay on his feet that tiny bit longer until the point where he physically felt as though he couldn't practice any more. As he lay on the floor having decided he'd had enough practice today, he felt a real sense of accomplishment, happy with the progress that he had made.

Once his muscles had stopped tingling, he put the hilt back in his bag before having a large drink of water. He went back to the changing room and got showered and dressed before heading to exit the Spirit Wardens, his body now feeling slightly jittery and a little bit numb from his training.

When he made it to the reception, there was still no one around. He looked down the corridor at the training room and towards the exit and a thought went through his head. He stopped walking and headed back to the training room and opened the weapons room. Inside, he picked up his macuahuitl blade. With everything going on, he felt like he would be that little bit safer if he had this with him. No one was around to stop him taking it out of the Spirit Wardens, so Arnold fastened its holster over his shoulder. He then put the macuahuitl against it and quickly headed back down the corridor and left the Spirit Wardens. Arnold knew he would be in trouble if he got caught, so he kept his head down and kept walking at a fast pace until he was well away from the Spirit Wardens and out of sight.

He headed back to Bramley Lock-up so that he could ensure Otto got some fresh air, given that he had been inside for a couple of hours now. He reached the container and looked forward to sitting down and resting. He felt exhausted. Placing his hand on the hieroglyph, he felt it begin to tingle and the container opened up.

"How are you –" Arnold stopped mid-sentence.

Otto was gone.

Arnold quickly looked around. Nothing seemed displaced, nor did it look like there had been any form of struggle. Arnold knew he was the only one who could unlock the container. Yet, Otto had simply vanished into thin air.

He pulled out his phone and rang Otto, but no one answered. Arnold continued to survey the container when he noticed something perched against one of the cabinets. He picked it up to find a card not too dissimilar to a business card. He turned it over to reveal a print of an old picture. Arnold recognised the image straight away: it was the head of a were-jaguar.

Arnold was certain he had seen this symbol somewhere before. He grabbed his grandad's journal straight away and flipped it to the page about the were-jaguar, and there it was.

The same picture that was on the card was in his grandad's book.

It was the symbol for the Order of the Aegis. Arnold's heart raced. Whoever they were, they had Otto, and they wanted Arnold to find them. Why else would they leave this card here for him to find?

Suddenly Arnold's world went dark as his head was covered from behind at the same time that someone grabbed his arms to stop him from moving or fighting back.

"Do not be afraid," came a softly spoken woman's voice from behind him. "Relax, we have your friend. Come with us."

Arnold un-tensed his muscles, and knowing he didn't have much choice, he allowed himself to be escorted from the lock-up and put into a car, which set off taking him to another destination. He was wedged in the back of the car with someone sitting on either side of him. He tried to tip his head back to improve his vision, but whatever had been put over his head ensured he couldn't see anything.

He sat in silence, choosing not to speak. He was pretty confident he knew who it was that had snuck up on him, given the card he had been left in the storage container. He sat calmly and quietly in the car until it eventually pulled up somewhere, and the engine stopped.

The door opened, and suddenly the pressure to his right side left as the hulking person got out of the vehicle. The person grabbed hold of his arm and led him out of the car. Arnold listened to his surroundings and could hear running water, like a stream. He followed the guidance he was being given before coming to an abrupt stop. Arnold could still hear the stream a little but could not feel any breeze on him, which indicated to him that he was indoors somewhere. Shortly after stopping, the hood that had been placed over him was removed, and Arnold squinted as he became accustomed to the light in the room.

The room was large and hollow, and Arnold quickly realised he was in a warehouse of some sort. He couldn't help but notice the smell of chemicals that faintly filled the air. The scent reminded him of hospitals.

A group of men and women stood around him in a large circle, each of them hooded by different animal hides. They appeared to be dressed in some form of armour that resembled bone mail, intricately bound together somehow. There were many shapes and sizes stood around him. He noticed two large, well-built men that Arnold presumed had been in the car with him.

His bleary gaze drew back to the masked figure that stood in front of him. He knew it was a woman by her delicate shape. However, he could not see her face due to it being covered with the hide of a jaguar. This all but confirmed to Arnold who he was dealing with.

"You're the Order of the Aegis," Arnold stated.

"Yes," she answered, her voice reassuring and soothing. She stood with her hands clasped together in front of her, her long, white gown draped down to the floor around her.

"Where's Otto?"

"He is fine. We have given him something that should help him with his transition into Night-Sun. Make it less painful in the future."

"What do you want with him?"

"For him to be safe and to be free from control," the woman explained. Her voice was so gentle.

"Then, we want the same thing," Arnold responded.

"We have been observing you for a while now, Arnold Ethon. Your loyalty and dedication to Night-Sun is to be admired." She paused. "Your grandad would be proud."

Her words piqued Arnold's interest instantly. "You knew my grandad?" he asked, their conversation suddenly becoming more intense.

The woman nodded. "Who do you think moved all his belongings to the lock-up for you?"

This did not make any sense to Arnold. "Why?" he asked.

"Because he willed us to do so, Arnold."

"What do you mean? Why would he ask for that?" Arnold didn't know much about the Order of the Aegis, but he knew enough to understand that they would not have been aligned with the Spirit Wardens in anyway. Elwood had been an Elder for the Spirit Wardens, so what was he doing with the Order of the Aegis?

The woman stepped forwards and took hold of Arnold's hands to reassure him. "Your grandad was a good man, like you are becoming. He came to see me shortly before he died and requested that if his time came, we remove his belongings to somewhere safe before the Spirit Wardens obtained them."

Arnold felt even more confused now.

"You have his journal, do you not?"

Arnold nodded.

"Then I recommend you read it to get some insight. That journal was always intended for you. Your grandad wanted to explain. For me to do so would be disrespectful of his wishes and all that he stood for."

The two solidly built men stepped forwards and covered Arnold's head once more.

"We wanted to show ourselves to you to show we exist. We will keep Night-Sun safe, Arnold, you can trust us. More than the Spirit Wardens." With this, the woman placed some salts underneath Arnold's nose. When he breathed in, he vision began to blur.

"Do not be afraid. We will guide you home, Arnold Ethon."

Arnold drifted into unconsciousness, and his dream took over.

He found himself standing in the same warehouse, but instead of people around him in a circle, he was surrounded by different spirit animals. In front of him stood a coyote, to the left of him a wolf and a hyena. To his right was a reindeer and a buffalo, all of which were entirely focused on him. He went to move his arms and noticed that they were wings; he was in his eagle form.

As he stretched out his wings, the surrounding animals began to buck and bow their heads towards him. Arnold felt as though they were saluting him, giving him the nod to say that they approved of him. He was sure that these were the spirit beasts of the people that had been gathered around him in the warehouse. This was the most bizarre dream.

When he woke, Arnold found that he was in his bed, and he couldn't help but wonder if the night before had been a dream or if it had actually happened.

He felt a little dehydrated and sat up in bed to see a glass of water next to his bed with the card from the Order of the Aegis balanced against it, thus confirming that last night had happened. He sat there, processing everything that had been said. How had they gotten him back to his bed without anyone noticing them? Then again, they had managed to move everything from his grandad's house to the lock-up without being seen, so this didn't really surprise him.

The woman had told him to read his grandad's journal. She'd also warned him not to trust the Spirit Wardens. But how could he not trust the Spirit Wardens? They were all he had ever known or wanted. More so, why would his grandad have been working with the Order of the Aegis?

Arnold looked at his alarm clock. It was four o'clock in the morning, and he was exhausted. His head was spinning, and his body was aching. Arnold knew that he had left the journal at the storage container, and he planned on going there to read it, but first, he needed to rest for a few more hours at least.

CHAPTER 19

Levent woke to a shrill scream, and his heart instantly began racing. He jumped out of his bed and headed out from his hut to see what was happening. Different members of the tribe had begun to emerge from their huts as well, some of whom had brought their weapons with them.

Strangers stood in the shelter in the middle of the village. They looked hostile, and he could see the shaman knelt on the floor in front of them facing away from them as though he were on parade.

Levent ran back into his hut and reached underneath his bed to pull out a roll of fabric that lay there collecting dust. He quickly unwrapped the cloth to reveal his ebony and ivory blade. He had never needed it, until now. He tucked it into the back of his pants before exiting the hut once more.

"This is what happens when you defy the will of the Spirit Wardens!" a voice called from behind the shaman. "Now, I suggest that if you want your shaman to live, then you will stand before us and listen to what we have to say, to offer."

Levent shuffled up before the crowd that had begun to form around the shelter. One of the three men stood there had hold of Kaliska. It had been her scream that woke the village. He wanted to rush forwards to help them, but feared what the consequences might be if he did. He had no choice but to listen to what they had to say, but seeing Kaliska in danger like this made him angry. It was a wave of anger he had managed to keep suppressed for some time, and he didn't want to release it. But he would if he had to.

"We have come to believe that there may be some artefacts here," the man in the middle shouted. He was wearing his sandy coloured pants and green khaki t-shirt. His sweat had formed a wet v down the front of it, such was the humidity here.

"You should be aware that the Spirit Wardens has issued orders to collect such artefacts to preserve safety for all."

"You wish only to preserve yourselves!" an older man called from within the crowd, to which some of the other tribesmen cheered in agreement.

The man laughed, then hit the shaman in the back of the head, knocking him to the ground. "See what you made me do?" he goaded. "Now, I don't want to come in here and have to start roughing people up. So, I am going to ask this once and once only. If there are any artefacts here, you have ten minutes to find them and bring them to us before we take things further."

"Give it to him, Kaliska," the shaman called. "No one needs to get hurt."

"But, Father!"

"No!" His voice was stern and full of authority. "It is my choice."

Kaliska pulled away from the man holding her. The leader of the group nodded for him to let go to allow her to fetch what they had come here for. She disappeared into the shaman's hut before returning with a chalice, which she held tightly to her chest as she walked back up to them to hand it over.

"Father, we can't let them – "

Before she could finish her sentence, she was slapped to the floor by one of the men. He laughed out loud to himself, and groans of disapproval rang out from the tribe.

The leader knelt to her level and lifted her head to look him in the eyes. "Now, don't be putting ideas in your old man's head. I'm sure he just told you to hand it over to me."

As he said this, a tremendous roar erupted from the darkness and the crowd parted between them and the shelter. Levent stood there with his fists tightly clenched. In his right hand, he was holding his dagger. On either side of him stood the two giant mane-less lions, ready to strike at any moment. An orange auro emitted from the dagger and around the spirit beasts, and Levent's hand glowed where he clenched his dagger tightly. Their roars echoed around the village, forcing some of the other villagers to shriek out in fear. He was furious at the way the shaman and Kaliska were being treated, and he would not allow these intruders to stay here any longer. He would not let them take from the tribe what was not theirs.

"How dare you!" Levent growled at the men. "You strike down Kaliska and our shaman, you dishonour whoever you represent." With this, his two lions set off running through the crowd and leapt through the air, instantly pinning the leader's henchmen to the floor. The lions stared them dead in the eyes, ready to bite down on their prey. All Levent needed to do was will it and they would.

Levent, however, only had eyes for one person. He ran towards the shelter and struck out at the leader, letting out his roar of frustration. The leader dodged Levent's attack and pulled out his own weapon. Levent held the hilt of his dagger so that the blade followed the flow of his wrist and down his arm.

The two of them stared into each other's eyes and it was as though time stood still as Levent's heart pounded against his chest, waiting for the man to make his move.

The leader lunged forwards and attempted to slice Levent, but he blocked this with his blade before striking out with his free hand against the man's face. The man was twice his age, and the strength of Levent's punch seemed to surprise him.

"You are stronger than you look, boy," the man goaded. A smile pulled on the corner of his mouth as if he were enjoying every second of this.

The man lashed out again with his knife. Levent dodged with ease before striking back, using his elbow to knock the man down to his knees. He kicked the leader's knife out of his hand, then slid his blade to the man's throat, just hard enough to draw blood.

"Get your men and leave," Levent growled at them. His breathing was heavy, his aggression rising.

"And if we don't?" The leader smirked. His arrogance was unbearable.

Levent's patience was running out and his frustration was becoming dangerously close to bubbling over right here, right in front of everybody.

The smaller of the two lions let out a roar and lunged forwards, biting down on the thug that it had pinned to the floor. The man let out a blood-curdling scream as the lion's teeth pierced his flesh and started to shake his head.

The leader grew furious. "Fine, we will leave," he fumed. Levent's lion instantly stopped its attack and the two of them stepped off their prey so that the men could return to their feet. Levent allowed the leader to climb to his feet, then pushed him across the shelter to his thugs. The three attackers retreated with their tails between their legs.

Levent turned to help the shaman back up to his feet. He had remained silent during the exchange between him and the invaders.

"That blade, where did you get that blade?" the shaman asked.

"I've always had it." The lie was easier to explain than how he had stolen it while in the spirit world.

"I know it. I know that blade."

Levent felt confused, thinking he must be mistaken. There was no way the shaman could have recognised the blade. He had spent most of his life in the spirit world, and he had only acquired the blade prior to being transported here. Until then, his mum had always had it in her possession for as long as he could remember.

"My great-grandad, he is the one who created that artefact. He is the one who controlled the lions of the Aether." The shaman reached out for the blade. "May I?"

Levent passed him the ebony and ivory weapon, not wanting to cause any offence, but he did feel uncomfortable not knowing whether the shaman would give it back to him, given that it appeared to be a long-lost family heirloom.

"This is by no means a coincidence. This blade has connected to you. You have no idea the power you possess because of this blade."

"Can you show me?" Levent asked, wanting to know as much as he could about the blade.

"You have shown great courage and restraint in fending off those Spirit Warden invaders. They roam the lands removing artefacts and hiding them away in London. They don't want any menials to wield their power. They are purists."

"I think I am a menial; without that blade, I have no spirit beast."

"That may be so. Without your soul, the lions of the Aether would not have anyone to connect to within this world. They need you as much as you need them."

The shaman passed the blade back to Levent. "This is yours. The spirits wanted you to be here at this time, at this moment. To protect us."

Levent took the blade back from the shaman, and an overwhelming sense of pride overpowered his emotions. He had a purpose, and he knew that from this day on he would protect this tribe and its people from the Spirit Wardens.

WEEKS TURNED to months and months turned to years. Before Levent knew it, twelve years had passed and he had become a central pillar within the tribe. His dark hair had grown long, his skin had become tanned, and his torturous past was just a distant memory. He had escaped that life and found himself in his version of paradise, one that he never wanted to leave. He was the protector of the tribe, and his ability to summon two spirit beasts had become legendary in the region, ensuring that no outsiders stepped foot within the tribe while he was there. They remained safe and undisturbed, able to live peacefully.

Levent spent his time with the shaman who had been training him for the last twelve years. The shaman's plan was for Levent to step into his shoes once he passed.

Levent had become even stronger, and through his hunting, gathering, and general working within the community, he had developed a muscular physique. His training was intense at times, but Levent become masterful at wielding his spirit blade. He had been told its correct name was the Blade of the Spirits, but Levent much preferred the shortened name he had become accustomed to using. He found that it rolled off the tongue much easier.

Levent lost count of the hours he spent training with the weapon. The shaman told him that to truly master the blade, he would need to practise with it for more than ten thousand hours. Levent felt that he must have been close to this figure, as he practised every single day. His combat ability was his strength, and he had proven to be the strongest and most skilled in the tribe. However, he was not yet skilled enough in the arts needed to be a shaman. He needed to be able to heal using his spirit beasts, needed to learn all the different remedies and potions that the shaman had developed and learned himself. The shaman even told him that one day when he had mastered his powers and abilities, he would be able to create artefacts himself. This was the highest skill a shaman could achieve, and it took an incredible amount of energy to be able to do this. Each time a shaman created an artefact, their life expectancy would shorten.

The shaman always told him he wasn't ready to learn this skill yet, and that ultimately, he would only show him reluctantly so that the power was passed on within the tribe. Being close to the shaman, it became Levent's role to be involved in decision-making within the tribe, and the rest of the people that lived in this community had nothing but respect for him. Levent was kind, caring, and compassionate, but the thing he was admired for was his bravery, which he showed time and time again, putting other people's safety and well-being well before his own.

It was through this bravery that the shaman finally gave his blessing to Levent to marry his daughter, Kaliska. The two of them had been in a relationship for twelve years now, and Levent was still as devoted to the shaman's daughter as ever.

Levent stood in his hut with two other members of the tribe, who were painting his body with different colours, creating symbols and drawings all over his skin, including hieroglyphs of his spirit beasts and Kaliska's. One of the tribesmen picked up a sash and placed this over the top of his head. It rested against his shoulders, and the leaves which formed part of the sash scratched his skin, but he was quickly able to ignore this.

"Are you ready?" the tribesman asked, his body also decorated in different colours. He was already prepared for the occasion.

"It is what I have always wanted," Levent said, nodding. He was incredibly nervous, the most nervous he had ever felt. His stomach was tied up in knots, and he felt as though he could vomit at any moment.

Today was a special day.

Today, he was going to marry the love of his life, Kaliska.

CHAPTER 20

No sooner had Arnold woken up, he got himself dressed and headed down to the lock-up to read through his grandad's journal like the woman had told him to do the night before. It wasn't as warm today as it had been the day before, with the weather appearing slightly overcast, and the clouds sat relatively low on the hills on the far side of Oswaldtwistle.

The town was eerily quiet with it being so early on a Sunday. Arnold couldn't remember the last time he had been up this early and out of the house at the weekend. His eyes were still bleary, and he wiped the dry sleep that had crusted underneath his eyelids, causing his eyes to water even more than they were.

By now he had become used to the aching feeling over his body from his physical training and training to spirit-wield, but today he could not help but feel that he had pushed himself too far the day before. As he made his way through the ghostlike town, he could see one of the many cafés that populated Oswaldtwistle was opening. The woman that owned it was setting everything up in the back of the open-plan kitchen, while one of the waitresses stood outside having a cigarette. The newspaper boy was exiting the newspaper shop just down the road, with his large paper bag looking filled to the brim. The paperboy looked over-encumbered, as though he could fall at any moment. He placed his paper bag in between himself and the handlebars while shuffling along with his feet. Apart from the paperboy, Arnold didn't see anyone else on his way over to the lock-up and by the time he reached it, he felt like the fresh air had cleared his lungs, and he felt revitalised.

He opened his lock-up and could see his grandad's journal sat on the side of the cupboard where he had left it. He grabbed the leather book and hastily opened it, wanting to learn what the woman had meant by what she had said to him. He skipped past the entry that he had read the night before and started to read the entries one by one.

It was fascinating to read, with each entry explaining the work Elwood had been carrying out for the Spirit Wardens, getting to travel all across the world in the process. The stories ranged from stopping robberies, thugs, and even a murder in the early nineties. Each entry he read showed how great his grandad had been as a Doyen and then later on in his career as the Elder.

One entry in particular caught Arnold's attention due to spotting the words *Order of the Aegis* early on.

April 15th 1995

I don't like the way that the Spirit Wardens store artefacts and keep menials from using them. It just does not sit right, and how the Spirit Wardens have acquired some artefacts has been questionable. It's why I have always stored some at home. I don't know whose hands are the wrong hands. Is it anyone wanting to use these artefacts, or is it the Spirit Wardens?

I've recently had contact from the Order of the Aegis. They are going to be here soon and have asked me to meet up with them. They have requested the artefact that I borrowed from them when we trapped Helen in the spirit world. I will have to speak to Edith. Hopefully, she will tell me where it is. After all, I did ask her to put it somewhere safe, somewhere where I did not know the location.

The Order of the Aegis and the Spirit Wardens, dare I write it, but I feel more drawn towards the Order of the Aegis at this moment in time. Maybe it's time I resigned as Elder. Something in their letter I received concerned me. They spoke of the Spirit Wardens crossing the line but did not tell me what. I am going to do some digging and see what I can find out before the Order of the Aegis arrives.

ARNOLD PUT the journal down to process what he had just read. It certainly came across to him that his grandad was not entirely on board with the Spirit Wardens. If that was the case, why had he never said anything to his dad, or himself for that matter? Arnold had always wanted to join the Spirit Wardens, to become a Doyen and protect his community as his grandad had done. Like his dad still did.

Arnold felt incredibly confused, but even more so, he was angry with his grandad for not being honest with him. If he had, would Arnold still have wanted to join the Spirit Wardens?

The container door moved, startling Arnold. He jumped to his feet but quickly calmed when he realised it was Marrok.

"Why are you here so early?" Marrok asked as he pulled

the container door to the side, the metal scraping on the rollers echoing loudly around the barren lock-up.

"I was just going to ask you the same thing," Arnold said.

"What are you doing?" Marrok asked.

Arnold was still holding his grandad's journal, his frustration rising. He threw it down on the side. "Well, I was reading," he spoke shortly. "Might want to read that."

"What does it say?"

"Basically that my grandad didn't fully trust the Spirit Wardens and was looking to get out."

Arnold sat perched against the cupboard, his frustration towards his grandad ever-growing.

Why couldn't he have just been honest? What had he been hiding? More and more questions entered Arnold's head.

"Right, okay." Marrok's shifted his body, sweat beading on his head. He seemed hesitant for some reason, which caught Arnold's attention.

"Everything okay? You seem edgy."

Marrok moved about awkwardly, shuffling through some old books that were in a box in front of him. "I'm fine, I mean, your grandad might have had a reason for wanting to leave the Spirit Wardens. Maybe the Order of the Aegis had more information, and that's why they wanted to meet up."

Arnold continued to watch Marrok who was squirming that much he looked as though he was about to combust spontaneously. "I didn't say anything about the Order of the Aegis wanting to meet up with him," Arnold said. His friend, it seemed, was not being entirely honest with him. Something he did not care to entertain today, not after learning of his grandad's dishonesty about the Spirit Wardens.

Arnold suddenly had a flashback to a detail in the

dream he'd had last night. A detail he had overlooked until now.

"You were there," he said. When he had dreamt that he was surrounded by spirit animals, the one to his immediate left was a wolf, a white wolf. Arnold thought nothing of this at the time, but now it stood out to him like a sore thumb. How had he not picked this up any sooner?

"You are with the Order of the Aegis, aren't you?"

Marrok nodded. "Yes." His nervousness seemed to subside as soon as he spoke, as if he were finally unburdened by the secret he had been hiding from Arnold.

Marrok had been lying to Arnold this entire time. It felt like he had just received a double blow of people not being honest with him, and it hurt.

"Why lie to me?" Arnold demanded. "Why not tell me why you were really here?"

"I'm sorry, Arnold, I really am. I was following instructions. Trust me. I wanted to tell you everything."

"Trust you!" Arnold barked back. He was less than impressed with Marrok's explanation; blaming someone else was the easy way out in his eyes. "Have you been following me?" Arnold felt furious at the betrayal and could tell he was losing his temper. First his grandad and now his latest friend, both with connections to the Order of the Aegis, the very organisation that had suddenly come forward to contact him yesterday. Arnold's world had been tipped upside down overnight, and he was struggling to process all this new information.

"They wanted to make sure of your allegiance," Marrok said slowly.

"My allegiance? I'm training at the Spirit Wardens. I want to be a Doyen. I'm going to be a Doyen."

"You need to calm down, Arnold, let me explain."

"Calm down!" Arnold tried to push past Marrok, wanting out of the container.

Marrok stood his ground. "You need to listen to me," he said.

Arnold felt incensed, his blood rushing to his head. His anger was dangerously close to spilling over now.

"Arnold, calm down, I am not here to hurt you. I am here to help you." Marrok's hands were up, showing his open palms, trying to de-escalate the situation.

"What is going on?" Everett scolded from outside the container. She and George stood outside, both still wearing their pyjamas underneath their coats.

"We only came down because Everett saw you power-walking through town," George yawned, given that it was still quite early in the morning.

"Looks like it's a good job that we did. You look ready to kill someone," Everett added, her words directed at Arnold.

Arnold clenched his fists. "Why don't you ask him? He's been lying to us this whole time. He is with the Order of the Aegis. They took Otto!"

"Well, right now you look like the only one capable of hurting anyone, so sit down, shut up, and let Marrok explain," Everett said, folding her arms.

Arnold sighed and reluctantly sat down. He didn't want to fight in front of Everett and George, so he opted to do as he was told. He breathed in and out through his nose to calm himself down. "Fine. This best be good, though." He sulked like a petulant child as he folded his arms, waiting to hear what lies would be spouted next.

Marrok smiled at Everett in appreciation, evidently amazed at her ability to calm Arnold down. However,

Everett looked less than impressed and had a face like thunder as she stood there with her arms crossed, scowling at the pair of them. George shuffled into the container and sat herself down, leaning her head against the container wall. She appeared almost vacant and not that interested in what was going on.

"As I was trying to say, I was told that I was not allowed to tell you that I am part of the Order of the Aegis. As you know, we have the belief that one day our deity would return in the form of the were-jaguar, or as we know him, Night-Sun. As you now know, something has happened to Otto. His body has somehow fused with that of his spirit beast. Which has given him the ability to transform himself into the were-jaguar."

"So, you think he is Night-Sun?" Everett asked.

"That is correct. We received information from Otto's family, who explained that he had become corrupted. I was sent here to get closer to Otto, and I thought the best way of doing this was through you guys. My plan had taken longer than I expected, given that you two were not talking when I arrived here in Oswaldtwistle and began attending your school. The Order of the Aegis was concerned when you two were not speaking and needed to trust that you would do right by Otto when you discovered his true identity. As expected, you did not fail, and you have satisfied the council that you share your grandad's compassion for others."

"What do you know of my grandad?" Arnold spoke shortly, unable to keep the anger from his voice.

"That he was a kind man, just as you are. He saved us. There are not many of the Order of the Aegis left, and the only reason we are still around is because of him. He came to see us shortly before he passed and told us that you were being allowed to join the Spirit Wardens, and this caused him great confliction. Do you remember, Arnold? It was when he and your dad had a falling out?"

Arnold thought back to the argument he had once heard between Bernard and Elwood in the middle of the night. The night that he had met Levent for the first time and rescued Charles Grey, who was a retired Doyen, one of the people involved in banishing his corrupted grandma to the spirit world.

"Are you saying that when he left for a while, he was with the Order of the Aegis?"

"Yes. That is exactly what I am saying. Your grandad, he asked us to do this for you when he was gone. To bring all of his belongings that he had collected through the years to here. So that you could keep them and learn from them. So that the Spirit Wardens would not take them for themselves."

"Why was he so against the Spirit Wardens? He dedicated his whole life to them." Arnold was beginning to calm down, but he was as confused as ever about what Marrok was telling him.

"I don't know all the answers, Arnold, but there are people from the Order of the Aegis that do, that knew your grandad far better than I ever did. Please, you need to work with us like your grandad once did."

"How do you mean?" George picked up on the conversation and had decided she would give her input.

"Something is happening, deep beneath us. There is a great amount of spirit energy within Oswaldtwistle. This is from a gateway. One that opened when your grandma was sent there for her safety as well as others. We think that someone wants to gain access to the mines beneath the town and delve deep enough to open a gateway to bring her back, and we can't let that happen. We now believe that this same person is now in possession of an artefact which can be used to help open the gateway. The one that was taken from your granny's shop, George." Marrok turned to look at George, his eyes saddened.

George sat upright, suddenly looking interested in Marrok's words. "But Otto broke in when he changed into the were-jaguar."

"Otto may have done this, but he was under the control of the dagger that fused him and his spirit beast."

“His dad, his dad has the dagger,” Arnold said. “Otto said so himself, when he became corrupted, his dad took the dagger to look for ways to free him from the bond.”

"Why would he do all this? Why would he steal from the shop, make Otto do these things?" Everett said, her face scrunched as she pondered on her thoughts. “It just doesn’t make sense.”

"He is desperate to separate Otto from his spirit beast,” Arnold said. “Who knows how far he will go.”

Despite Everett’s hesitance, Arnold was sure of it. The more he thought about it, the more it made sense.

"What do we need to do?" Arnold asked. “How do we stop him? How do we get Otto’s life back?”

"We have Otto where we’ll fight to keep him safe. With us, he is well protected. We need you to keep the final piece of the puzzle safe, no matter what."

"The final piece, what is that, then? What am I going to be looking after?"

"Not what, Arnold. Who."

Marrok turned to face George, who suddenly looked incredibly uncomfortable herself and began to squirm in the corner of the room where she sat. She stood up, looking perplexed at what Marrok was saying.

Everett walked over to George and held her trembling hand to reassure her. "This doesn't make sense; what does George have to do with any of this?"

"Her blood. It's about her blood."

Arnold looked back at the confrontations that he'd had with the were-jaguar, and he kicked himself for not picking up on the link. The first attack was directly on George. The second was right outside the storage container. Both times it was Arnold that had stood against it, both times Arnold had been successful in this. But he was not the target; George was, on both occasions. The third time they faced off, when Otto transformed in front of their very eyes, Otto was trying to escape them, he was fighting them off, desperate to get away. To get his target, which must have been the artefact that he had ransacked Rushton Remedies in search for. The last question that remained was why.

"George, I am sorry. It was your granny, you see. You share her blood and her abilities. You have it in you to be a shaman."

"But why me? Why our blood? I don't understand." George continued to tremble. None of this was adding up.

"Your granny was the spirit weaver who opened the gateway that banished Arnold's grandma. Her spirit is linked to opening a new gateway to bring her back, and her energy lives on in you." Marrok picked up the journal that Arnold had been reading and took this across to her. "Read this. It will explain everything. She is mentioned many times. She helped Arnold's grandad and Charles Grey with their work within the Spirit Wardens, and quite often was key in them succeeding."

"What about you? Why can't the Order of the Aegis keep

her safe? Surely that's the best place for her if she needs protecting," Arnold pointed out.

"No!" Marrok raised his voice. "Whatever happens, they cannot be together; that is what he wants, that is what they need to open the gateway. You need to protect her, Arnold. You cannot let them take her."

"What do you mean?" George asked. "What happens if we are together?"

"If you are together then so will be all the components to this ritual. As soon as your blood is spilled," Marrok replied, his expression serious.

"My blood?" George said, her skin turning almost translucent. "I wish I never asked now." She sat down on one of the boxes.

"What are you going to do?" Everett said.

"I need to report back to the Order of the Aegis, but if you need me, call me, and I will get to you as soon as I can." With this, Marrok headed to exit the storage container. "I'm truly sorry for this burden, George." He left and disappeared into the courtyard, heading back to wherever the Order of the Aegis had set up their camp.

The three of them sat silent for a while, each of them trying their hardest to comfort George who was crying her eyes out. She had only just lost her granny and was still coming to terms with this, and now she had learned she was in mortal danger.

"This isn't fair," George cried into Everett's arms. "Why me? Why does it have to be me?"

Arnold put his arms around Everett and George tightly and hugged them, not wanting to let either of them go. It was his job to keep her safe, and that was what he intended to do. He wouldn't let any harm come to her, not while he was still breathing.

"I'm going to keep you safe, George, I promise," he told her.

"I'm going to hold you to that." Everett squeezed his hand tightly, fully aware of the burden that had just been placed on him.

CHAPTER 21

The sun was especially harsh with the humidity making the air feel sticky, the moisture feeling like his body was wrapped in skin-tight clingfilm. Levent stood with the other two tribesmen, momentarily taking in what was due to happen that day. His body was highly decorated, and the tribesman had done everything they needed to prepare him, in appearance, anyway. There was still a long way to go just to settle his nerves.

"Good luck, my friend."

"Not that you will need it."

The two tribesmen patted Levent on the shoulder before leaving his hut.

"Shall we go?"

Levent nodded and took a large breath in to try and steady his nerves, but at this moment in time, he felt as though he could collapse at any moment. He followed the two men out of his hut and through the village. As he walked, the other members of the tribe began to sing and chant as they joined his procession and continued on their journey through the densely wooded area. The crowd grew larger and larger as the whole village was participating.

On this momentous occasion, the shaman's daughter was getting married.

Levent felt dazed as he continued to make his way to the ceremonial stones where the ceremony was due to take place, concentrating on not tripping over any roots that lay hidden on the ground. He was sheltered from the sun, but sweat still pooled on his head. He pushed on through the heat and the terrain, eager to get to his destination as quickly as possible. He was soon to marry Kaliska, and in all truth, he just wanted the ceremony to be over and for them both to be man and wife after all these years.

It was not too long before he could see the ceremonial stones in the distance which were a series of millennia-old ancient blocks that lay on the ground in no particular order. There were five overall, varying in sizes and shapes.

The stone monument was often a place where the shaman would come to meditate. He had always told Levent that the area had a great connection to the spirit world and that their tribe had been conducting ceremonies here going back many generations. Now it was the turn of Levent and Kaliska to be married here, and Levent could not think of a more beautiful place than he had ever come across in his life.

When they reached the stones, the two tribesmen stepped to the sides and allowed Levent to walk through between them. Levent obliged, and once he made it past them, he could see the shaman sat atop one of the stones with his legs crossed while he meditated. Levent could hear him humming and chanting to himself as he made his way over to the part of the ceremonial site he had been instructed to when practising.

Levent watched intently as the shaman continued his meditation and waited for him to acknowledge his presence. He could feel his legs trembling beneath him, and his heart began to beat harder as his time to marry Kaliska drew ever closer. After a few minutes, he began to feel uncomfortable at the shaman not acknowledging him.

Levent cleared his throat. "Any advice before we get started?" he asked.

"Yes, don't interrupt the shaman that is blessing your marriage." The shaman opened his eyes and smiled down at Levent, who was stood feeling incredibly nervous below him.

Levent cracked a smile back but could not tell whether the shaman was joking or not, which in turn made his stomach feel as though it had just turned inside out. Had he just offended the shaman right before he was to be married to his daughter? What if he decided to curse him now rather than bless him, or even worse, withdraw his consent to them getting married?

"Relax, Levent. I am only joking with you." The shaman's words failed to reassure Levent of his worries, however. "It is not very often a shaman gets the opportunity to conduct the ceremony of his daughter getting married. Allow me that moment to wind you up. You can relax now. However, you look as though you are ready for a funeral, not your marriage."

Levent laughed, and the knot in his stomach changed from a feeling of worry to one of apprehension. What was taking Kaliska so long? Why was she not here yet?

"She will be here at any moment. You are making me nervous, calm down, my boy."

Levent felt he best do as he was told and tried to steady his nerves. Regulating his breathing better, he stood there with his hands behind his back as he awaited Kaliska's arrival. He did not have to wait long before he could hear the soft tone of some of the tribeswomen singing as they escorted Kaliska to the ceremonial stones.

Levent's heart fluttered in anticipation of her arrival, and as soon as she appeared behind the escorting women, his nerves disappeared in an instant. Her beauty was like none that he had ever seen, with her dark skin complemented by the reflecting light from the stones. It was as though her skin was shimmering in the sun. She looked truly radiant, and when the two of them crossed eyes, they cast smiles at one another. Levent caught sight of the enchanting tribal dress that she was wearing and could not help but wonder the time that the tribeswomen must have put into creating such a mesmerising dress for Kaliska for her wedding day. He knew that Kaliska and her closest friends had been working on this dress for several years in preparation for this day.

Levent stood there wishing to savour this moment truly. Kaliska looked astonishing, and the smile on her face was the happiest that he had ever seen her. He just wanted her to be standing with him now so they could share this magical moment. He loved her with all his heart. She had saved him when he was at his lowest and his most desperate. He would never forget falling in love with her the first time that he had met her, her kindness like nothing he had ever experienced. She accepted him straight away, accepted his horrific scars, never once being fazed or afraid by them. She calmed him when he had nightmares about his past and reassured him that everything would be okay. She had given her heart to him, and in return, he wanted to provide her with his soul.

He continued to look towards Kaliska, entranced at her smile when he felt an unexpected force against his shoulder. It caught him off guard and offset his balance. He looked towards Kaliska as he began to fall to the floor, and her smile had turned to horror as she screamed out towards him.

He slammed against the floor, and a shooting pain went down the entire right side of his body. He looked at his shoulder and could see an arrow protruding out of it. Screams rang out around him as people realised what had just happened. Someone had just tried to kill him, but why? His first and only thought at this moment was that he needed to get to Kaliska, to make sure she was safe. As he pulled himself quickly back to his feet, panic was all around him. Women and children had started to run to safety as the tribesmen readied themselves to fight to protect them. Levent frantically looked around, but he could not see Kaliska anywhere.

“Spirit Wardens!" the shaman bellowed, pointing out towards the trees.

Levent followed the direction he was pointing where some men and women had emerged from the trees. They wore different coloured robes with differing crests on them. There must have been about twenty of them which was more than double the number of the tribesmen that stood ready to face them.

"Where's Kaliska?" Levent called out to the shaman. Her safety was his priority and all that he could think about.

"She was ushered back towards the village for her safety. Are you okay?"

The tip of the weapon had exited the back of Levent’s shoulder. He grabbed hold of the arrow and snapped it.

Wincing slightly at the pain, he looked towards the large group before him, searching for whoever had shot the arrow at him. "Why are they here? Why now?" he questioned, hoping that the shaman would have the answers.

"They have come for artefacts, like before. They have come for your blade. We will not allow that." The shaman pointed towards the attackers, and his entire body began to glow a cyan colour as he channelled his auro. Before he could do anything, another arrow flew by Levent and buried itself deep within the shaman's chest.

"No!" Levent cried, and he pulled out his blade, his anger taking hold of him. It was a rage that he had not felt before, not even when he was tortured in the spirit world by his mum's dragon. He could feel the rage building up inside him, and he let out a mighty roar of his anguish and pain. The shaman had been like a father to him, had been struck down so needlessly.

Levent's cry was drowned out by the roar of his lions as they formed at either side of him. The beasts instantly rushed out and dived towards the Spirit Wardens, taking two of them out immediately. Enraged by the attack on their shaman, the rest of the tribe let out a collective battle cry and ran at the robed men and women who were all channelling their auros to summon their spirit beasts. A rainbow of colours lit up the trees as each of the tribespeople began drawing on their own auros in their time of need.

Levent scrambled to the shaman's side and tried to sit him up. Blood was leaving his body at an alarming rate, pooling beneath him.

"You need to find Kaliska. You need to save her," the shaman said as his auro began to fade from around him.

"But what about you?" Levent didn't want to leave him, but could not stay if he were to honour the shaman's wishes.

The shaman grabbed hold of Levent's hand, and Levent felt a strange sensation coming over him. The pain in his shoulder dulled and his anger began to clear like a fog being moved by the wind. Everything became clearer to him.

"There's more than one way that I can live. I am channelling my auro to you. This will help you become stronger and to understand. Please, you need to save Kali . . ." He closed his eyes as the cyan glow around him began to fade before he slumped into Levent's arms. His body became motionless. His life had faded away, taken away for no apparent reason.

The roars and shouts from men, women, and spirit beasts in combat echoed all around him. None were louder than Levent's lions, whom he could hear but not see. Levent lowered the shaman to the ground before gathering himself. He stood up and ran towards the battle, his fist clenched and his blade outstretched. He needed to make sure that whoever these attackers were, they did not harm any more innocents.

Two robed people stepped into his path and attempted to block him. Levent slammed his fist into one of the men's chests, and the man crumpled instantly from the brutal force. He swung his blade out at the other attacker who was not fast enough to block the blow, and Levent felt the blade pierce the man's flesh as he continued his run back towards the village.

Levent sprinted as fast as he could. He could hear the trees rustling behind him and glanced over to see that it was his lions catching him up, wanting to aid him in finding Kaliska.

Even though the shaman had helped heal his injury, blood still seeped down his shoulder like a crimson stream. Levent didn't know if it was magic or his adrenaline, but the wound did not faze him. He had hardly noticed any pain and was pushing himself through the light-headedness that hit him in wave after pulsating wave.

He finally reached the village, manically trying to spot where Kaliska was. His chest was pounding and his breathing was heavy, his worry unimaginable. He did not know what he would do should anything happen to her.

There was a scream from just beyond Levent's hut, and Levent ran towards it.

Three men from the Spirit Wardens stood there in their robes. They had hold of Kaliska as well as two other women from the tribe.

"Kaliska!" Levent called out. He did not care for his safety, he merely wished for hers. One of the robed men turned towards him, and Levent's anger rose even further as he realised who it was stood before him. It was the man that Levent had faced off against twelve years ago when he had summoned his lions in front of everyone for the first time.

The man had a bow hanging over his shoulder, and Levent knew instantly that he was the one who had shot him, who had so callously and needlessly killed the shaman. How was he going to tell Kaliska that her father had been killed, and that he had been unable to stop it from happening?

Levent's fury took over, and he walked towards the men with his blade in his hand, his intent stare focused purely on the leader of the group. He did not care that he was outnumbered, and he didn't need his lions for what he was going to do. He wanted to deal with this himself, and there was no way that he would let them get away with what they had done to them.

"Stop right there!" the leader called out. "Come any

closer, and I am going to have no choice but to kill this pretty little thing."

Levent stopped in his tracks. The leader was holding a blade against Kaliska's throat.

"Now, those lions over there are quite the problem, let's put them away, eh?"

Levent called his lions back towards his blade. He didn't want to use them, anyway; he wanted to savour ending this man's life with his own hands.

"What have you done! I told you to let me handle this!" A man stepped out from within the thick trees of the forest. His robes were torn and his head bloodied, but he was most certainly part of the Spirit Wardens. He looked older than the others, and wearier. "Capture not kill, that is our way. It's our fundamentals."

"Well, the old man shouldn't have got in the way. I was aiming for him." The leader nodded towards Levent and smiled at him, trying to goad him into a reaction. "This is personal; it's between him and me, Elwood. This does not concern you."

"Please just let her go. I beg you." Levent held his hands up as a peace offering. He just wanted Kaliska to be safe.

"She does mean a lot to you, doesn't she?" he teased further.

"Let her go!" the robed man commanded. "I am your Elder, now let her go!"

The man smirked and pushed Kaliska towards Levent. Levent felt he could stop holding his breath as she began to walk towards him. She was all that mattered.

Suddenly her face became contorted with shock as an arrow burst through her chest from behind. She let out a whimper as she began to fall.

"No!" Levent roared as his rage consumed him. Why had

he done this, why would he fire an arrow into someone defenceless? It was cowardice at its worst. Without hesitating, Levent launched his dagger through the air, but the man was sharp to this and pulled one of the robed men into his path who took the full force of the blade as it embedded in his chest, his breathing gurgled as he drew his last breath. The man grinned at Levent as he set off into the woods. Levent wanted to give chase but heard Kaliska call out for him.

"Levent!" Her struggling speech cut him deeper than any weapon could. He couldn't bear to lose her, couldn't believe what was happening. This was supposed to be their big day. They had wanted this for so long. His entire existence was down to her, and how she made him feel whole, made him feel human again.

The robed man had summoned his spirit beast, and a large elk stood over Kaliska.

Levent felt a flicker inside his brain, like a rubber band snapping. "Stay away from her!" He ran towards the body on the floor and removed his blade from his chest, then raised it, ready to fight.

"Please, let me try and heal her. I can ease her suffering." The Elder held his hands out and began to channel his auro.

Levent's anger was rising to a new level as his auro coursed through his body like electricity. He had never felt power like it, and he wanted to use it to punish everyone from the Spirit Wardens. His power surged as the orange energy from his blade engulfed his entire body.

Then he noticed something that he had not seen for a long time. An area just before the trees to the side of the shelter had become distorted. He recognised it straight away as a gateway, a portal to the spirit world which he had travelled through so many years ago and had not seen since.

He was pulled towards the portal like a magnet, and he knew what was happening. It was drawing him in, and he had no control over it.

"No, I can't. Kaliska!" He fought against the pull as hard as he could, but before he knew it, it was too late, and he was dragged through the distorted energy, screaming as he tried to fight against it, but his efforts were pointless. The last thing he could see before being pulled through was the robed man knelt over Kaliska who lay on the floor motionless, her life drifting away from her.

He was back in the spirit world. He knew it straight away because the air felt different, and there seemed to be no breeze, no heat burning down from above like when he was in his village. He crawled around frantically on the floor where he had landed, desperate to go back through, to get to Kaliska, but the portal had vanished. His frustration manifested in a scream of anguish. He had just seen the shaman killed, who had died in his arms, his auro now a part of him. The shaman had been like a father to Levent, and he didn't know how to process his death.

And Kaliska was gone.

"It should have been me!" Tears streamed down his face and dampened the dry floor where he knelt. He had never experienced grief before, and he had no idea how to deal with it. He began to punch the floor in frustration, pounding the ground over and over until his hands began to bleed. He gritted his teeth, his face distorted with rage and fury. He needed to find a way back, he needed to get back to his tribe to help Kaliska, but the problem was, he had no idea how he was going to do that. The few times he had transported through had been sporadic, and he'd never had any control or understanding of why these portals opened for him. The portal had so cruelly torn him away from Kaliska when she needed him most.

Levent continued to scream into the air with prolonged anguish. He knew there was nothing he could do to save Kaliska.

And finally, the anger inside him took over.

CHAPTER 22

For the first time, Arnold could not turn to his dad for help or advice on their current situation, and it killed him.

George and Arnold remained holed up at the storage container, not knowing what to do. George looked increasingly pensive about the plan. The weight of this looked as though it was taking its toll on her.

Everett had left the container to get some supplies for them from the shop, but she had been gone longer than expected. Arnold and George had started to worry something had happened to her when Everett calmly appeared in the doorway with a carrier bag full of sandwiches, crisps, and drinks. She seemed completely oblivious as to why they were both looking at her with their eyebrows raised.

"Took your time! We were worried, Everett," George said, racing over to Everett to give her a tight hug.

"What? I decided to grab a shower while I was home. Arnold is with you," Everett pointed out.

"You do pick your moments," Arnold joked, trying to make light of the situation.

They spent the entire morning at the storage container, pacing around and trying to come up with a plan on how to keep George away from Otto. So far, they had managed to come up with nothing. They tucked into their sandwiches quietly while each of them tried to think of what to do next. Arnold was munching down on his tuna and sweetcorn sandwich, which was his favourite. He was pleased that Everett had remembered.

Arnold wished he could call his dad, but he couldn't turn to the Spirit Wardens given that they would discover all his grandad's belongings. They would surely figure out that Elwood had somehow been associated with the Order of the Aegis, a group that actively worked against the Spirit Wardens. Elwood would be deemed a traitor and his mark would be removed from the temple, removed from the carvings meant to honour his sacrifice and dedication to the Spirit Wardens.

Arnold couldn't bear the thought of bringing shame to his grandad's legacy. They would have to find another way.

But what Arnold still couldn't understand was why his grandad might have been working against the Spirit Wardens in the first place, and this was causing him great conflict. He couldn't discuss this with his dad for fear of how he would respond, and he wanted to protect his grandad's name. For now, Arnold had no reason to disbelieve the information that Marrok had given them, as it correlated with what Arnold had figured out for himself. The Order of the Aegis had Otto in their protection, George was with him, and Mayor Redburn had the artefact that they needed. As long as Otto, George, and the artefact remained separate, whatever this ritual was couldn't happen.

"We can't stay in here forever, guys. It's not practical,"

Everett pointed out. She was becoming bored of being holed up in one place.

"That's easy for you to say, it's not your blood he is coming after," George fired back.

"Come on, you two. There's no need to fall out," Arnold said. However, he agreed with Everett, and was merely trying to play peacekeeper with the three of them beginning to develop cabin fever from their prolonged time in the storage container. "I do think we need to come up with another plan. We're sitting ducks here."

"Well, it's the best idea, in my opinion," said George.

"What else can we do? If we stay here, we might as well just hand her over to Mayor Redburn."

Arnold thought about what Everett had said for a moment. "That might not be such a bad idea."

"What?" George squealed. "What a stupid idea that is, that's not going to happen!"

"Hear me out, George." Arnold could understand her initial reluctance, but a plan was forming in his mind. "What if we let him take you?"

George and Everett were in a combined state of disbelief at Arnold's words.

"I think you have taken one too many blows to the head," George told him.

"Let's face it, there is no one we can go to for help with this. The Spirit Wardens might even be involved, remember? I've seen Mr. Whittaker speaking with Mayor Redburn about opening the coal mines. What if we went somewhere and allowed you to be taken? I'll follow and let Everett know where you are, and she can let Marrok know. If they bring the Order of the Aegis, we could stop Mayor Redburn before anything happened." He knew it was a long stretch, but what else could they do?

"Absolutely not. No way, Arnold. We will get ourselves killed," George protested.

"The other option is we wait around looking over our shoulder until he appears or sends someone else to get you for the sacrifice."

"I hate to say it, George, but I think Arnold has a point. Mayor Redburn would not be expecting Arnold to be so bold, and technically he does need Otto too for whatever his plan is to work."

"Seriously, you too?" George demanded. "What if it goes wrong?"

"Would you rather be looking over your shoulder or would you rather we try and catch him off guard and get the upper hand?" Arnold asked. He was sure that the plan could work; they just needed to find somewhere away from the lock-up, so its location remained hidden from everybody else.

George still did not look impressed, but she looked like she was beginning to give his wild idea a second thought rather than dismissing it outright. "Why don't we tell Marrok the plan?"

"Because they wouldn't want us to do it," Everett said immediately. "I think this is the best way we follow you, and we catch him."

"What could possibly go wrong?" George asked sarcastically. "And where are we going to hatch this plan then?"

The three thought for a moment, and then Everett smiled. "Where do teenagers hang around at the weekend? It's certainly not old, dusty storage containers."

Arnold didn't know the answer, as he spent all his weekends training at the Spirit Wardens. Arnold and George both looked at Everett waiting for her to tell them where they would lay George as bait.

"The nature reserve at Foxhill Bank," Everett explained.

Arnold agreed that this was a good idea with its location away from the general population. Hopefully, this would help to prevent anyone from getting hurt. The nature reserve sat just outside the centre of town and was a short walk from the lock-up. All they needed to do was draw Mayor Redburn out by making sure they walked down all the main roads on their way there and hope that he would see them.

"Right, it's decided then," Arnold confirmed.

The others nodded in agreement, but George looked more nervous than ever.

"I won't let anything happen to you, George. I promise," Arnold told her. The three of them readied themselves to leave to put their plan in motion.

Arnold grabbed his macuahuitl and placed its harness over his head. He shut the container and held his hand against the elk hieroglyph that decorated the side and waited for the locks to kick in before the three of them left the lock-up and began their journey towards Foxhill Nature Reserve.

Their dangerous plan had been set in motion. Arnold knew there was a lot that could go wrong, but it gave him the chance to catch Mayor Redburn and stop all of this, to save his friends.

The streets seemed uneasily quiet, as though the town knew of the showdown that would ensue should their plan work. They made their way across the overgrown field that sat in front of the nature reserve and disappeared into the trees where they escorted George down the path towards the central bank. Locals did visit here from time to time to walk their dogs or come and feed the ducks, but it remained quiet today, which was a good sign.

Once they got to the bank, they readied themselves to leave George.

Everett wrapped her arms around George and gave her a lasting hug. George looked like she was going to have her breath hugged out of her as the two of them remained in their embrace for some time, Everett becoming tearful.

"We will be right over there." Arnold pointed to some trees that were surrounded by bushes and shrubs to keep their location hidden. "If anything goes wrong, I will be out straight away."

"You better be," George finished before hugging him. Arnold and Everett headed to their hiding point and removed themselves from sight, sitting on the floor next to one another. They waited awkwardly like something should have happened straight away.

Hours passed. They remained at the nature reserve, waiting for Mayor Redburn to make a move against them. It was surely just a matter of time. Boredom had well and truly set in with the two of them waiting in introspective silence while George remained out in the open on her own.

Arnold was crouched in the undergrowth with Everett leaning into him.

“I hope she’s okay,” she said.

“I will do everything I can to keep her safe, but I can’t think of any other way for us to stop Mayor Redburn.”

“I know, Arnold,” she replied, giving him a nervous smile.

Maybe it was because of the danger but Arnold felt a moment pass between them and he did something that surprised himself. He leant into Everett and gave her a kiss.

He was so startled by his own action that he almost drew back to apologise, but then she kissed him back.

It was a moment Arnold wished would last forever.

Arnold's phone suddenly vibrated in his pocket, bringing them back to ground. Smiling sheepishly, he removed it to see that Marrok was calling.

"Hello," Arnold whispered, not wanting to draw attention to Everett and himself who remained under cover of the trees and bushes.

"Arnold, it's Otto. He got out!" Marrok said hurriedly over the phone.

"What do you mean 'got out'?" Arnold hissed. If Otto was loose, it could destroy their entire plan.

"He's . . . stronger than we anticipated. He hasn't shifted into Night-Sun fully, but he is not in control, Arnold."

Arnold realised that their plan must have worked, but with unintended consequences; Mayor Redburn had taken the bait, but regained control of Otto through the use of the blade he was linked to.

Everett poked Arnold to get his attention, and he looked up to see someone heading down the path towards George. "I'll call you back, Marrok." Arnold hung up and used his enhanced vision to focus on the figure that was heading through the nature reserve.

It was Otto. He had not transformed into the were-jaguar, but his eyes looked considerably paler than usual, and it was the vacant expression that Arnold had become accustomed to whenever Otto was under the control of his father.

Otto's pace was quick, and as he drew closer, George spotted him, and Arnold could see the panic on her face.

Everett went to stand up, but Arnold grabbed her arm and pulled her back down towards him.

"We can't let those two be together, that's what Marrok said," she spoke with conviction.

"I know, but if we intervene now, we won't get another

chance to find Mayor Redburn. This is our best chance of catching him and ending this."

Otto grabbed hold of George's arm who tried to pull against him, but he was far stronger than her. She reluctantly gave in and began to follow him. They exited the nature reserve together, disappearing out of sight.

"Ring Marrok, find him. I will follow and let you know where we end up." Arnold stood up and began to follow the two of them out of the nature reserve and up through town. They continued to walk at a fast pace, and Arnold was trying his hardest to remain out of sight from them. They walked past a derelict factory which used to be an old chemical plant, through the overgrown grounds and across the field behind. Continuing his pursuit, Arnold was able to easily keep them in sight with the help of his enhanced vision while keeping a safe distance.

Once across the field, the two of them disappeared, and Arnold instantly recognised the location. It was where the entrance to the coal mine was.

As Arnold sped up his pursuit, he quickly pulled out his phone and typed out a text to Everett to tell her where they were.

With Otto and George now together, their initial plan had changed. Arnold knew that he could no longer wait for backup to arrive in the form of the Order of the Aegis as they had initially agreed. He needed to get inside and prevent any harm happening to George as he still didn't know how Mayor Redburn planned to use her and Otto. He reached the entrance to the mine and saw that the usually flooded entrance had been drained. The large machine that had done this was still switched on and running off its internal motor, the noise of which sounded like a chugging car engine.

He wanted to end this. He wanted to save his friends. He just hoped that his training had paid off and that he was strong enough to do it.

CHAPTER 23

Arnold stood at the entrance to the cave, his senses heightened. He needed to stop Mayor Redburn from opening a portal to the spirit world no matter what. It was dusk, and the birds were now settling into their nests for the night. There was a refreshing breeze in the air, and Arnold took a large gulp of it, knowing that once inside the tunnel, he would find nothing but stale air until he resurfaced.

He stepped into the muddied entrance, recently unearthed after decades of being submerged underwater. He trudged his way through the thick sludge and grabbed hold of the copper-coloured rusted handle. It was rough to touch, and Arnold pulled the door open with force, nearly pulling the whole thing off its decrepit hinges. He dreaded seeing what it was like inside if this was the condition on the outside. Knowing it would only get worse, he bit the bullet and stepped forwards into the pitch-black tunnel.

Arnold concentrated and illuminated a slight glow before his eagle manifested in front of him. The blue light from his eagle engulfed the immediate area so that Arnold could see clearly down the winding mine tunnels for a short distance. The tunnel was narrow, meaning his eagle wouldn't be able to fly.

A slight splatting noise could be heard from the eagle's feet skipping through the bog-like floor next to Arnold. Arnold continued to concentrate, trying to use his enhanced vision, but with the darkness ahead, it was hard to see clearly. He needed to keep calm so that he could think rationally when he confronted Mayor Redburn.

He continued through the tunnel slowly, trying to make as little noise as possible. The further he delved, the thinner the air felt. A stale taste lingered in his mouth from the musty air that he was breathing in. Arnold pressed down the narrow tunnel for some time until eventually he could see light up ahead.

Voices echoed faintly down towards him, which gradually became clearer as he approached.

"Let me go!" George cried. "I can't believe it was you all along!"

"If you don't start talking, I will have to bind your mouth again."

Arnold froze. The voice did not belong to Otto – or Mayor Redburn.

He felt lifted his hand to the hilt of his macahuitl and kept it firmly in his grasp, prepared to draw his weapon at any time. When he drew level to the chamber, he knelt behind a rock so that he could survey the area and devise a plan of action. Gazing over the top of the crescent, uneven surface of the dirt-covered rock, he glanced around the room.

George was tied up next to what looked like a mineshaft that went even further down below. Otto stood beside her with a vacant expression on his face.

Opposite them stood a man with his back turned, the sight of whom hit Arnold in the pits of his stomach, knocking him sick with shock.

Mr. Higgins was wearing armour, the patterned skin of a tiger lining his tunic. He had a weapon strapped to his back, and when Arnold focused his eagle vision on it, he realised it was a morning star. A short, wooden handle was attached to a chain with a solid metal ball on the end of it, with more spikes protruding from it than Arnold dared to count.

Mr. Higgins had his hands outstretched and appeared to be holding a chalice in one of them. He was moving around the room, waving the chalice in the air when he stopped suddenly.

"It's here, this point. This is it," Mr. Higgins said. His hands began to glow, the energy generating a powerful force around him, like a swirling storm. "It's directly below us, but this is the point can you feel the energy."

He turned to Otto. "Get her ready to take her down," he commanded. Otto grabbed hold of George's arm and began to walk towards Mr. Higgins. He looked emotionless, like he wasn't truly present.

"Get off me, Otto!" George barked. "What are you doing?" She attempted to dig her feet into the ground, but Otto was much stronger than her, making her attempts to stop him meaningless. He dragged her across the chamber and pinned her firmly in place.

Mr. Higgins started chanting. When he had finished, he said, "We are done here. Bring her with me down the mineshaft."

Siezing his moment, Arnold stepped out from behind the rock and pulled out his macuahuitl from its holster.

"Let her go," he growled, gripping the hilt of his ancient weapon with both hands.

"Ethon," Mr. Higgins hissed. "I have to do this. It's the only way."

"I don't know what it is you intend to do, but whatever it is, I'm not going to let it happen. Not when it involves my friends." His eyes did not shift from Mr. Higgins, anger rising within him at his betrayal. "Let George go. You don't need her."

Mr. Higgins laughed. "But I do, Ethon, I do. She is the key."

"What are you on about?" Arnold said.

"To the portal!" he said, his voice elevated with a tinge of aggression that Arnold was not used to. "She is a spirit weaver like her grandmother was. Edith was the spirit weaver that helped trap your grandma in the spirit world. Her essence is in the girl, and I need to extract that essence to release her."

"Why would you do all this?" Arnold asked, confused as to why Mr. Higgins would be involved. Where was Mayor Redburn?

"I didn't want to have to do this, but I have no choice," Mr. Higgins continued. "You have no idea what being a menial is like. If I can free her, if I can release her from her prison, then she will be indebted to me. Perhaps even help me find a way to finally harness the power of a spirit beast."

"I've already told you, I am not going to let that happen." Arnold took a step forwards, but Otto released George and moved to block his path.

"How could you do this to Otto?" Arnold roared, furious for what Mr. Higgins had done to his best friend, what he had made him do. "How are you even controlling him when his dad had the blade?"

"That part was easy. You see, Mayor Redburn came to me for some advice about the old mines. After all, I am a historian before a teacher. It didn't take long for me to grow suspicious of his questions. I did some digging of my own and found out the real reasons these mines were shut. The real reasons the Spirit Wardens lied about it. Mayor Redburn had inside information and it didn't take long before he confided in me everything that had happened."

Mr. Higgins smiled to himself, holding the dagger tightly in his hand. "But in truth, I already knew about Otto and the dagger, just not to the extent of his corruption. I simply had to bide my time, had to wait for the right moment. I convinced Redburn to hide the dagger, but unbeknownst to him, I followed him and replaced it with another. And so I gained control of Otto, and as such, had him do my bidding for me, helping me to remain unnoticed."

Mr. Higgins let out a laugh when he saw the upset on Arnold's face. "Now, now, Ethon," he said, "if it wasn't me, it would be someone else. That's why I keep the dagger. I need it to release him from his spirit beast so I can use it to open the portal. Can you imagine the energy that it will create?"

"But how?" Arnold asked. "How did you already know about the dagger? How did you know you could control him with it?" Up until now, Arnold had been certain it was Mayor Redburn who had been controlling Otto.

"Foolish boy. Do you think Raine and Levent were the only people that night at the tower?" Mr. Higgins's face turned into an aggressive snarl, so far away from the friendly teacher Arnold had come to respect.

"You were there?" Arnold's mind started to whirl, consuming his every thought.

"I helped Levent and Raine that night. I have been watching you for a while, Ethon. Why do you think I teach at that wretched place you call a school?" Mr. Higgins turned his nose up as if the mere mention of school repulsed him. "The night that Otto broke the most sacred rule of the Spirit Wardens, the night he took Raine's life, I watched it all. I watched him break her neck from the shadows. Then something strange happened. You see, Raine tried to take Redburn's spirit beast. Levent had gifted her a blade, similar to his own, something he had failed to bestow me with."

Mr. Higgins grew notably more frustrated as he continued to speak. "I never understood why he showed more faith in her than me. I have achieved so much more than her . . . When she used the blade, she started to consume it. That was, until Redburn stopped her. But afterwards . . ." Mr. Higgins's eyes widened as he drew on his memory. "Afterwards, something strange happened, something that at first, I did not understand. You see, he managed to stop Raine from stealing his spirit beast, but part of Redburn's soul became trapped in the blade, along with his jaguar. As he lay unconscious on the ground, I contemplated ending his life, and I nearly did," he hissed.

"You were helping me! You were helping me to learn how to spirit-wield. Why?"

"My boy, it was simply too much of an opportunity, helping to sow the seeds of mistrust between you and the Spirit Wardens with all that nonsense I filled your head with. Tell me, has the relationship with your father fractured? Would it pain him to know that his son didn't trust him in his time of need?" Mr. Higgins's eyes lit up and he smiled a wicked smile. "Imagine my delight in seeing you become more distant and in so, more isolated. True, I did not expect you to turn up here and find out it was me all along, but it is what it is. You will not survive to tell anyone anyway."

"You're a monster," George cried, interrupting Mr. Higgins. "Otto, you don't have to do this!"

"He can't hear you," Mr. Higgins sneered. "Not while I am commanding him." He paused. "The thing is, I don't want the boy. I just want his beast. And I will rip him away from it!"

"And turn him into menial like you?" Arnold scolded, raising his macuahuitl as he moved into an offensive stance. "I won't let you go any further. You will answer to the Spirit Wardens for what you have done. For what you are trying to do."

"And how do you expect to stop me," Mr. Higgins said, "when I have him?"

Otto dropped to his knees and began to contort, letting out a howl of pain. The cracking noise of his bones breaking into shape echoed throughout the chamber as Otto's body began to change. A green glow emitted from his body and within a few moments, he had turned into the were-jaguar. He stood up tall and let out a low-pitched grumble as he stared down Arnold, that wild, feral look taking over his eyes. He did not move, though. He just stood there, blocking Arnold's path to George.

Last time they had gone toe to toe, Otto had thrown Arnold around like a rag doll. This time, however, Arnold had his weapon, and George's life depended on him. He couldn't fail.

"Take care of him and meet me in the pit," Mr. Higgins ordered. He quickly began to walk towards the mineshaft, dragging George with him.

"Let me go!" George cried.

Otto swung a razor-sharp, claw-filled hand, but Arnold quickly brought his macuahuitl upwards to shield himself from the blow. Otto spun and swung his other hand around with Arnold parrying this away, then continued swinging his claws wildly at Arnold over and over again, relentlessly trying to shred him.

Arnold parried each blow while stepping back each time, meaning that Otto was gaining more and more momentum as the two of them duelled. Arnold desperately wanted to refrain from hurting his best friend, but one thing was clear: Otto was not in control, and he was trying to kill Arnold.

This time when Otto raised a hand in the air to swing at Arnold, Arnold used his momentum against him. He ducked and stepped underneath the attack, turning his macuahuitl to the flat side of the panel and smacking it against the were-jaguar's ribs with as much force as he could muster. Otto went crashing face-first into the wall beside them.

Arnold jumped away to put some distance between the two of them, but the beast had pushed itself from the wall and thrown itself at Arnold, diving at him with its mouth wide open as it attempted to lock its brutal jaws around his arm. Arnold shielded himself with the top of his macuahuitl, but the were-jaguar's jaws were gnawing at it as it wrapped its mouth around the weapon. Arnold rolled backwards and lifted his feet into the beast's chest, then kicked over the top of it before quickly jumping back to his feet.

Otto continued to growl ferociously, and he paced around Arnold as if he were prey that he was stalking. Arnold's eagle flew out from behind the rock into the open space. It sunk its talons into Otto's side and attempted to lift off and knock him into the wall again. Otto grabbed hold of the eagle with both hands and bit down onto one of its wings. The eagle let out a shrill shriek as Otto began shaking his head violently, attempting to detach the eagle's wing from its body. Arnold cried out in pain as what felt like fire erupted inside his shoulders. Panicking, he rushed forwards and swung his macuahuitl against the back of the were-jaguar's head, making the beast let go of its prey. It spun and hurled the injured eagle straight at Arnold, which smashed into his chest and knocked him to the ground.

Arnold gasped, attempting to regain his breath from the blow. The force had taken him by surprise. His eagle now lay on the ground injured, so Arnold focused his auro and it began to dissipate within him. He didn't want it to experience any further harm. His shoulder throbbed intensely from the pain his eagle had experienced with that last blow.

The space was too open for Arnold to get the upper hand against Otto. Otto was simply too large and too strong in this form.

Arnold glanced around the room looking for any kind of opening. A darkened tunnel just past the mineshaft where Mayor Redburn had taken George wound its way into the darkness. He made a run for it, setting off at pace to get as much distance between Otto as he could. Otto immediately gave chase, roaring as he snapped ferociously at Arnold's heels.

He ran through the darkness, unable to see each bend and curve of the mine until the very last second. The snarling beast was right behind him, baying for Arnold's blood, and he put everything he had into keeping the minuscule gap between them.

The tunnel walls were flying past him, and Arnold continued to dodge rocks and posts, some of which flew past him a little too close for comfort. He was running off instinct now, and was amazed that he had not clattered into anything yet.

When he passed another post, he swung his macuahuitl into it. The post splintered in half, instantly causing it to drop in front of Otto, giving Arnold that split second extra as Otto was forced to smash through the debris.

In front of Arnold was a dead-end which he was fast approaching. He was out of space and out of ideas, and he needed to act quickly.

Jumping from a large rock in front of him, Arnold threw himself at the wall, kicking off of it to catapult himself at the pursuing beast.

The were-jaguar was leaping through the air with its claws outstretched.

It was him, or Otto.

Arnold slammed his macahuitl into the side of Otto's head with incredible force, giving it everything he had. Otto went hurtling to the ground, his head bouncing off the rock before he slid eerily to stop as he reached the wall. Arnold skimmed across the floor like a thin stone projecting across a lake, rolling repeatedly until he ground to a halt. He let out a laboured groan as he pushed himself up from the floor.

The feral beast lay motionless on the floor, but after a moment, Arnold could see that it was breathing. The beast was unconscious, and Arnold had beaten him. However narrowly he had won, they were both alive.

With a heavy heart, Arnold knew he didn't have time to tend to Otto, and hoped that his best friend would be okay. He turned and set off running back towards the mineshaft. He was exhausted from the confrontation, but he knew there was more to come.

He needed to stop Mr. Higgins before it was too late.

CHAPTER 24

The taste of iron engulfed Arnold's throat. His shoulder was red hot with pain, and he was covered in cuts and grazes. The ache in his body was tremendous, but George's situation kept him going. He needed to get to her no matter what, and as soon as possible.

He made it to the mineshaft where they had travelled below, and not wanting to draw attention to himself, he decided to climb down rather than calling the lift up to him.

He placed his macuahuitl back within its holster, then began to lower himself slowly onto one of the beams that were planted within the wall. He dropped down to the next section, grabbing hold of another beam, continuing this process until he was on top of the elevator. He opened the hatch on the roof and slid through as delicately as he could without making any excess noise. The gate to the elevator was already pulled to one side. Arnold exited it and carried on down the darkened tunnel in the only direction he could. The air felt at its thinnest here, and despite not being claustrophobic, he certainly understood how those who suffered from the condition might feel.

The tunnel was incredibly narrow compared to the ones above. The ground beneath him was sloped, and the tunnel spiralled as if he were on an ancient staircase. When he reached the bottom, he could see a faint glow growing brighter as he edged ever lower beneath the surface. He reached a door opening and crept through slowly.

George was tied up in the centre of the room. She made eye contact with him and tried to shout towards him, but her mouth was gagged, and all that Arnold could hear were muffled cries. Her eyes grew large, and at this moment, Arnold knew it was too late.

He felt a blow to his head, and everything went dark.

WHEN HE CAME TO, he found his hands had been bound behind him and interlocked around some chains that were bolted to the floor. He attempted to pull away, but the bindings were fastened tightly around his wrists, making it almost impossible to move.

Arnold looked around the room and found Mr. Higgins standing with George by his side. She was no longer gagged and was still trying her hardest to pull away from him, but her attempts did not get her anywhere.

"Arnold! Are you okay?"

"Never better." A sarcastic groan was slowly coming from his mouth. A dull throbbing pain engulfed the side of his face where he had been knocked unconscious. He had no idea how long he had been out.

"Quiet!" Mr. Higgins commanded.

Before them, the air appeared distorted as though Arnold was looking through frosted glass. He knew what was happening straight away; he recognised the distortion from when he was at the tower the night that his grandad was murdered. The portal was there for them all to see, and after a moment, a powerfully built man stepped through.

The newcomer stood face to face with Mr. Higgins, his large, black overcoat moving with the energy that was emitting from the distortion behind him. His heavily scarred face was easily recognisable as he cracked a crooked smile, showing his delight at the current situation.

Levent.

Arnold's rage built inside him. This was the monster who had turned his life upside down, the person who had kidnapped him, taunted him, goaded him into summoning his spirit beast so that he could steal it for himself. Arnold had known deep down that Levent would show himself again, one way or another. But he could not believe that Mr. Higgins had been working with him this entire time.

Arnold tried to pull his hands free so that he could show them both exactly what he thought of them, but his efforts were pointless, as his bindings restrained him tightly. All the hatred he had for Levent came rushing back, and he could feel his body trembling with pure rage.

"Do you have it?" Levent asked, his rasping voice echoing around the mine.

"Here." Mr. Higgins passed him the chalice that was in his hand.

Arnold's eyes widened when he realised he had seen this chalice before. He thought he had broken it at George's granny's shop. It seemed to pulsate in Mr. Higgins's hands who cradled it delicately as he passed it to Levent. Arnold felt a surge of confusion overcome him. Why would they need such an old chalice? Why would it be key to all of this?

Levent took the chalice from Mr. Higgins and inspected

it closely. Then he nodded towards George. "I presume this is the girl?"

"Yes, she is the granddaughter of the spirit weaver. She has also shown herself to have similar abilities to those that Edith possessed."

"Let me go!" George started pulling away from Mr. Higgins.

Levent lashed out and backhanded George across the face, busting her lip. If not for being gripped by Mr. Higgins, George would have been launched across the room from the force.

Arnold felt powerless, and another wave of fury erupted from within. How could Levent hit someone so much weaker than him?

"Get off her!" he screamed. "I'll kill you. I'll kill both of you for this."

Levent grinned at Arnold. "Sit tightly, boy. I'm sure you will have your chance soon enough."

Levent pulled out his blade from within his jacket and grabbed hold of George's arm, yanking her close. George struggled and shrieked as Levent drew the blade across her arm, turning it crimson instantly. She let out a shrill scream from the pain as Levent squeezed her forearm tightly, causing her blood to come gushing out of the open wound. He placed the chalice underneath and collected her blood within it. Levent then set the chalice on the floor and used the same blade to cut his hand before clenching his fist and dripping his own blood into the chalice as well.

"I share the blood of the dragon trapped within the spirit world. You share the blood of the spirit weaver who trapped her there." Levent looked around the room. "Where is he?"

Arnold knew straight away that he meant Otto, and felt happy that in some way, he had slowed down this process.

He smirked at his small victory, but this was short-lived as no sooner had Levent spoken, Otto appeared at the entrance to the cavern.

He had changed back to his human form. His head was heavily bleeding where Arnold had hit him and his face was swollen.

"All we need now is for the girl and the were-jaguar to drink this," said Levent, looking thrilled. "Then they will be parted from their spirit beasts. That sacrifice combined with the consumption of our blood will be enough to create a gateway strong enough to pull her back into this world."

Otto began to stagger towards Levent, his feet shuffling as he walked in an almost zombie-like fashion.

Levent's eyes were open wide with anticipation.

"And when he does this, he will be back to normal? He won't be tethered to this blade anymore?" Mr. Higgins interrupted.

"Seeing as he would no longer have his spirit beast, I would assume so."

"His beast will be mine?"

"Do you doubt me?" Levent asked furiously.

Mr. Higgins bowed his head. "No, not at all," he muttered.

Glancing down at the floor, Levent's dark, sunken eyes landed on Arnold's macuahuitl cast to one side. "You have gotten careless," he said. "Leaving your grandad's things lying around like that. This was his weapon of choice, was it not?"

Arnold didn't answer him, choosing to simply stare him down, not wanting to show any signs that he was intimidated by him.

"What about the chalice?" Mr. Higgins pressed impatiently.

"Ask me again, and I will remove your tongue. Now hold this."

Levent passed the chalice to Mr. Higgins and walked over to the macuahuitl that lay on the ground just ahead of where Arnold was restrained. He picked it up with one hand and inspected the details of the carvings, as if admiring the craft that had gone into it. He then began to swing it around in the air back and forth as he figured out the weight of the weapon. He moved it with much more ease than Arnold could, using only one hand to wield it, whereas Arnold needed to use both of his.

"It is a thing of beauty, isn't it?" Levent teased.

"Put it down. You don't deserve to hold it. You're a coward!"

Levent smiled, appearing unfazed by Arnold's words. He was toying with him, like a lion playing with its food. After continuing to wield the weapon for a few minutes, Levent shrugged and rested the macahuitl against one of the large rocks in the chamber.

"Now, where were we?" He grinned. "Shall we continue?" He started walking back towards Mr. Higgins, who was still standing next to George while Mr. Higgins held the blood-filled chalice. He stopped for a moment as if thinking about something carefully. Then he stared Arnold dead in the eye.

Spinning on his heels, Levent ran back towards the macahuitl and jumped into the air. He stomped on the weapon, snapping the blade from the hilt.

"Oops," he goaded.

"No!" Arnold yelled. He had put so many hours into practising with the macahuitl precisely so that, one day, he could face Levent and beat him in honour of his grandad.

Levent's laugh echoed around the chamber. He did not care for the pain he had caused Arnold. It was as if he thrived off being able to tease him while Arnold was unable to do anything about it.

Levent took the chalice from Mr. Higgins and began to hum and chant quietly under his breath. The ancient artefact began to glow, illuminating Levent's scars in a green light. "Open her mouth," he commanded.

"I'm not drinking that!" George cried. Mr. Higgins kicked her in the back of the knees, forcing her to drop to the floor. He then pulled her hair pack and grabbed her around the jaw, holding it open.

Levent stepped forwards and tilted the chalice slightly, allowing the blood within to drip down into her mouth and down her neck. Mr. Higgins then pulled her jaw up and held his hand firmly over her mouth until she had no choice but to swallow the contents. After he let go of her, George dropped onto all fours, coughing into the ground trying to spit out what she could, but Arnold knew she was too late; she had already swallowed Otto's and her blood.

A cracked, yellow glow of her auro coated her. "I don't feel right," she said. "I feel funny."

Her fox spirit beast appeared in front of her, but it wasn't its usual colour. Instead, it glowed green, matching the power from the chalice.

A surge of power erupted besides George and a blast of energy threatened to bring the cave in on itself. It was as if the fiercest of storms had started as the energy swirled around in a circular motion until a gateway formed in the centre, growing in size until it matched George's height. The energy swirled around the outer edge at speed, gaining momentum.

Without warning, Levent grabbed hold of the fox and threw it behind him towards the emerging gateway.

However, the fox's trajectory changed as a purple blur barged into it, knocking it away from the portal.

"George!" Everett cried, having made her way down the mineshaft. Her boar nuzzled into George's fox, then positioned itself defensively in front of it.

"The gateway is opening. We just need to feed it enough energy so it can sustain her passing through it." Levent grinned. "Do not be fooled into thinking I need her beast specifically. It was her blood I needed to start the process."

Levent charged at the boar, and it ran to meet him. He sidestepped it just in time as he grabbed one of its tusks, thrusting the boar towards the portal. Everett's spirit beast let out a shrill shriek as it hit the portal. It disappeared, the echoed noise of its cries slowly vanishing.

Everett dropped to her knees, her eyes wide with shock. Her purple auro faded from around her, and tears began to form in her face.

"No!" Arnold screamed in harmony with George. His heart was breaking for her. Everett's spirit beast had been ripped away from her and tossed to one side like it was nothing, its energy absorbed by the gateway never to be seen again. Just like that, she had been turned into a menial, someone without any spirit world energy, someone without a spirit beast.

Everett looked up at Levent, tears streaming down her face. She curled up on the floor in agony. "Why would you? Is she –"

"Gone? Yes. Don't worry though, that energy is being put to good use."

Levent then passed the chalice to Otto who took hold of the artefact, grasping it with both of his hands.

"Once you drink this, I will use my blade to draw out your spirit beast within you. We will then use the combined energy of yours and the boar to open a gateway strong enough to let it pass through to this side."

Mr. Higgins stared at the chalice in Otto's hands, then placed his hand on his dagger and commanded, "Drink from the chalice, Otto. Drink, and we can end this. He can free you."

Otto had slowly begun to raise the chalice to his mouth when Arnold noticed something in the background. A noise echoed down the tunnel that led to the chamber, and it was growing louder.

A bright orange glow burst into the room, and a loud howl echoed throughout the chamber as Marrok's white wolf sprinted into the chamber. It immediately jumped into Otto, sending the chalice flying out of his hand and onto the floor. The area around the floor grew red as the mixed blood curdled with the dirt beneath them.

"What!" Levent roared, his anger there for all to see. "Who is this!"

Marrok entered the room wearing bone mail armour beneath a thick cloak with a wolf pelt hood. His shoulder pauldrons were spiked, adding to his menacing appearance.

Marrok's amber eyes first landed on the vacant Otto before switching to Levent.

"The Order of the Aegis," Levent stated furiously.

"I am here for Night-Sun," Marrok declared, his stare still firmly planted on Levent. His white wolf had bounded around the room to stand next to him, the light emitting from it reflecting off his bone armour. "You bring dishonour in trying to destroy Night-Sun. I won't let that happen. You will be punished. The council wills it."

"Your council have no laws that bind me," Levent hissed in response. "They send a pup into a lion's den." With this, Levent summoned his giant mane-less lion with the power from his blade. As it materialised, the lion let out an ear-splitting roar and ran straight towards Marrok, its face as angered as Levent's. It bared its teeth, going in for the kill.

Marrok's white wolf rammed into the lion, just barely giving Marrok enough time to dive out of the way before the lion's paw could make contact with his head.

Mr. Higgins released George and made a run for it. George immediately rushed to where Everett lay on the ground in shock from the trauma of being torn away from her spirit beast.

As Mr. Higgins tried to run by, Everett kicked out her leg, hooking it around his shin. He lost his balance and slammed down onto the floor, dropping the dagger that he used to control Otto.

"You coward!" Everett screamed, picking up the dagger from the floor.

The realisation struck Arnold. "Everett," he yelled, "you need to command Otto! You have the dagger. He will listen to you!"

Everett looked down at the dagger, then at Otto. Otto was fixed to the spot while the lion and white wolf continued to maul each other. The lion's far superior size had already given it the upper hand.

Levent made a move towards Marrok, and the two of them entered combat. Marrok threw punches and kicks at Levent, who repeatedly dodged these before brutally punching Marrok to the floor. He jumped on top of Marrok and started to rain down blows from above. Marrok raised his arms above his head, trying to protect himself.

"Everett!" Marrok's muffled voice called. "You must get Otto out of here, you have to keep Night-Sun safe!"

Everett wore a panicked look as she turned to face Otto,

gripping the dagger tightly to her chest. "Otto, you have to listen to me. We need you back. You have to help Marrok."

Levent broke through Marrok's defence with his relentless, ape-like onslaught as he continued slamming his fists into his head and chest.

Otto suddenly snapped back into the room. His vacant look was gone, and he immediately ran towards Marrok. Mid-stride, he began to change form once more as he dived through the air, completing the transition into Night-Sun as he grabbed hold of Levent and threw him off the top of Marrok, growling ferociously.

George ran across to Arnold and used the dagger to cut through his bindings.

"You need to get Marrok out of here," Arnold told her. "He's badly injured."

George nodded and scrambled towards Marrok, only to be intercepted by Levent's monstrous, roaring spirit beast. Judging by the colour draining from George's face, she felt like her time was up.

Otto dived on the back of the lion and pierced its skin with his claws. He then jumped from the lion and landed in front of Everett. Now that he had the full attention of the lion, George ran to help Marrok.

"Come on, Marrok, get up!" She pulled Marrok to his feet and the two of them began to make their way towards the tunnel with Everett close behind.

Levent was back on his feet and moving towards them. Arnold set off running across the chamber, wanting to get to him before he got to George and Marrok.

"Get out, you three!" Arnold yelled. "Quickly!"

He jumped and planted a dropkick on Levent, knocking him to the ground as he ricocheted off the floor. He looked up just in time to see George helping Marrok exit the chamber and into the tunnel. Everett was just behind them clutching Otto's dagger, its soft green glow illuminating the darkness in front of her.

Behind him, Otto and the lion were taking it in turns to maul each other with their claws. Otto had managed to grab and pin the lion's two front legs as the two of them roared, the noise of which made Arnold's heart beat even harder than it already was.

Arnold climbed back to his feet at the same time as Levent, and they stood facing each other. Levent looked as furious as ever, and Arnold had both fists tightly clenched, equally angry at everything that Levent had done.

"You think you can fight me? You think you are strong enough to kill me? You have no idea!"

"I'm not going to kill you."

Arnold ran at Levent and began with a quick one-two punch combination that Levent was able to palm away before returning his own punch, making contact with Arnold's cheek. Arnold tried again but Levent managing to block these before Arnold attempted to catch him with a kick. Levent jumped forwards and struck Arnold in the face multiple times before kneeing him in the stomach, the force of which took Arnold's breath away.

Arnold dropped to his knees as Levent grabbed hold of him by the hair and struck him twice in a row.

"You thought you stood a chance?" Levent raged. He pulled Arnold to his feet and slammed his fist into his stomach, causing him to drop to the floor again. Arnold spat a mouthful of blood out onto the floor as he stared down at the dirt beneath him.

The lion had managed to make contact with Otto's leg, causing him to let out a roar of pain. It then took a swipe at Otto's head, sending him crashing through the air and into the wall beside them. The lion was quickly over the were-jaguar, slamming its giant paws into his chest repeatedly. When it attempted to bite down on him, Otto grabbed the lion's jaws and held them tight, preventing it from clamping down.

Blood began pouring from Otto's hands where the lion's teeth had pierced his skin.

Arnold couldn't pick himself up in time, and Levent kicked him with tremendous force, catapulting him to the side. He couldn't keep this up. He was taking a hammering. Arnold had not laid a punch on Levent. He was nowhere near strong enough to face him, and didn't know whether he would be able to continue the fight.

Arnold needed help. Despite being weakened and unable to fly from the injury it had sustained from Otto earlier, Arnold summoned his eagle, desperate for aid. The bird emerged, standing in front of Arnold with one wing outstretched as though protecting him.

Feeling a second wind, Arnold brought himself back to his feet, a wave of courage coming over him. He might not be as strong, but he was going to give Levent a good fight nonetheless.

Bloodied and bruised, Arnold stood up straight and braced himself for another round.

Levent grinned maniacally at him as he retrieved the Blade of the Spirits from his pocket, then removed his over-coat and tossed it to the floor.

A wave of panic overcame Arnold; he was weapon-less, and he knew his eagle would be vulnerable to Levent's blade.

It was over. He couldn't match Levent in hand-to-hand combat. At least the others had gotten to safety. Maybe he could distract Levent just a little longer to allow his friends to escape the mines.

The eagle slammed its wing down to the ground, as if trying to get his attention. Arnold followed the eagle's line of sight, his gaze landing on the broken hilt of the macuahuitl.

Clarity unclouded his mind, and he knew what the eagle was guiding him to do.

"I've had enough now!" Levent screamed as he ran towards Arnold with his blade outstretched.

Arnold dived for the macuahuitl hilt and focused, trying his hardest to keep his mind clear. His blue auro began to glow around him as he held onto the hilt. He pictured the macuahuitl in its full form, and pure energy from the spirit world re-forged the blade exactly how it had been before. From its paddle-like shaft to the blades that ran around the outer edge, Arnold now had a weapon to defend himself with.

After hours of practising with Mr. Higgins, he had finally spirit-wielded.

Levent slashed down towards Arnold, but Arnold was able to parry the attack away just in time with the newly forged weapon in his hand.

Arnold couldn't believe how light the macahuitl was in this form, having grown used to the weight it was before. The pure spirit energy now flowed through the weapon and himself, making it seem almost weightless in comparison.

"You can spirit-wield? You do surprise me. Still, the result will be the same," Levent sneered.

He began swinging a flurry of blows at Arnold, but Arnold was able to continue to parry his attacks. Behind Levent, Otto was still holding the lion's jaws tightly, which was attempting to bite down on him. His arms were beginning to buckle from the prolonged grapple.

Levent then came at Arnold again, and the two of them began swinging their weapons against each other. With the lighter macahuitl, Arnold was able to move so much faster than he usually did.

Levent and Arnold slammed their weapons against each other and drew face to face. Arnold focused on keeping his spirit energy up through his auro while Levent growled at him with pure hatred.

Arnold could see the lion's jaws getting closer to Otto. Sensing he didn't have much time, he went at Levent with a flurry of blows which Levent blocked. Each blow knocked him back slightly further. Arnold quickly swung out his other arm and made a satisfying connection with Levent's face. He hit his macuahuitl repeatedly against Levent's blade, then spun the other way and swung the blade downwards towards his leg. Levent screamed as Arnold cut through the back of his achilles, forcing him to the floor.

The lion flinched as it shared Levent's pain. Otto pushed back against the lion forcefully and twisted its jaws. The lion attempted to fight back, but sensing the upper hand, Otto continued to twist the lion's jaws until it eventually cracked and dropped to the floor.

"Nooo! You can't do this!" Levent screamed as he fell to the floor, unable to balance with his leg injured. "I can't stop her. I can't take her dragon unless she is in this world! Sixteen years! It has taken me sixteen years!"

Levent had dropped his blade, and Arnold quickly kicked it away from him, then dropped to his knees, exhausted from the battle.

"Go on, finish it," Levent seethed. "Have your revenge. It's over now."

Arnold lifted his macuahuitl above his head. He had

wanted this revenge since the day Levent had murdered Elwood.

"Death would be too kind." Arnold slammed the hilt of his blade into the side of Levent's head, rendering him unconscious.

Arnold stood over Levent's unconscious body as Otto limped across the room in his were-jaguar form. He did not appear aggressive, however, and seemed to be more in control of what he was doing.

Otto reached down and picked up Levent, chucking him over his shoulder. Levent's leg was bleeding, but only slightly; the raw spirit energy of Arnold's blade appeared to have cauterised the wound upon contact.

Otto began to leave the room with Levent cast over his shoulder, grumbling towards Arnold as an indication for him to follow.

As they began their journey to the surface, Arnold realised that they had won. He had defeated Levent.

And he had avenged his grandad, once and for all.

CHAPTER 25

Arnold and Otto left the coal mine side by side. Arnold immediately began looking around for Everett, George, and Marrok so he could check that they were all okay.

They found George sitting on the ground outside, holding Marrok who looked pretty beaten up. Everett was staring off into the distance, a blank look in her eyes.

"Is he okay?" Arnold called over to George.

"I think he will be. He just needs patching up." George was channelling her auro onto Marrok, trying to ease his pain.

Everett saw that Otto was carrying Levent and looked at a nearby tree. "Take Levent over there. Do no let him out of your sight until the Spirit Wardens get here."

Otto obliged and carried the unconscious Levent to the tree, then shifted out of his were-jaguar form.

"You control Night-Sun now, Everett," Marrok told her, wincing from his injuries. "You wield the dagger."

"I don't want to control him. Otto, are you okay?"

Otto looked disorientated as he came around from his

transformation, his bones resetting into their natural position. "I'll be fine. How is everyone else?"

Everett's eyes filled with tears. "My spirit beast, is she gone?"

Marrok shuffled up to a seated position and took hold of Everett's hand. "I'm afraid so. I arrived too late. She was absorbed by the gateway. I think her spirit energy became a part of it."

"So I am a menial now?" Everett stifled a sob.

"I'm so sorry, Everett," George said, trying to console her but with little effect. "If you hadn't saved my fox –"

"Don't," Marrok cut her off. "You will torture yourself with what-ifs."

"Where is Mr. Higgins? Did anyone see where he went?"

"I don't know. When we came up out of the mine, he was already gone."

Across the field, Arnold could see a group of people approaching, and he knew from the animal hides they were wearing that they were the Order of the Aegis.

"Night-Sun, how are you feeling?" the leader of the group asked as she dropped the hood of her coyote hide to rest on her shoulders.

It seemed to take Otto a few moments to realise that she was talking to him; he was not used to going by that name. "Please, call me Otto," he told her. "I am okay, thanks. I don't know what to do now though, now that Mr. Higgins is not in control of me. What should I do with the blade?"

"This is still a difficult situation that you find yourself in," said the woman. "You see, you cannot hold the blade. To do so would risk your corruption worsening and you fully losing control of your humanity. Someone needs to look after that blade. May I recommend that we do this for you?

Night-Sun, you are our deity, and as such, we are here to help you. Our culture exists to serve you."

Otto looked taken aback by this. Arnold could tell from his face that this was not what he had asked for, nor was it what he wanted. "Does that mean I am stuck this way?" Otto asked quietly.

"Yes. There is no way to reverse corruption. You and your jaguar's souls are now intertwined."

Otto turned to Everett. "Everett, I want you to hold on to that for me and protect it. It's hard to explain, but I felt like I could read your soul when you asked me to help against Levent. All I could see was kindness and selflessness, and I know I can trust you with it."

Everett looked surprised at what had been asked of her, and Arnold didn't blame her. "I will, for you, Otto. I will never command you to do anything again as long as I hold it. I promise you. You will not be a slave to this blade."

Otto smiled at her, but Arnold could see that he was saddened at learning that he was stuck this way for the rest of his life, that he would never be able to command his jaguar spirit beast again.

"Does this make me your spirit beast?" Otto tried to make light of the situation in front of the audience around them, a flicker of his old self.

"Weirdly, I guess so," Everett answered. She looked at Levent, who lay unconscious on the ground. "What are we going to do with him?

"He is coming with me to the Spirit Wardens," Arnold explained. "He murdered my grandad, and he will face the consequences for that."

"We will not interfere with your business, Arnold," said the leader of the Order. "Should Night-Sun wish it, that is."

Otto looked nervous at the position he had been put in.

Arnold knew that Otto had harboured his own hatred for Levent, as it was he who had created the artefact that was used on Otto's spirit beast. It was Levent's actions that had made Otto this way.

Otto looked to Arnold as if seeking reassurance, and an understanding seemed to pass between them.

"He needs to go to the Spirit Wardens," Otto declared. "He needs to go with Arnold."

The woman looked disappointed by Otto's choice, but she didn't argue. Her eyes were filled with sadness as she stared at the unconscious Levent, and Arnold couldn't help but feel that there was something she was not telling them. There was a pain in her eyes, and a great sadness.

"Very well. We will leave him in your care." The woman lifted her coyote hide hood and turned to leave. "Marrok, are you coming?"

"Yes, Mum," Marrok said as he struggled to his feet and dusted himself down.

Arnold was stunned. "Your mum is –"

"The leader of the Order of the Aegis," Marrok finished.

Battered and bruised, he limped over to the Order of the Aegis, readying himself to leave. "I guess I will see you around."

"Thank you." Arnold knew if not for Marrok's interjection in the cave, the story may have been different.

They began to leave but not before the woman left Otto with some parting words. "If you ever need anything, we will be there to help. But you need to be wary of the Spirit Wardens. If they learn of you, they will try to catch you, and they will want that blade. Everett, you can't let that happen."

"I won't," Everett said.

The woman turned to leave, but Arnold had a burning question. "Wait!" he called, and she turned around slightly, peering at him over her shoulder. “What's your name?" Arnold finished.

The woman smiled at them all, the moonlight illuminating her natural beauty. "My name is Kaliska."

She waved them goodbye, and the Order of the Aegis began to leave, fading away into the darkness.

Arnold couldn't help but feel that they would stick around, to keep watch on Otto and try and maintain his safety. He liked that there were people out there that would do that for his best friend, and he knew that he felt the same. He wouldn't let anything come between them again, and he would also do his best to try and ensure no harm came to him, even though this now put him in direct conflict with the Spirit Wardens.

"I promise to protect your secret, Otto, no matter what happens with the Spirit Wardens," Arnold told him.

"I know you do, mate.”

Arnold glanced at Levent. "I'm going to have to call my dad. He’ll have to bring the others, which means –"

"I need to leave and stay low for a while, just while the dust settles," said Otto in understanding. Arnold was relieved that he didn’t seem offended.

"I'm going to head home. Text me later. All of you." With this, Otto left them at the coal mine with Levent.

Arnold pulled out his phone and rang his father to explain what had happened.

CHAPTER 26

It was not long before Bernard and some other Doyens arrived. Levent was taken to the hospital while in custody, and Arnold, Everett, and George were escorted to the Athenaeum by the Spirit Wardens. Once there, they were expected to give detailed accounts of what had happened that night.

They relayed almost everything that had happened at the coal mine, but as agreed on beforehand, they omitted Otto and Order of the Aegis being there, pinning everything on Levent and Mr. Higgins. They explained that he had tried to use George's spirit beast to open a gateway, but they said they did not know why.

After what felt like hours, Arnold found himself sitting in the reception area of the Spirit Wardens, waiting for his father to come and tell him what was to happen next. He stared down at the floor and for a moment contemplated lying down on it and having a little sleep. He was that tired.

He heard a door open, and he looked up to see George being escorted out of Mr. Whittaker's office by her dads. She cast him a small smile and waved at him as they walked past and out of the door.

"Arnold, can you come in please?" Bernard stood by Mr. Whittaker's office with his hand outstretched, directing him to enter.

Arnold obliged and walked into the office, wondering what they wished to discuss with him now. He just wanted to be in his bed now, and to remain there for the next week.

"Please sit down, Ethon," Mr. Whittaker's well-spoken voice directed Arnold.

"You have managed to capture a highly dangerous wanted man and bring him back to the Spirit Wardens," Mr. Whittaker began. "In doing so, you have proven your ability in combat as well as your aptitude. Not only this, but I am led to believe that you were able to spirit-wield a weapon while in combat against Levent. Is this all true?"

"I guess so." Arnold wanted to stay modest about his actions. He had done what he had set out to do. He had captured the man who had murdered his grandad in front of him, and he had protected his friends.

Except for Everett. A knot of guilt formed in Arnold's stomach. Everett had lost her spirit beast, and he didn't know how to comfort her. He couldn't imagine having his eagle ripped from him so callously.

"Your actions have brought great honour to the Spirit Wardens. Your grandad would be proud," Mr. Whittaker finished.

At this point, Arnold felt conflicted. He knew his grandad would be proud of him. However, as far as Arnold knew, Mr. Whittaker didn't know of Elwood's affiliation with the Order of the Aegis. Or that deep down, Elwood hadn't been fully on board with the Spirit Wardens and their ways.

"What will happen to Levent?" Arnold asked.

"He will be detained in London at the maximum-security prison, Glyckeria. He will remain under constant supervision there."

"And his blade? The Blade of the Spirits?"

Mr. Whittaker shuffled some papers on his desk before answering. "The Spirit Wardens will keep the blade to stop it falling into anyone else's hands." His response was quick and short, and he looked a little bit unhappy that Arnold was questioning this.

"Now, there is something that I would like you to see. If you would follow your father, I believe he would like to explain this next part to you." Mr. Whittaker gestured to Bernard for him to take over from this point.

Bernard nodded away from the room. "Come on, son, this way."

Arnold followed his father to the elevator in the centre of the Spirit Wardens. The last time Arnold had entered the elevator, he had undertaken the Boodbound Ritual, his initiation into the Spirit Wardens. The ritual had set him on the path he needed to follow to become a Doyen. The experience had felt like a dream, but he remembered how nervous, intimidating, and scary the experience had been.

Bernard seemed to sense his nervousness, because he smiled at Arnold in an attempt to ease his anxieties. "Don't worry, its nothing like the ritual."

When he pressed the button to the lift, it illuminated straight away, and within a few seconds, the lift doors opened and the two of them entered inside.

"What about Otto, Dad? We can't let anyone know about him." Although Arnold had omitted Otto from their official story about what happened that night, he knew his father was aware that Otto had been involved somehow.

"I won't say a word as long as he is in control. I won't

have any choice otherwise, Arnold. I can't let anybody get hurt."

"I understand, thanks, Dad. Where is it you're taking me?" He had seen his father press one of the four buttons in the elevator, each with a different symbol on it that Arnold did not understand. The last time he had been in here, his dad had pressed the very bottom symbol, but this time he had touched the second one.

"I want to give you a bit more insight into your spirit beast, into your eagle. I am taking you to an area where you now have permitted access to, given that you have captured a highly dangerous criminal and proven yourself to the Spirit Wardens."

Arnold's eyes lit up in excitement; he felt he knew what was coming but wanted to seek assurances that his idea was correct. "Am I about to receive my first ranking?"

Bernard just smiled at Arnold as the elevators opened to reveal a large armoury. Weapons and armour lined each side of the room, ranging from ancient and old-fashioned weapons to the more modern ones. There were many sets of ancient armour, each crafted from unique materials. It was truly mesmerising for Arnold, who could not believe the ancient relics that lay hidden on this floor. He never knew this room existed.

"As you are aware, there are many ranks within the Spirit Wardens, and currently I carry the rank of Doyen, which translates to protector," Bernard explained as they walked down the centre of the long room. "I wanted to show you something incredible, given what your spirit beast is and what Otto's was before his transformation." Bernard pressed the button of a small remote that he had picked up, and two sets of armour lit up on the opposite side of a glass case. "Look at the armour and tell me, what do you see?"

Intrigued, Arnold began to examine the two sets of armour. The one on the left was the hide of a jaguar. He could tell by the markings and the similar shape of the headpiece to Otto's spirit beast. The one on the right was adorned with perfectly placed feathers. Parts of the chain-mail armour could be seen underneath what looked like finely polished gold that bound the breastplate together. It did not take Arnold long to recognise the eagle feathers on the amour.

Arnold's eyes shone in the light as he stood in awe of the ancient set of armour on display before him. Each set of armour had individual lights fitted into its cabinet, shining on the magnificent details in the armour and showcasing the mastery and craft that had gone into making them.

"An eagle and a jaguar," Arnold said, amazed.

"That's right." Bernard smiled at Arnold's reaction. "You have shown a tremendous amount of bravery in what you have achieved, and I am so incredibly proud of you. You have protected those that needed your help without hesitation, demonstrated courage and strength beyond your years. As well as this, you have captured a powerful foe who has caused us great pain and anguish, without allowing your anger to consume you. You accepted the guidance of your spirit beast and have proven yourself."

Bernard pressed another button on the remote he was holding, and the glass casing opened on the eagle armour. "This is yours now, son. You need to get dressed, and then I will take you to the ceremonial chamber."

Arnold picked up the armour and was surprised at how light it was. "What's going to happen?"

"You will receive your rank. I'll wait for you at the elevator."

Bernard walked over to the elevator and walked in, shutting the doors behind him to give Arnold some privacy to get dressed. "I'll come and get you when you are ready," he called as the elevator doors closed.

At this point, Arnold couldn't tell who was more nervous, his dad or himself. After around ten minutes, Arnold had managed to figure out how to put the armour on.

"It feels itchy," he said when Bernard returned, pulling at the collar.

Bernard laughed and stepped to the side to allow Arnold into the elevator. "That's because it hasn't been worn in over two hundred years."

The doors shut as Bernard pressed to go down to the ceremonial chamber where Arnold had completed his Bloodbound Ritual.

This time, the chamber was much better lit, and Arnold could see the solid stone walls that had been untouched since the place had been built. He recognised the stone casket in the centre of the room.

Mr. Whittaker stood in front of it, dressed in his ceremonial robes.

But others had gathered as well. Arnold didn't recognise some of the other men and women that stood around the room in different coloured ceremonial robes. By looking at the various symbols on each person's robe, he quickly deduced that they were most likely representatives of Spirit Wardens from different parts of the country.

"Go on, son." Bernard prompted him to step forwards into the ceremonial chamber.

Arnold suddenly felt nervous. He hadn't expected any of this, and he was baffled at how all these people had gotten here so quickly.

And they were here for *him*.

This was something that Arnold never could have imagined in his wildest dreams.

"Step forward, Ethon." Mr. Whittaker beckoned him to stand in front of him.

Arnold followed the instructions, amazed at how easily he found it to manoeuvre in this armour. It felt as though it was weightless, as light as a feather almost.

He stopped directly in front of Mr. Whittaker, who began to address the room.

"Arnold Ethon has proven himself in his ability to protect others. He has also proven himself in battle as well as demonstrating the rarest of abilities of spirit-wielding. His power runs through his bloodline. With his spirit beast, he has shown he has nothing but commitment to the ways passed down in the Spirit Wardens. Given his age, this is unheard of for someone to be able to demonstrate the skill that he has shown consistently. He stands before you in armour not worn for two hundred years in this very Spirit Wardens.

"The last person who wore that armour set also had an eagle for their spirit beast. Arnold, this armour was crafted over a millennia ago. It is imbued with incredible power. When wearing this armour in training or battle, your abilities to spirit-wield as well as your mastery with your spirit beast will become less strenuous on your body. It will allow you a greater connection with your auro."

"Thank you." Arnold nodded his head to Mr. Whittaker, feeling a bit dazed. This all seemed so surreal, he could pinch himself. Here he was, standing in a room full of Elders from across the country, adorned in an ancient armour set made out of eagle feathers.

"You are not of an age where I can grant you the rank of Doyen; however, I do have the authority to give you an incredible rank which I now have the pleasure of granting you. This rank within the Spirit Wardens is rare, and it is a testament to the skills you have shown with your mind, body, and spirit. I do not doubt that you will bring great honour during your time in the Spirit Wardens."

Arnold felt he might faint at any point because of how fast his heart was pumping. He waited nervously through the moments of silence that followed.

"I now grant you the rank of Eagle Warrior."

Stunned, Arnold turned to face the room of Elders who had begun clapping and applauding. His father stood at the back of the room, clapping the hardest and the loudest, his eyes filled with tears.

Arnold had earned his rank. He had his official role within the Spirit Wardens, and he felt truly honoured to be accepted in this way. He was one step closer to the future he had always dreamt of.

But this did not stop the conflict that Arnold now felt in his heart.

His grandad, even as an Elder of the Spirit Wardens, had been working with the Order of the Aegis. He may have even held rank with them for all Arnold knew. The Spirit Wardens and the Order of the Aegis held different rules and views on how spirit beasts should be wielded, how auros should be channelled. The two of them had opposed each other throughout history.

The Order of the Aegis was thought not to be around anymore, but Arnold knew the truth.

As he began to leave the ceremonial chamber, he could not help but feel that soon, he was going to have to make a choice.

He was going to have to choose between the Spirit Wardens or the Order of the Aegis.

EPILOGUE

Far within the confinement of the darkness that engulfed the coal mines, nothing could be heard. Not an animal nor nature. There was no wind blowing down the tunnels nor the echoing sounds that might have travelled from outside. All that existed within these tunnels now was darkness. Where the lion spirit beast that had been slain by Otto lay, a slight wind appeared to ruffle the beast's fur as it lay motionless on the floor. There was no wind present, and the force that was creating this movement was unnatural, gradually getting more powerful. The energy within the room began to rise. The lion slowly began to slide along the floor towards the point where the unnatural force was coming from. The lion was raised into the air and disappeared as it was absorbed in the same manner that Everett's boar had been when Levent had sacrificed it to the gateway.

The room began to shake violently as the energy levels continued to rise.

A distorted portal appeared, much larger than the one that Levent had used to travel through to this world. The gateway had opened, and nobody was around to witness it. The power was immense. The chamber continued to shake with sections of the mine beginning to crumble because of the disturbance.

From within the gateway, a figure could be seen on the other side as it moved closer towards the distorted opening that had formed, illuminating the room and fighting off the darkness that lived here.

The figure leant forwards, and a hand emerged from within. The fingers began to move as it tested what the area felt like. A moment later, a foot emerged from the gateway, followed by the other. Taking a huge gulp of the thin air, the woman wondered where they were but at this moment in time, she did not care.

They had finally escaped from the spirit world. She smiled as she summoned her powerful spirit beast to guide her from this dark place. Her beauty became distorted as her sinister expression was revealed. She had waited for this moment for a very long time indeed. For now, they were free. They had escaped the prison where they had been held for over forty years.

And they were ready for their revenge.

ABOUT THE AUTHOR

A.P Beswick, a devoted parent and a passionate writer, embarked on the wonderful journey of storytelling when his children expressed a desire for an original bedtime story. This story.

In 2023 A.P Beswick went full time as an author, he looks forward to sharing more of his enchanting tales with his read- ers. He hopes you find as much enjoyment in reading his stories as he does in creating them.

www.apbeswick.com

ARNOLD ETHON WILL RETURN IN.....

Spirit Beasts Revolution

Made in United States
Orlando, FL
22 November 2023